Hollie Porter Builds a Raft

Welcome to the RAFT. ♡

Eliza Gordan ⭐

Welcome to the
KGL. ♥

Hilingdon A≡

Hollie Porter Builds a Raft

Sequel to Must Love Otters

ELIZA GORDON

WEST 26TH STREET PRESS
NEW YORK CITY

Hollie Porter Builds a Raft © 2015 Jennifer Sommersby Young / Eliza Gordon. All rights reserved.

www.elizagordon.com

Cover art © 2015 Sarah Hansen, Okay Creations (www.okaycreations.com)

E-book ISBN-13: 978-1-63064-016-3

Paperback ISBN-13: 978-1-63064-017-0

First edition, September 2015

Published by West 26th Street Press, NYC, 21 W. 26th Street, New York City, NY 10010

No part of this publication may be reproduced in any manner in any media, or transmitted in any means whatsoever, without the prior written permission of the publisher. The publisher has made every effort to ensure the accuracy of the information contained in this publication. Any errors brought to the attention of the publisher will be corrected in future editions.

This e-book is licensed for your personal enjoyment only and may not be resold or given to other people. Please respect the copyright. Piracy hurts.

This is a work of fiction. Names, characters, businesses, places, events and incidents are either the products of the author's imagination or used in a fictitious manner. Any resemblance to actual persons, living or dead, or actual events is purely coincidental.

Contents

Dedication ix

1. Kiss-Cam Carnage 1
2. YouTube Famous 5
3. Ode to Etta James 13
4. Oh, Anxiety, You're So Cute 25
5. Our Raft, Our Rules 35
6. Surprise! 39
7. Apocalypse Now 47
8. Family Disunion 53
9. Caipirinha Coupons for All! 71
10. Only Cake Can Save This Day 83
11. Letter of the Law 97
12. Save the Date 103
13. Embrace Thy Enemy—Because Drowning Them Is Illegal 117
14. Silk, Organza, and Satin—Oh My! 147
15. My Uterus Has Left the Building 167
16. Fire ... and Fizzle 181
17. I Shall Call Her Squishy and She Shall Be Mine 193
18. Love Is Spelled O-T-T-E-R 209

19. High Roads Are Full of Stones 223
20. Pretty Corvus 239
21. Full-Service Concierge 249
22. Hollie Porter, Goat Whisperer? 259
23. Tragic Kingdom for the Win 271
24. It's a Dress, But... 279
25. "O! for a muse of fire ..." 289
26. Water, Water, Everywhere 307
27. Sugar and Spice and Everything Nice 317
28. Serenity, Where Art Thou? 333
29. It Means Bright 339
30. Enhydra lutris, Bridesmaid Edition 357
31. Epilogue: A Raft--or a Clan? 367

Acknowledgments 373
A Special Note 377
About the Author 379
Must Love Otters 380
Neurotica 382

Dedication

To the readers who wanted more of Hollie and Ryan's adventures.
Thank you for asking so politely.

1

Kiss-Cam Carnage

If a hot dog looks dodgy, don't eat it.

Otherwise, the following could happen to you:

Your dashing boyfriend of almost one year decides it's a brilliant idea to spend a few days in Portland to watch the Winterhawks as they battle and bulldoze their way into the Memorial Cup playoffs. It's a big deal. There will be lots of people. Lots of loud, drunk, excited hockey fans.

While you're in Portland, you'll stop by Dad's. *Hey, Bob, how are you, how's work at the hospital, oh wonderful, I see you still have that demonic goat, sure come along with us we're going to a hockey game but first I'm really hungry because the float plane we flew down on had only a duffel of liquor and expired granola bars, sure I will have a hot dog, how old do you suppose these are?*

And you will get ready, wearing a custom Winterhawks jersey that says FIELDING across the back, because you want more than anything for your dashing boyfriend to know the vast expanse of your love for him and that you're so proud of his rough-and-tumble past in the N-H-L because it has given you access to a world you didn't know existed. (Namely one that involves a little money and a tiny bit of fame among the hockey crowd.)

Then after braving the huge, rural yard where Mangala the Demon Goat lurks, you will drive with your dad, Nurse Bob, to the Moda Center and while you're en route, your tummy will feel a little weird but it's probably fatigue from working long hours at the resort and maybe a little hunger because really, you shouldn't have helped yourself to so many of those wee little liquor bottles while aboard Miss Lily the Floatplane. She's a lovely plane—don't mind the duct tape.

Inside the Moda Center, you will find your seats, comp tickets, of course, for Ryan Fielding: Local Hero. The folks sitting around you are stoked to meet a real hockey star and you smile while Ryan shakes hands and signs programs, and you bob your head when people ask if you're the girl who saved him from the cougar, even though moving your head makes the world a bit spinny and maybe it's just best you sit still and watch the crowd and the promos on the Jumbotron.

After the second period, your team is winning—Go 'Hawks!—and that pesky Kiss Cam will shine on you, although your stomach is REALLY not feeling great *at all*, but instead of leaning over to kiss you, your boyfriend pulls you to your feet and then the entire arena sort of quiets down as the announcer calls attention to "former Vancouver Canucks defensemen who works hard year round with hockey charities to raise money for kids in sport, please give a rousing welcome to Misterrrr Ryaaaaan Fieldinggggg!" and then there are cheers and hollers and beer is spilled, but not much, because it is beer after all.

Followed by your tall hunk of a man getting down on one knee and offering up a little box with a sparkly thing shining out of it.

Accompanied by oohs and ahhs, and some words you think sound pretty but really all you can hear is the roar in your head because your stomach is going into full revolt, all you can do is smile, put your hand on his cheek, and then barf all over your seat. As if that weren't enough, your knees buckle and you last remember hitting your head on something very hard. Likely concrete. Just don't think about your cheek against the sticky dirtiness from the aforementioned spilled beer and forgotten hockey arena snacks.

You've waited your whole life for your Kiss Cam moment, and this is what you do with it?

Also: it was definitely the hot dog.

2

YouTube Famous

"Hollie? Hollie Cat, wake up, sweetie. Look at me. Look at Dad. Come on, kiddo."

Ryan holds my hand, leaning over the seat in the row in front of us, while my dad, a nurse (yeah, yeah, my dad is a nurse) pats my cheeks to bring me around. I smell barf. Which makes my stomach want to give a repeat performance.

Why am I on the ground?

A new voice. "Step aside. Excuse us. Oh, hey, Mr. Porter. And Ryan! Wow, hey! Wait—is that Hollie?"

No. No. No.

I did not just pass out in the middle of the Moda Center. They did not call the paramedics. And that is not Keith, my paramedic ex-boyfriend, standing over me with his stethoscope around his neck. This is too rich.

I have to sit up. I've made enough of a spectacle of myself.

"Nooooo, you don't. Stay put, Hollie," Keith says. Just perfect. His moment to shine. There are hundreds of paramedics in the city of Portland, and I get THIS one. Further proof that I did something really terrible in my last life, and now all the important deities are giggling and nibbling on appetizers at their collective golden table in the sky.

Blood pressure is low. Duh, I could've told you that. Just ask the stars floating around my peripheral vision.

A hundred questions about what's going on, answered by my dad and Ryan taking turns. "Could she be pregnant?" Keith asks. This pisses me off, even if he is just going through the EMS 101 cards.

"NO," I say loudly. "It was the hot dog. Why are you even here?"

"We're the team on call in the arena tonight. Hockey's a brutal sport. But I don't gotta tell you that, do I," Keith answers, flirting with Ryan. I'd be embarrassed for him, except vomit.

The arena announcer tries to return everyone's attention to center ice because the weird girl in section 103 is going to be okay. Like show biz, the game must go on. I don't want to be responsible for a delay-of-game penalty.

It doesn't take much longer for stadium security and Keith plus cohort to load me onto their little board and get me the hell out of there in case I have something communicable, most probably because I'm throwing up and it's really gross.

"I'm so sorry about my new jersey," I say.

"Porter, we can get you a new one." Ryan winks and squeezes my hand.

If only I'd known the hot dogs were bad, I could've fed them to Mangala and then waited for the humanitarian awards to fly through the mailbox, like letters from Hogwarts, in thanks for my contribution to making the world a better, safer place for humankind. Then again, hundreds of milligrams of codeine didn't kill him last year—the radioactive hot dogs probably would've given him superpowers and he'd have turned into the Goat Hulk. Or a Republican.

Ryan is so wonderful. He doesn't let go of my hand and pushes my hair out of my face, even as the bumpy gurney ambles toward the waiting ambulance.

"You went almost an entire year without having to be in a hospital, as patient or visitor," Ryan says next to my ear. "I'm impressed."

"Reset the DAYS SINCE GENIUS HOLLIE'S LAST MEDICAL INCIDENT board."

He laughs. I throw up again.

Ryan gives Dad the keys—he'll follow in the rental car to Emanuel Medical—and makes him promise to stop apologizing about the hot dogs.

"It's fine, Dad. It's just food poisoning. I wish you guys would let me get up. This is stupid."

"You lie still, Hollie," Keith reprimands. Oh god, he is so loving this. "Are you sure you're not pregnant?"

I answer with my middle finger.

"Such a classy girl," Keith says to Ryan, who at this

point, even under his playoff beard, looks a little green around the gills himself. Thank heavens he didn't eat the hot dogs too. One geyser of goo is plenty.

In the ambulance, Keith makes a show of explaining every little step to Ryan, though not missing an opportunity to speak in a manner more appropriate to a room full of kindergartners: "This is the IV, full of fluids that will get our girl back on track." *I'm not your girl. I'm Ryan's girl.* "And I'll give her medicine so her tummy will stop hurting and the pukies will slow, although it's best to get that stuff out, right, Hols?"

Don't call me Hols.

"Ow! Jesus!"

Keith smiles. "Squeamish with needles, this one."

"Because you're supposed to aim for a vein, not the bone, idiot," I say, trying to yank my arm away.

"Don't make me use the restraints." Keith smiles. I want to stab all the needles in the ambulance into his dumb face. I also hate noticing that he looks better than I remember—the tire around his middle is gone, his dumb face thinner and the angles sharper. I'd almost say handsome, but knowing him like I do, let's not get carried away.

Ryan leans close to my ear. "Almost there. You okay?"

I nod. He smells so much better than I do. I'd yank his face closer but I reek like gastric juice and discarded putrid foodstuffs.

At the hospital, my dad is in his element. The cougar mishap made Ryan and me—and my dad—minor celebs among Dad's hospital crowd. Bob Porter's little girl Hollie saves a famous hockey player from certain death, and then they fell in love. Awwwww. As such, his cronies gather round to check on his barfing baby girl. People shake hands with Ryan and ask about his arm, if he's ever going to be able to play his beloved game again.

Thankfully, Keith disappears when his phone screams out "Karma Chameleon," the same stupid ringtone he's had the whole time I've known him. Blood tests are done—confirming finally that I am *not* pregnant, as if there were any doubt—and it's agreed that it's nothing more than a rather excitable case of bad hot dog, likely caused by *Staphylococcus aureus*, based on its very quick onset. Fluids, a preventive course of antibiotics, medicine to stop the diarrhea (I told you this was fun), and because it's a slow night at the ER, they're going to let me stay in an isolation room all by myself until someone worse shows up and boots me out.

Ryan, the dear, runs water in the room's tiny stainless steel sink to soak my jersey. "You've seen enough of my bodily fluids for one night."

"I love your bodily fluids," he says, kissing my forehead.

"There is something definitely wrong with you, then. Go back to the game and catch up with your friends. I'm so sorry I screwed up your night ..."

"Don't be silly. My friends can find me another time when you're not puking out your kidneys."

"Then go to the hotel. My dad will bring me around when this is all over."

"Hollie ..." He's got one hand in his pocket.

Where the ring box is.

I shake my head. "Wait. Not yet."

When I started this little episode, he was proposing. To me. On the Kiss Cam. In front of my dad and thousands of crazed hockey fans. And I threw up and fainted. Surely that cannot be a fortuitous way to start a life together?

We've talked about getting married, and we both know now it's not a matter of if, but when. I wanted this day more than anything, and a tiny hope bubble in my heart had her tiny bubble fingers crossed that Ryan would use this special trip to Portland to pop the question.

But now I feel awful that I've foiled not one but two attempts to get the ring on my finger, his face looking a bit disappointed as he pulls his hand out of his pocket.

"I'm so sorry, Ryan. But not like this. I don't want to ruin this amazing moment any more than I already have. I want it to be perfect, for you. The world's greatest concierge deserves a vomit-free moment in the sun."

He nods and looks down at his feet, chuckling.

My dad moseys into the room and interrupts the weirdness.

"How are we doing in here?" He steps in front of Ryan and squeezes the IV bag, drops a hand across my forehead. "If you're not feeling dizzy anymore, you can have a shower. Get the vomit out of your hair."

Wonderful. Ryan was going to drop to his knee again whilst I have regurgitated hot dog in my hair?

Ryan's phone rings. "Hey, Mom …" He turns away and talks quietly into the phone. "Porter, I'll be back in a sec. Can I get you anything?"

I shake my head no and watch him step out into the bustle of the ER. I hope Miss Betty isn't mad at me for screwing up her darling son's big moment.

My dad is helping me to my feet when the door to the room opens again. "Keith, what? You did your job. Go away."

He's smiling again—he's had his teeth whitened. Someone is definitely playing the Keith Skin Flute. Gotta be the only reason he's so manicured and tidy. I had to remind him about regular dental hygiene and changing his underwear when we lived together.

As he steps into the room, I clench my fists and jaw, a Pavlovian reaction. Which makes me want to punch his lights out. I could plead not guilty by reason of being goaded by my annoying ex.

Without saying a word, he crosses the short distance from door to bedside, his outstretched hand cupping his phone. He presses play and holds it up before me.

I'm throwing up on YouTube as my gorgeous boyfriend is down on one knee. And then I disappear from the camera while everyone scrambles around to gawk at the dumb dirty-blond who ate a bad hot dog and is face down in her own sick.

When I joked to the Ouija board in seventh grade about being famous? This was definitely not what I had in mind.

3

Ode to Etta James

It's our last full day here. Ryan's brother, Tanner, is meeting us at Seattle's Lake Union early tomorrow morning for the trip back to Revelation Cove, British Columbia. Our own private island with grass and trees and beaches and golf and swimming and Miss Betty's famous jam.

Well, a private island we share with the guests who come stay at the resort owned by Ryan, Tanner, and a couple other silent partners, former NHL players and friends of Ryan's. It's a good life—I still pinch myself daily to make sure it's real, even if I'm pinching myself while helping the maid staff clean rooms or scrub toilets or helping unload the floatplane after a fresh supply run or while trying to get a bunch of rambunctious kids to listen as we meander the grounds on a nature walk. Which is really what my job entails now. Wildlife Experience Educator. That's my official title. I even have business cards.

It's a long way from the confining basement dungeon of the emergency dispatch center. No more Polyester Patty, no more Les and his Book of Death, no more trying to wash my brain of the images of what Les and Candida the Troll Lady are doing to each other's body parts in the oversized handicapped bathroom. Oh. God. Stop, brain. Just stop.

But today is brighter, I am no longer throwing up from bad processed meat, and we have the whole day to ourselves to hang out in Portland.

I roll over in bed, hiding my morning breath behind the sheet draped across my lips. "Ryan, get me out of this hotel room."

"As your concierge, I think that can be arranged," he says, twisting to face me, his dark brown curls appropriately messed after slumber. "First, however, I need to do an inspection."

"Of?"

"Everything. I need to make sure you're fully healed and healthy and ready to face the world."

"And that would involve ..." Ohhhhh, that. His scruffy face tucks under my nightshirt, an old Red Wings T-shirt stolen from his vast collection, and he blows a raspberry between my boobs. Which, of course, leads to laughter and the blowing of raspberries on other important body parts.

It does not matter how many times I see his nekked bod—I still cannot believe I get to touch it whenever I want.

Once fully inspected and deemed fit for consumption, I am cleansed. Head to toe. Ryan is nothing if not thorough in his duties as concierge and boyfriend. Sharing a shower with me is always a win-win for Mr. Fielding, except he's taller than I am, so he has to drop to both knees to have his curls washed. Oh, what a tough job this is.

I'm careful when I bathe the scarred patchwork decorating his left arm. Though it's been almost a year, Ryan likely has another surgery or two to deal with nerve and tendon damage from Chloe the Cougar's handiwork. And while he's self-conscious about the fact that the arm is now weaker and smaller than the right one, I try to make him forget by kissing all the bits the doctors sewed back together.

Most importantly, his arm is still attached to his body, and it still functions mostly the right way, and I've told him a hundred times that it lends itself to his softy-wrapped-in-a-tough-guy shell. Scars are badass, as is wrestling a cougar one-handed. Then he kisses the scarred lines on my left wrist—the same badge of honor earned when stabbing the cougar in the shoulder to save both our lives. That did not make Chloe the Cougar very happy at all. If I could see her again—my body safely ensconced in claw-proof glass—I would apologize for getting in her way. It was her wilderness, not mine.

Nothing further has been mentioned about the incident at the Winterhawks game two nights ago (we won, by the way). No mention of the almost-proposal. I haven't seen the ring box, although I have sort of looked. Not too hard—curiosity kills cats and honestly, I don't need to poke Fate in the chest. Ryan hasn't razzed me once for screwing up his important night, or for making a fool out of us via YouTube. Keith gained far too much pleasure from shoving his phone in people's faces at the ER, stopping only when my dad threatened to call his supervisor.

Clothes on, camera bag in the trunk, caffeine on board, it's time for fresh spring Portland air. Ryan takes a detour through downtown and we stop at an amazing diner called Piewalker's—total retro-meets-*Star Wars* thing going on, the best cherry turnover I have ever eaten, so good that Ryan strikes up a convo with the owner, cute guy named Luke Walker, and they exchange info, especially as it pertains to the resort. Seems Luke and his fiancée will be looking at wedding venues. We have just the place!

Calories consumed, we're off for an adventure. Although what that adventure will entail, I am still unsure. When Ryan turns the wheel onto Highway 26 West out of downtown, I know we're going to the Oregon Zoo.

One of my favorite places in the whole world.

"I figured your buddies might like to see you again," he says, holding my hand across the console. By my buddies, he means the southern sea otters who live there—Eddie (who plays basketball to help relieve his arthritis), Thelma, and baby Juno, who joined the older two otters in 2014.

And that is another reason why I love Ryan Fielding. Despite the fact that I have spent the last ten months filling his head with every fact I know about *Enhydra lutris* and *Lontra canadensis* (river otters need love too), he still listens, he still surprises me with adorable otter trinkets and collectibles—he even built me a gorgeous cabinet out of maple and glass that we keep in our shared apartment at Revelation Cove so I have a place to keep everything. We invented a game where, for every otter or sea creature fact I feed him, he gives me one in return about hockey.

I tell him that otters are the largest members of the *Mustelidae*, or weasel, family; he tells me that the Seattle Metropolitans were the first American team to win the Stanley Cup, in 1917 against the Montreal Canadiens. I tell him that sea otters don't have blubber but rather the densest fur in the animal kingdom; he tells me that Maurice Richard, aka "The Rocket," has his name on the Stanley Cup eleven times as a player. See, kids? Romance can be educational! Who knew?

Ryan has checked his phone twice since we pulled in. Once since we parked. And again as we're making our way through the epic parking lot toward the front gates.

"Got a hot date, Fielding?"

"Only with you," he says, grabbing a handful of ass.

"Mind your manners. There are small humans lurking about."

It's a weekday, so the front terrace of the zoo teems with school-aged monkeys, running around touching and sneezing and punching and stuffing their germy faces with whatever the harried teacher or parent guardian shoves into their grabby hands. Humans of the world who make teaching their life's mission? I salute you.

"They're more interested in their elephant ears than what my hand is doing." Ryan's right. More than one face we pass is smeared with a buttery mixture of cinnamon and sugar. I'll need to make a stop at the café for one of my own before this fine day concludes. An elephant ear, not a grimy child.

"Otters first?" As if he has to ask. Steller Cove, where the sea otters live, is not far from the entrance. I know the zoo houses lots of other beasts, but this ... this is my favorite spot.

When I found myself at Revelation Cove the first time, it was to cash in the Sweethearts' Spa & Stay package my dad had gifted me. Well, gifted me and Keith, the loser paramedic-classless-voyeur-ex-boyfriend you met earlier. But I dumped Keith, got drunk, made the reservation for the Cove, and managed to get myself into all kinds of mischief for about a week.

I might have fallen flat on my stupid face in love that week too.

It didn't take long. Have you met Concierge Ryan?

Once we decided that our hearts beat better when they shared the same atmosphere, I applied for a work permit, packed up my tiny Laurelhurst apartment, and moved to O Canada. (Did you know they have healthcare and they're actually grateful for it?)

But just before I made the big move north of the 49th, I spent two weeks with some amazing otter people in Monterey, with Friends of the Sea Otter and the scientists and animal behaviorists at the Monterey Bay Aquarium. We went into Elkhorn Slough and counted otters and I cried when I saw new babies clinging to their mommies, and the researchers and otter enthusiasts were so gracious with their knowledge and science. For the first time ever, I felt ... whole.

Another unexpected side effect fell out of the otter experience: I picked up a camera. One of the guys working with Friends of the Sea Otter loaned me a DSLR for a few days. Who knew I could take pictures of otters and make them not half bad?

During the two weeks away, I sent Ryan and my dad copies of my photos. When I stepped off the plane in Portland, Nurse Bob presented me with a gift card to a camera store and a one-year subscription to an online learning academy where I am still taking classes to learn how to take better pictures. At the resort, I assist the wedding and event photographers, carrying equipment and holding reflectors and changing out batteries and moving lights. It's grueling and makes me sweat like a dude, but in exchange, the pros teach me hands-on stuff I could never learn from a classroom.

Like I said, it's been a good year.

We're through the admission gates; Steller Cove is in the Pacific Shores section just ahead. Steller sea lions bark at their fish-toting trainers; the mid-May sun burns through what's left of a misty morning. Excited whistles and chatter from kids, squeals from those of the human larval stage strapped into strollers and on parental torsos, the haunting call of peacocks hovering around garbage cans and along the edges of the picnic area, one fellow with his fan on full display as a disinterested peahen grooms herself atop a concrete table.

Ryan checks his phone again.

"Everything okay?"

He seems jittery. I should've vetoed that second espresso at Piewalker's.

He pulls me against him, his arms lovingly around my front, and kisses the top of my head. Stopped in front of the otter enclosure, I press my hands against the glass like I used to do as a kid at the aquarium in Newport—wanting to let the beautiful beasties inside know that I love them better than anyone else. Childhood habits die hard.

Juno, the baby abandoned sea otter rescued in California, is giving Thelma a good game of chase over an urchin. Thelma's an old girl, but little Juno chases and dives and bobs around the pool, keeping her older friend on her otter toes. Thelma floats along the glass, urchin guts atop her belly, and I swear her little brown eyes are staring into my soul.

Stop laughing at me.

I really love otters.

Violin music trickles in above the din of the local crowd. Faint at first, I look around for speakers in the nearby man-made rock structures. Ryan takes my hand and we move to the glass half-wall overlooking the otter pool. The violin music grows louder. And nearer.

"Is that live music?"

Ryan looks in the direction of the melody. "Sounds like it."

And then the sea of people parts, and there's my dad, and two women stroking violins tucked under their chins, and Miss Betty and Ryan's brother Tanner and his very pregnant wife Sarah, followed by a gathering crowd, smiles on everyone's faces.

When I turn to Ryan, he's on his knee.

Again.

And in his hand, the same little velvety box.

"Hollie, a year ago, I was manning the check-in desk late at night, looking at hockey scores and pretending like I wasn't really alone in this world. Then I get this call from a newly single drunk girl who sounds like she needed a vacation almost as much as I did. Little did I know that when you arrived on that dock in Victoria, wondering where the real pilot was for Miss Lily, that you would change my life in immeasurable ways. It quickly became obvious that you were unlike anyone I'd ever met—from almost falling out of the plane midflight to streaking through my hotel in nothing but your birthday suit to getting lost in a remarkable storm during which you swam with orcas—I knew I was done for. Whatever had been missing in my life up to that point all of a sudden wasn't missing anymore.

"I love how you love otters, how you love all the animals—well, except the demon goat—and that you were brave in the face of certain death when you saved us both from that rather large angry cat." He flexes his left arm, and kisses my scarred forearm. "I love that even when you're having a really rotten day, you try to make all the people around you laugh. I love that you love with your whole heart, even if it means you might get hurt." Ryan swallows his emotion, voice wavering. He's in double vision because my eyes are clotted with tears. "I don't mind the fact that you snore, or that you never change the toilet paper roll in our bathroom, or that you root for the Anaheim Ducks even though you should be a Canucks fan because of where we live." The crowd chuckles. "I don't even mind that you barfed your way through my first attempt to do this and that we are now YouTube stars. I always knew I'd make it to the big time, one way or another."

More crowd giggles.

"You told me that otters will float together in the tide, holding hands so they don't drift apart. That they make a raft so they can stay together. Hollie Porter, my otter girl and best friend, if you'll have me, I'd like to make a forever raft with you. Float with me in the tide so we don't drift apart. Marry me, Porter. Marry me so that I can have the tax deduction, and so that I can wake up to your funny-looking toes every day for the rest of my life."

Wow.

And all these people are staring at me, and I should use this time to answer, but instead I am running my fingers through his curls and through his playoff beard that gets thicker every day that his team doesn't get eliminated.

I lean forward, my lips inches from his. "Yes," I whisper. He smiles, kisses me harder and longer than is appropriate with so many applauding bystanders, and stands, wrapping us both in his wondrous embrace and then we're both crying and kissing and the whole crowd is cheering and even the otter trainers are clapping and someone is singing *At Last* in a voice that would make Etta James jealous and then he's returning my feet to the ground although they're not really touching anything but clouds.

    Hollie Porter is engaged.

4

Oh, Anxiety, You're So Cute

We almost got kicked out of the zoo for taking too much time in the one-stall-fits-all family/universal bathroom—hey, we just got engaged! We have to consummate the engagement, don't we? Isn't that a rule or law somewhere? Yes, I know your baby just shit up its back and I'm sorry for that, but maybe fewer prunes next time, and I'm sorry to the other lady who needed to breastfeed her darling screamer but *I just got engaged and I needed to do what engaged people do* (and ew, gross, why are you feeding your baby in a toilet room where people have pee-peed on the floor and where Concierge Ryan and I just had sex?). Also, playing Hollie Hides the Sausage on the open lawn during the Birds of Prey show is generally frowned upon. It apparently excites the golden eagle.

But omigod, there is a not-so-wee rock made of time and pressurized coal gleaming from my left fourth finger, and the man who gave it to me said a bunch of really sweet stuff that I wish I could remember and he looks gorgeous in his button-down shirt that is now misbuttoned and his brown curly hair that is messier than it was fifteen minutes ago and those Levis that hug his ass like they're involved in an intimate relationship of their own and seriously? Would you not want to tap the hell out of that after it got down on one knee and said I LOVE YOU MAKE ME YOUR HUSBAND?

That's what I'm sayin'.

After we said our polite goodbyes to family and friends who came to share the happy moment—the engagement, not the part in the universal bathroom (perverts)—we made one stop before heading to Seattle for the night: a newsstand where I bought every bridal magazine the smelly, throat-bearded dude had to sell, despite the fact that he also tried to talk me out of getting married because his ex-wives were sucking him dry "like piglets on a sow's teat" and that's why he had to work three shit jobs and if I knew what was good for me, I'd run as fast and as far away as possible. I instead handed over my credit card to pay for an armload of outrageously priced glossy magazines I swore I would never, ever buy and asked him if he hates women so much, then why does he have Match.com open on his computer screen. He grunted and gave me a free "Keep Portland Weird" bookmark.

And then Mr. Ryan Fielding, *my fiancé*, and I checked

into a hotel in downtown Seattle so we could violate one another's body parts in real style and comfort, and after my newly engaged girly bits were thoroughly exhausted, I lay awake next to Ryan's lightly snoring form, staring at the sparkly bauble's reflective properties in the light spill sneaking into our room through a split in the gauzy curtains, like a love-drunk girl is supposed to do, but the ring on my finger is kinda sorta freaking me out because Hollie Porter wasn't voted Most Likely to Marry the Man of Her Dreams—not even close. Getting married? Me? That's something grown-ups do.

And then they screw everything up and get divorced, like my dad—twice, first with my absentee mother and then with Dr. Aurora (although by law, they're still married—Dr. Aurora thinks that ET's cousins run the court system so she won't file the papers). Or look at the dispatch center and all the lives ruined because of illicit romances born of a strange occupational brotherhood—dealing with dying people and life's worst tragedies for a living does something to a person's head. Rumor has it that Troll Lady and Les finally got caught playing porn stars in the handicapped bathroom and Troll Lady's very large, steroid-juiced husband broke Les's nose so badly, he will never breathe properly again. Hell, even Throat-Beard Guy at the newsstand warned me against taking the stroll down the aisle.

But here we are, and a scarred, beautiful arm just wrapped around my middle and as he pulls me closer, my concierge lightly smooches my cheek and burrows in my hair and whispers that he loves me and he thinks I broke his penis, and all is again right with the world, and I don't have to worry about failing as a wife yet because maybe we can have a really long engagement and since we live at Revelation Cove, we have a chef onsite so it's not like I need to really learn how to cook for *real*.

Because isn't that what wives do? Cook and stuff? Will everything change if we get married? Is he going to want to have kids, like, next week because I saw that baby's back at the zoo today, the poop oozing out the top of his little outfit, and no one can deny how uncomfortable Tanner's charming wife is with her very pregnant belly and ankles that look infected with elephantiasis and I just don't know—I don't know if I can do that. Getting married is *one* thing—finding the dress and ordering a cake and flowers and pretty invitations and having a sundae bar so guests can gorge on ice cream—but babies? Ryan wants kids. I know that. When will he want them, though?

Soon? Because I'm only twenty-six and the battery bay in my biological clock is totally empty, and the idea of having to: a) grow something in my body, like a little alien leeching the calcium from my bones; b) push said alien out of a hole that nicely fits a heavy-flow tampon; and c) be responsible for a tiny human being who poops out the top of its tiny T-shirt and sucks on my body parts for nourishment—

I sit ramrod straight, pushing Ryan's arm away, heart thudding a primal beat against my eardrums.

Why are my fingers tingling?

"You okay, babe?" Ryan says, though his eyes aren't

open and before I can answer, his breathing tells me he's still asleep.

I look at him, how the scant light dances across the profile of his very crooked nose, and I know that any babies would be adorable because look at their potential father with his curly hair and his strong forehead ... but maybe the best thing to do right at this very second is stick my head between my knees and count to twenty, finish what's left in the champagne bottle, and go to sleep.

"Baby steps, Hollie Cat," my dad's voice whispers in my head.

Please don't say babies, Dad.

~ ~ ~

Tanner, his wife Sarah, and Miss Betty are already at the floatplane terminal when we arrive. As Ryan returns the rental car, the girls pull me aside to gawk at the ring. Even though they've already seen it, it is kinda fun to watch Miss Betty pull one of her monogrammed hankies out of her sleeve to dab at her eyes.

"I didn't think that boy was ever gonna settle down," she says, kissing my cheek.

I've been on the floatplane enough in the last year that I no longer have to breathe in and out of a paper sack upon take off and landing—and my darling concierge even had the door fixed on Miss Lily so I won't almost fall out. Aw, what a sweetie.

But this plane isn't Miss Lily—it's her bigger cousin we use to transport guests—so there is plenty of room for Sarah to recline in her seat and for Miss Betty and I to sit on each side and massage Sarah's poor sausage-swollen fingers.

"That ring is never coming off," she says, eyes closed, a smile on her lips.

"Oh, just wait. Once this little peanut is out, you'll be so busy chasing him or her around the pounds will melt off. After I had my third one, the doctor put me on a diet to gain weight because I was run so ragged. Tanner and Hailey were crazy toddlers, so when Ryan arrived, I was done."

"And yet you did it again?"

"Brody was an oops," Ryan teases from the front. "We remind him every chance we get."

"Don't listen to him, Hollie," Miss Betty says, shaking her head. "Their dad would've had a hockey team if I hadn't put my foot down."

Sarah's eyes open. "I think I'm good with one."

"Are you sure there aren't twins in here?" Miss Betty says, patting Sarah's belly, already in love with her new grandbaby.

"Bite your tongue, Grandma," Sarah says, turning to look at me. "What about you, Hollie? You want kids?"

I can't help but look up at Ryan, to see if his head is turned, if he heard Sarah's question. Is this how things are going to go now? We've not even been engaged a full day yet.

"Ahhhh, I've freaked you out. Okay, question rescinded. Don't worry, Hollie. You guys have lots of time. Well, as long as your eggs aren't scrambled like mine were,"

Sarah says, squeezing my hand. I'm so grateful I don't have to answer her question.

"So, have you and Ryan thought at all about when you'd like to get married? I'm assuming you'll want to have the ceremony at the Cove, yes?" Miss Betty squeezes more lotion onto Sarah's hand, the cabin filling with the scent of peach mango, and continues massaging.

"No idea yet. We haven't really talked about any of that stuff ..."

"Well, I know the summer is very booked, depending on how big a wedding you kids want. If you want a long engagement, that would be doable. Get married next summer maybe?" she says.

A year ago, getting married was so far off my radar, and although Ryan and I have both been quietly confident that this relationship would be our forever, I don't have a ready response for Miss Betty.

I twist the engagement ring, still unfamiliar with the sensation of jewelry on my usually bare fingers. It really is the most gorgeous setting, though. Ryan did so good. Shall we take wagers on how long before I break it?

But Miss Betty is one step ahead. As per usual. Hands wiped clean of the lotion, she's got her iPad out. And she's scrolling through her reservations app. I will have a word later with Ryan about why introducing his mother to technology was probably not the best idea. I fear that she will next Google "secret recipes to help your son impregnate his new wife on their wedding night."

I should maybe stop eating Miss Betty's food for a while.

Also, where is the duffel of booze? This flight isn't nearly as accommodating as it should be. I'll have to have a word with the copilot.

Miss Betty taps Ryan on the shoulder—and then looks between him and me before returning her sparkling eyes to her screen. "How do you kids feel about a weekday wedding?"

"Mom ... we haven't had this conversation yet," Ryan says, pushing his spongy mic thingie aside.

"But do you want a long engagement?"

Ryan and I lock eyes, shoulders shrugging in unison. "Mom, please—"

"Because if you want a weekend, we're looking at possibly November, which could be lovely if you want a holiday theme, but Ryan, so many of your friends won't be able to make it because hockey will be in full swing and then what about Hailey and the kids, and Brody—we have to think about when they'll be able to fly out if it's during the school year, and then Brody needs enough notice to be able to take his vacation time. But," she almost sings the word, "we could pull something beautiful together for a summer wedding—Hollie would look so lovely in a summer gown—in the next four to six weeks? Last weekend in June might work, if you do a Friday—Canadians will be busy with Canada Day and the Americans busy with 4th of July—"

"MOM!" Ryan is joined in chorus by Tanner and Sarah. Thank heavens for backup as my mouth is fixed open and I think I forgot how to breathe and those pins and needles have retaken my fingers and maybe the plane door opening right now wouldn't be such a bad thing. Plan a wedding in four to six weeks?

"Hol," Sarah says, pushing her rounded girth more upright in her cushioned airplane seat, "hand me a few of your magazines. Let's look at pretty dresses and find one that will make your boobs the envy of this modern sexist society, shall we?" Into my palm, she slides a tiny bottle of gin, seemingly from the ether, and winks.

I mouth "thank you" and bury my terror in the glossy pages of emaciated models drowning in lace and tulle, turning away long enough to guzzle the bottle and hope that Miss Betty doesn't next Google "signs your future daughter-in-law is a drunk."

5

Our Raft, Our Rules

"Four to six weeks? *Four to six weeks?*"

Ryan stops rubbing my shoulders and tilts my head so he can kiss me upside down, like that scene in *Spiderman*, only without Spiderman and the rain and—never mind.

Four to six weeks?

He mutes the hockey game and pulls me up so we're facing one another. "She's just excited. Mom gets like this when there's a big event on the horizon."

"But isn't an imminent baby enough to spazz about? Sarah's going to explode if she gets any bigger. I was watching her belly today on the plane. It's like *ALIEN*—the baby rolls and her whole belly does the wave." I shudder. "Like it wanted to punch its way out and then eat everyone on the plane. And then we would've crashed and the mutant baby would've swum to shore and eaten all the people."

"I'm canceling Netflix. It's warping your imagination."

"You didn't see her belly."

"Hollie Porter, how many babies did you deliver in your prior career?" Ryan smiles and tugs on my earlobe.

"It's different when I don't have to witness the actual event. Usually just a lot of screaming and the hee-hee-hoo breathing they teach at birthing classes, which can be remarkably loud in the telephone speaker. The paramedics or cops or whoever gets their first—they do all the dirty work. Emphasis on *dirty*."

"But, Auntie Hollie, that's your future niece or nephew in there. And he or she is gonna think the world of you." Ryan's eyes twinkle with an alarming amount of hope, a wistfulness that suggests he's daydreaming about the future fruit of his own loin. And while a nice loin it is, let's leave the fruit dreams for later.

"I don't even know what I want in a wedding. Do you?" I have to get this conversation away from babies.

"You being there is important. Also, it would be nice if I get to peel you out of a dress at the end of the night ..." He slinks his hand under my shirt and springs the clasp on my bra, but I slap him away and push his shoulders back with both hands.

"Ryan, I'm serious. If we don't give your mother something to chew on ..."

He cradles my ring hand atop his fingers. "Do you like it?"

"A little."

He smiles, clenches my hand, and kisses my bejeweled finger.

"These two smaller diamonds are from one of my mother's anniversary rings, from my dad."

"Ryan ..." I examine the setting with new eyes—the almost embarrassingly large center diamond offset by the two smaller but no less brilliant stones—a gift from Ryan's father to the woman he adored, and now shared with me?

"She didn't offer these before ..." With Alyssa, he means. Alyssa, the beautifully perfect, model-fit former girlfriend who was almost Mrs. Ryan Fielding but bailed when she realized that the hockey-wife life she sought was not to be if she stuck around. "My mother—she knows this—us—it's the real deal. She adores you, Hollie Porter, so whether it's four weeks or six weeks or a Friday or a Tuesday or the last day in November four years from now, I want you to be happy. Whatever you want, I want. No pressure. Okay?"

But by this time, those big sloppy tears only sissy girls make are sliding down my face and then our lips are crushed together and Ryan whispers against my head, "Remember—our raft, our rules," just before he returns his hands to freeing the girls from the confines of their lace and satin imprisonment.

(P.S. I'm grateful to share with you that they have fully recovered from the Great Sriracha Debacle of Burning Doom. Ryan and I have also discovered that whipped cream is wholly appropriate topping for use in bedroom sports.)

6

Surprise!

A week later, Miss Betty has grown bolder with her hints, casually leaving printouts in our office mailboxes from stationers she's found online ("This place does the loveliest save-the-date cards and invitations! And a coupon!"), leaving cake samples from the Joseph the chef on the counter with Post-It notes ("Hollie, what do you think about these? The red velvet is SO yummy!"), sliding honeymoon destination pamphlets under our apartment door ("Very private! Perfect for ... *hint hint*" <smiley face>), and taping lists of potential openings in the not-too-distant Revelation Cove schedule where a wee wedding might squeeze in "with enough time to get family and friends here AND before hockey starts again!"

When Tanner and Ryan did this week's supply run, they had specific instructions—that I did not know of beforehand—to pick up floral samplers from Miss Betty's favorite florist in Victoria. WHO KNEW there were so many bloody flowers in the world?

Bottom line: Miss Betty is not known for her subtlety. Although I have to say, in terms of cake, I'm leaning toward tiramisu. Me and that sample were inches away from getting a room so we could whisper sweet nothings to one another.

And then *The Oregonian* jumped on our story like a bull shark on an oil-lathered tourist and did a follow-up article to last year's sensational headline about the cougar attack—"Local Heroine to Marry the Hockey Player She Saved"—complete with a photo my dad submitted of Ryan on his knee in front of Steller Cove, me looking the part of the surprised girlfriend. It's led to lots of congratulatory emails and messages on the Revelation Cove social media sites (and a spike in the number of views of the Winterhawks barfing video, the gift that keeps on giving—thanks, Keith!). Even Moonstar (Tanya) my Non-Sister has offered her culinary support via a multitude of messages on the RevCove Facebook page, not so quietly advertising her wildly successful cupcake company with irresistible pictures (my mouth waters thinking about it, to be honest—please don't tell her), promising "the wedding cake to end all wedding cakes, full of organic goodness just for my darling sister Hollie!" Dad says she means well. I will only invite her to the wedding if she has gained two hundred pounds, sprouted a third eye, and developed a terrible case of adult acne. Because no one is supposed to look hotter than the bride, and when Hippie Barbie walks in, I might as well be wearing a mascot uniform.

To keep Miss Betty calm, I started a Pinterest account. And I thumb through the wedding magazines with Sarah, dog-earing page after page of cake styles, bouquet arrangements, dresses, bridesmaids' dresses—even though I only have two humans who would serve that purpose, Sarah, and Tabby from the spa, and Sarah is already worried enough about fitting into her only pair of maternity pants that still fit. But I want Miss Betty to at least see I'm making an effort to get into this wedding stuff, even if Ryan and I still haven't settled on a date. Neither of us is in a huge hurry—Miss Betty sort of is, reminding us that she's not getting any younger and she wants to live long enough to see all of her babies happy. I never knew mothers could be so good at guilt. So it's not just a single-dad thing.

And Sarah must've said something with regard to not pressuring me about babies—Betty's cooled off on that, which means the panic button in my head hasn't been pushed for almost a full week.

Sarah wastes no time outlining options for bridal shops we can hit in Victoria, Vancouver, Seattle, and Portland, not because she's impatient for a new sister-in-law but because she's so swollen, she can hardly move, and thinking about my future wedding dress gives her something to not cry about. Because she cries a lot lately, even though she's been staying here with us at the resort instead of at their cabin, just in case since Tanner's out a lot flying guests back and forth, and even though she still has at least four weeks to go, and even though Smitty's General Store continually brings in fresh shipments of those juice freezer pops she craves and even though Tabby and I give her foot and hand massages every other night, to keep the swelling down and her spirits up. In fact, the more time I spend with Pregnant Sarah, the more convinced I am that maybe I will remain Childless Hollie.

But thankfully, today's a work day, and my duties include escorting a group of other people's loin fruit around the island's shores, teaching them about the local birds and sea life and bribing them with post-tour cookies if they will listen and not bite or kick me. If the weather holds and the group is full of nice children and not holy terrors that should've been eaten at birth, I've been known to wrangle Tabby so she can help and we take them out on the boat to look for otters and other local critters. Always a crowd-pleaser. Plus other people's children are easier to corral on the boat—if they're little jerks, I tell them the local Daddy and Mommy Orca really like small packages of fresh meat to feed their new baby. (I've only had one kid report me. But I would've fed him to the orcas given the chance.)

See why me being a mother is probably not the best choice for humanity?

Hair in a pony. Snazzy Revelation Cove-embroidered black polo shirt and freshly laundered khaki cargo pants. Windbreaker tied around my waist. Breath fresh. Smile on. Camera bag over the shoulder.

Hand on the doorknob, my phone rings. Ryan. Awww. "Yo, hot stuff, you miss my boobs already?"

"Naturally," he says. "Hey, you busy?"

"Just coming downstairs. Are my junior adventurers assembling yet?"

Ryan is quiet.

"You there?"

"Yeah. Um, the kids are trickling in. There are only supposed to be five in your group today."

"Did the parents sign waivers for the boat?"

"Ummm ..." Shuffling of papers. "Maybe no boat today."

"Ryan, what's up? You sound off."

Quiet for a beat. "You're coming down now?"

"Yeah."

"I'll see you in a sec."

"Fielding ..."

He hangs up. The last time he sounded weird like that was when a cougar tried to eat his head.

I usually go the long way around, past the other employees' living quarters to say hello to anyone on break in the common area, but not today. What could be waiting for me that would make Ryan sound so strange? Oh, maybe Roger Dodger has pulled in on his yacht with his latest chippie. Philandering jerk. Or maybe Miss Betty has arranged for a male stripper to come and dance for a surprise bachelorette party—oh god, that might make Sarah go into labor. I bet she'd be the girl trying to shove dollar bills in the dancer's G-string. Then if her water breaks, he could help deliver the baby. What a story that kid would have for show-and-tell: "I was delivered by a stripper!"

Or maybe my dad's here and it's meant to be a surprise!

That would be so cool. It's only been a week since we saw him but I miss my dad. He makes the best pancakes.

I push through the door that will shortcut me around to the front of the resort, past the brisk spring air that ripples the water on the so-blue pool, around the sun patio and down to the front concrete walkway where the cherry trees are at the tail end of another gorgeous snowy bloom, and finally through the huge main doors.

Ryan stands behind the check-in counter, green eyes widening when he sees me, his bearded face a little paler than usual. Miss Betty is next to him as they talk to two guests, a man with greased-back black hair and a sport coat that doesn't match his slacks, a woman with a red scarf wrapped around her head and a zebra-print coat that reaches almost to her knees, the duo newly arrived if the tattered Samsonites at their feet are any indication.

"Good morning," I say, rounding the check-in desk.

I stop next to Ryan. His face has lost the rest of its color.

"Ohhhhh, there she is!" the woman in the red scarf exclaims, clapping her hands together, pulling heavy sunglasses off to reveal garish blue eye makeup and bright pink lips that do nothing for a face that has seen one too many baby-oil-soaked beach days.

And then she's pulling off her leopard-print gloves and skittering around the end of the counter like she's meant to be behind here, her very high-heeled shoes clicking in rapid fire against the hardwood floor, arms extended.

She pauses, arms still stretched. Is her coat mohair? "What, no hug for your mother?"

I'd choke, if there were any spit left in my throat.

Oh no.

No.

"I'm sorry?" I squeak, feeling Ryan's comforting hand against my low back as he quietly takes my camera bag.

"I know it's been a while, my darling girl, but it's me. Lucy Collins in the flesh! I couldn't let you be alone in your hour of need, could I?" From her pocket, she slaps a copy of *The Oregonian* onto the counter, folded so the picture of our engagement moment shines up at me in black and white pixels. "Every girl needs her mother when she's planning her wedding!" She claps like one of those creepy wind-up cymbal monkeys with fresh batteries.

And then her arms are around me, and I'm gagging on a plume of cheap perfume and a faint odor of mothballs, trying not to sneeze as coarse, bleached-blond hairs sticking out from under the red scarf tickle my nose shoved firmly against her head.

My mother?

7

Apocalypse Now

Apparently they have a reservation. But it was made under her male companion's name—Ernesto Finklestein—so it didn't trigger any flags last night when I printed out the day's incoming room charge sheets.

Because seeing Lucy Collins's name on a reservation would definitely have caught my attention.

I push past Ryan, through the small door that goes into the front office that Miss Betty has decorated to look like an old English tearoom and not the administrative headquarters of a resort destination.

He's right behind me, and then he's right in front of me, hands on my shoulders. "Hollie, I had no idea. She told me who she was. I would've said something when I called but she was standing right there—" Ryan tries to tip my head to meet his eyes but I'm shaking too hard. I push away.

"She can't stay here. She has to leave. Can someone get her back on the shuttle boat and get her out of here?"

Ryan quietly moves to my side and rubs my shoulders, the furrow of his eyebrows communicating that he is just as flummoxed as I am.

"How long is their reservation?"

"A week, I think?" he says.

"No. She can't be here."

Miss Betty pops her head through, eyes wide with a total uncertainty about what she should do.

"Hollie, sweetie, she's asking for you again. And your nature kids are waiting at the concierge desk."

Ryan hugs me, kisses my temple, and walks out at my shoulder, ducking through the low doorway, his strong fingers twisted with mine in solidarity.

Miss Betty processes Ernesto's credit card. Ernesto—that's a Spanish name. Finklestein is not. And he definitely looks more Finklestein than Ernesto. Maybe his parents watched a lot of Telemundo? Maybe he's an out-of-work magician and Ernesto looked more romantic on his banners than, say, Elliott or Ezekiel? Maybe he's in the witness protection program and this is the name they gave him?

I'm not sure if it's the haphazard hair plugs stabbed in a poor recreation of a widow's peak or the charcoal-colored evidence of a recent dye job smeared behind his ear or the gaudy, stuffed-full money clip that he sets on the counter for everyone to see—all the *RUN AWAY* flags flap in my head as if caught in a haboob.

Once again on the proper side of the check-in counter,

Lucy Collins flattens her hands against the marble. Some of her nail polish has chipped off and her cuticles have been gnawed and all but one finger bears a ring. She looks like a caricature, like a little girl who went on a midnight raid at Goodwill and cleaned out the Halloween section.

"So, Hollie Porter—although technically, you should be Hollie Collins Porter or Hollie Porter Collins—"

"Hollie Porter is my name," I say. "Why are you here?"

She looks genuinely hurt for all of three seconds. "I know you must have so many questions, but we have all the time in the world to talk, don't we?" Ernesto, finished with his paperwork, steps to Lucy's side looking disinterested.

"Let's get to our room, Luce. I need a drink."

Pleasant.

"Ernie, allow me to properly introduce you to my daughter. Hollie, this is Ernie; Ernie, this is my Hollie."

I'm not your Hollie.

"Nice to meet you." Ernie bobs his head and looks down at my boobs. "Come on, sweet cheeks. I'm not kidding about that drink." He grabs her ass and holds on longer than necessary.

Wait—I know what this is. This is one of those prank TV shows with hidden cameras and my dad is going to pop out from behind that plant and we're going to see that this Ernesto isn't a misogynistic, tit-ogling, ass-grabbing prick, and this woman is not MY mother because how could I be related to *her*—it's all a joke, right?

I look at Ryan.

His face does not say anything that would lead me to

believe that this is anything other than the freak show it's shaping up to be.

"Ernie, tell her the good news!" Lucy says, tugging on the arm of his mismatched sport coat, almost stepping on the toe of his scuffed white loafer.

"Nah. She's your kid. You do it." He picks up the suitcases and exhales his impatience.

"Well, Hollie—and Ryan? You're Ryan, yes?" She nods at his name embroidered in his shirt. "When I saw the article last year about how my brave Hollie saved you from that terrible cougar, I just had to keep tabs on what she was doing. I'm so proud of you!" Pinches my cheek. "And I tell absolutely everyone that you are my daughter!" Lucy digs into her ginormous snakeskin purse that looks like it's going through its own molt and holds up the article Jake Stephens did on us last year, post cougar attack.

(Side note: This woman's insult to fashion, and the animal kingdom, is legendary and terrifying.)

She refolds the paper and shoves it into her bag. "I wanted to come find you in Portland but I was in a bit of a fix last year ..."

"By fix, she means jail." Ernesto smiles with too much glee, revealing teeth that could use a good cleaning. I shudder.

"It was a misunderstanding about some unpaid parking tickets." Ernie laughs under his breath, met with Lucy's fist landing a solid punch to his arm. "*Anyway*, when I saw the latest article about your engagement," she shrieks so loud, I swear she's awakened the bats who sometimes roost in the building's eaves, "I just HAD to come find you! I tried to get in touch with your father but he wouldn't return my calls—obviously he's not over me yet—"

"Lucy, do you have a point? I have work to do," I say. My five charges are now squirming alongside their parents at the concierge stand behind us.

Her smile withers a little. "Yes. Well, me and Ernie, we thought it would be a hoot if we came up here to see you. We were thinking that maybe since you two are getting hitched, we could make it ... a double wedding!" She shoves her left hand in front of my face, wiggling the ring finger sporting a bauble that is too big to be real. "Wouldn't that just be the best? Mother and daughter, together at last, celebrating their newfound relationship as they tie themselves to the men they love?"

Miss Betty shoots tea out her nostrils. After a stunned beat, Ryan hands her a box of tissue and pats her back as she coughs the rest of her Earl Grey out of her breathing passages.

I ... I ...

What just happened?

"If you'll excuse me," my mouth says and then my feet are moving toward the little kids and somehow, my brain knows that autopilot is a good mode here and I'm smiling at the five children waiting for me, several decked out in coordinating beige explorer shirts and shorts. One little blondie even wears a wide nylon belt with enough gadgets to survive an apocalypse, which, in this context, is wildly helpful. We can never have enough first-aid kits or flashlights or canteens or specimen boxes. I'm hoping she has a knife or maybe an atom bomb tucked around the side I can't yet see.

Because it is a very real possibility that the end of the world has arrived, and instead of plague or pestilence or locusts, it has taken the shape of Lucy Collins.

8

Family Disunion

"Does everyone have their binoculars?" Small human faces stare up at me before tugging the straps on their Revelation Cove-provided, kid-safe binocs and planting their eyeballs against the forest-green plastic eyecups. I cannot hold my own lenses up yet because my hands are vibrating hard enough to power a small engine.

Don't think about Lucy Collins.

Ryan will figure it out.

The little kids are staring at you.

Say something, Porter.

"Okay! First, eagles! Over in those trees on the bigger island across the way is a big group of eagles. Do you know how they call a group of lions a pride?"

I can do this. *Focus on the moment.*

"I saw *Lion King* on Broadway for my birthday," says the kid with the stuffed utility belt—her name is Melody, "eight and three-quarters years old, thank you very much." In the walk from concierge desk to the edge of the far lawns adjacent to the golf course, she has emerged as alpha of our juvenile pack.

"I have *Lion King* on Blu-Ray!" Easton, age six, raises his arm and jumps up and down.

"This wasn't the movie, kid. This was a live stage play, in New York City. Have you ever even been to New York City?" Melody crosses her arms and stands as tall as she can stretch, staring at a diminishing Easton who clearly has no idea what Broadway or New York City is. Little Mel doesn't even flinch when a quick breeze slaps her blond pigtail across her lips.

"Don't you worry, Easton. I've never been to New York City, either," I say next to his head. "SO," attempting to resume control only this is really a sham because my blood cells are trembling like they've sucked down a banquet-sized carafe of Red Bull and honestly, why is Lucy Collins here and is she insane? A double wedding? "Like a lion pride, there is a special name for a gathering of eagles. Does anyone know what that is?"

No one knows.

"It's called a convocation," I say.

"That's a weird name for a group of eagles," Melody says, hoisting her own superior set of binocs.

"When you're looking, you might see some young eagles. You can tell because they'll have chocolate-brown feathers with a little white mixed in. You can really see that when they're flying. They also have a black bill, which is different from their moms and dads who have what color bills?"

"White?" "Orange?" "Rainbow colored!" "Purple!"

"Yellow. Adult bald eagles have yellow bills." Melody's binoculars hang from the strap around her neck and in her hand she holds a pristine, fingerprint-free tablet that she shoves outward for the other kids to see like a librarian who hates her job.

"Right, yellow. Thank you, Melody. Hey, what do you say we put the technology away so we can see some real birds in real nature, okay? Does that sound like a good idea?"

My suggestion is met with stink eye. "Daddy says that we should always be inquisitive about the world around us and that is why I have a tablet—"

"Your daddy is a smart man but we can see real eagles in real life, right now."

"This says that the bald eagle has been the national bird of America since 1782. But we're in Canada, so did Canada steal the bald eagle from America?"

"Nope. No, bald eagles live wherever they want to. They've been in Canada just as long as they've been in America."

"How do you know?"

"Bald eagles are a very important part of cultures both in America and Canada, which tells us they've been a part of both countries for a long, long time."

"My dad says America is better than Canada because Canada is socialist and your taxes are too high."

I am not going to have this conversation with an almost nine-year-old.

"Well, Melody, I am an American and I live in Canada, and I think both countries are very nice."

"Why do you live in Canada if you're American?"

"Because I work here at Revelation Cove teaching charming little kids like yourself about nature." I hope she can't hear the grit of my teeth.

"Don't you have your own kids to teach nature facts to? Mommy says that women who don't have children of their own are selfish and—"

"Melody, a lot of women choose not to have children and that doesn't make them selfish. It shows they are making the autonomous choice to be childless. Do you know that a lot of women travel instead of have babies? And there are some mommies who have babies and then leave when their babies are a month old and that means the daddy has to raise the babies all by himself." This conversation is totally inappropriate. I cannot work out my anger at Lucy Collins's sudden appearance on this bossy little girl.

Pull your shit together, Hol.

Fake smile pasted on. Lots of teeth. To show my aggressive nature. Like a chimpanzee. "How about we continue on with our nature walk so we can go inside and have our snack?"

"I can only eat gluten-free. And I'm allergic to peanuts," Melody says.

Then I'll be sure that you get a fresh batch of gluten-stuffed peanut butter cookies.

Turning to the other kids who have now started throwing pine cones at one another, "Does everyone have their binoculars pointed at the trees over there?"

Pine cone ammunition dropped, they reposition their binocs.

"I see one! I see one!" Easton shouts, his excitement parroted by the other three junior adventurers as they spot the raptors.

Melody is not looking at the birds. Her glare at me pauses only long enough to recite a list of facts about the bald eagle: size, territory, eating habits, mating habits.

"What are mating habits?" Easton asks.

Awesome.

"Mating habits are how the birds have sex to make baby birds—"

"Okay, thank you, Melody! Moving on! How about we go down to the shoreline and see about some tide pools? Who knows what animals we might find in the tide pools along the British Columbia coastline?"

Our ninety-minute tour du nature continues on much as it started, Melody spewing facts from her tablet about anemones and sea stars (the other four love that some of our sea stars are purple) and hermit crabs and urchins and barnacles. I try to ignore her, dodging touchy sea-creature reproductive facts so I don't have extra explanations to provide to perplexed parents later, taking the required photographs of each junior adventurer that we will then provide to the family free of charge, hoping with every click of the shutter that when I get back to the main lodge, Lucy Collins and Ernesto Finklestein will have spontaneously combusted and I can then use a ShopVac to suck up their earthly remains.

"How many of you have ever seen a sea otter at an aquarium?" Three of five hands go up. "Sea otters are my very favorite." I pull up the sleeve of my light windbreaker and show them the tattoo of Oliver Otter.

"Mommy says tattoos are dirty. And Daddy said that sea otters are nothing more than sea rats, that they chewed up the seats on his new boat when he was moored in San Francisco."

I am not too proud to admit that this kid has finally found the right buttons.

"Sea otters are not sea rats."

"Yes they are."

"Technically, they're an endangered species, and not rodents at all. They're members of the weasel family—"

"We had a ferret in Mrs. Gardner's class! Is a ferret a weasel?" Easton offers.

"Sort of. A ferret is actually the sea otter's cousin," I say.

"I have a cousin but he broke his arm when he fell off the roof of the McDonald's."

"McDonald's is a terrible place to eat. Their food will kill you," Melody says.

"I like McDonald's," Easton says, looking a little like Melody has just dimmed the light of his childhood.

"They do have good fries, don't they, Easton?" I offer him a high-five, giving Melody my best challenge face.

"They cook their fries in soybean oil and Mommy says

that soybean farming leads to deforestation and is threatening animal populations and making more greenhouse gases."

"She said gases," Easton says, ripping a pretend fart with his mouth. The other three eagerly join in until we have a raucous chorus of farting junior adventurers.

I bend down on one knee. "Melody, I must say, you are very, very smart. But maybe we can keep politics out of today and just enjoy how beautiful it is here," I sweep an arm like a Showcase Showdown model, "and maybe stop freaking out the other little kids with so many facts, hmmm?"

"Daddy says that a person who doesn't like to learn will always be dumb."

"Daddy sounds like a real peach, but you're with me right now, and I think we're going to have more fun if maybe we turn our brains off for a few minutes and just relax. What do you think?"

She bites her lip and quietly replaces the tablet into her pouch. I'm confident I have Melody wrangled and consider patting myself on the back for a brief moment, and then ...

"Daddy says that Mommy turns her brain off sometimes too and that's why he put a lock on the wine fridge."

Okay, whoa.

I am a wildlife educator, not a child psychologist.

"Excuse me, Miss Hollie, but I have to go pee-pee," Easton says.

I stand up, still unsure how to respond to Melody's very weird revelation. "How bad?"

"Pretty bad." He proceeds to bounce.

"I gotta go too!" Another little boy—Jack—sidles up next to Easton and mimics his bouncing, the two boys hopping and giggling, which almost certainly will make them pee and we will go back with pee clothing. I could always push them in the inlet "accidentally" ...

I look around us. We're too far from the pool house for them to hold it.

An idea blossoms. "Have you guys ever peed in the woods?" Gleeful cheers. I fear Melody's eyeballs will pop free of her skull. "What? They're boys," I say. "You must know, Melody, that boys have different equipment than we do. Easier for them to pee in the woods."

"Boys have penises, and girls have—" I break protocol and put my hand over her mouth, turning to Easton.

"Penis! Penis! Penis!" Jack sings.

Easton stops bouncing for five seconds. "My nanny says that mommies don't have penises. They have baby holes."

"It's called a—"

"NOPE. Stopping you right there, Mel." I kneel down eye to eye with Easton. "Hey, how old are you?"

"Seven," he boasts, puffing out his chest.

"How old are you, Jack?"

"I'm six but almost seven."

"Okay, this is what we're gonna do." We walk up the beach to where the grass meets the sand. I point at a cluster of trees about fifteen paces from us, far enough from any edges or cliffs that unless a kid gets picked up by one of those eagles, no one is in mortal danger. I then give Easton instruction that he is in charge because he's older, and that he and Jack are to scramble over to the trees, make their business, and come running straight back.

I've never seen two kids more excited to do anything *ever*. I should definitely see about adding, "Your child will have the opportunity to urinate against a real tree in our beautiful natural setting!" to the tour blurb.

As we wait, the remaining two girls chat about My Little Pony or some small pony-like animal—little kids have such facility with new friendships—but Melody has her tablet out again, her little fingers flying across the screen.

"You okay, Melody?"

Her fingers stop moving and a not-altogether-friendly smile creeps across her mouth. "Fine."

"You sure?"

Before she can answer, the Pissing Partners are rushing toward us, the amusement of what they've just done plastered across their little faces. We move on through the rest of the walk, Easton and Jack the best of friends now that they have shared such an awesome experience, the other two little girls picking wildflowers against the walkway edge that abuts the golf course, Melody oddly quiet but still with that smug grin.

As we approach the main lodge, Ryan rushes out toward me. "What did you do?"

"Wait, what?" He wraps a firm hand around my arm. "Kids, wait here for a sec while I talk to Concierge Ryan." We step aside and turn so our backs are to them.

"One of the kids—her mother just came tearing down to

the front desk demanding to know what is going on. You let some of the kids pee in the woods?"

Oh. My. God. "Are you kidding me?" I whisper, almost too loud. When I look over my shoulder, Melody's demon glare is fixed right on my face. "Two of the little boys had to go and we were too far on the other side to make it to the main building without one of them having an accident. So *yes*, I let them pee behind a tree. They loved it! Look at them!" I cast an arm toward Jack and Easton, still horsing around.

"Well, the parents are pissed. They want an explanation."

"It's *urine*, Ryan. I didn't allow them to smear each other with feces."

"You know how some of these guests are, Hol," he whispers.

"Who wants snacks?" I say to his face, effectively ending this conversation.

So that's what Melody was doing: texting her mother to let her know about the horrifying debauchery happening on our nature walk.

Inside the main doors, the shitstorm blows mightily. Miss Betty is trying to talk to Melody's very unhappy mother, perfectly toned arms flailing, red-faced despite the photo-ready makeup.

"Mommy!" Melody hollers and runs to her mother, as if she's just been the last child rescued from the *Titanic*.

"Honestly, what were you thinking?" The mother storms at me.

"Ma'am, really, I think you're blowing this out of proportion. I had two little friends who needed to go to the bathroom—"

"Which in civilized society happens in a proper restroom, not behind trees in full view of other children! What kind of sick person are you?"

"Not sick at all. Just didn't want to bring home two junior adventures with urine-soaked pants."

She glares at me for a beat longer and then bends to one knee. "Melody, honey, are you okay?"

Melody sniffs. "Miss Hollie said that you're wrong about women who don't have babies and she has a tattoo and she called Daddy a peach and she said that boys can pee in the woods because they have penises."

Hammer, meet Nail. Our coffin is near complete!

Melody Senior's face has lost any hint that we are going to laugh this off. She turns to Ryan, jaw set, the hand not hanging onto her demon spawn curled in a white-knuckled fist. "Mr. Fielding, I don't know what you were thinking when you brought *this woman* in to care for the precious children of your *paying* guests, but I demand an apology, a refund for the nature walk fee, and some effort on the part of management to compensate my family for this egregious misstep."

Just for fun, I slide the sleeve of my jacket up again so my tattoo is in full view. Melody Senior sees it, squints, and flips her tight, shoulder-length chocolate bob away from me.

"Absolutely, I will do whatever you request to keep you

happy, but I can assure you, Miss Hollie is a trained, certified educator who is also licensed in advanced-level first-aid—"

A clicking sound echoes from the hardwood-floor hallway extending to the right. "Hollie! Hollie, honey, it's Mommy!" Oh god. Oh god *no*. "Yoohoo!" Lucy Collins waves at me—wearing little more than a leopard-print cover-up over a brilliant tiger-striped bathing suit that shows far too much mammary, her leathery tanned legs jiggling like a half-drained waterbed as she shuffles toward us.

Dear Jesus, if you're real, and listening, now would be a good time to take me into your loving arms. I can bring the wine?

"Do you see anyone bleeding here?" Melody Senior hollers, not missing a beat. "No. I asked for ninety minutes of quiet time where my daughter could learn about the flora and fauna of your island and instead she returns with tales of public indecency and inappropriate lessons in the male anatomy and commentary about how I'm [air quote] wrong about a woman's obligation to reproduce?"

"Whoa, okay, stop right there—an obligation?" I can't stand here and listen to another second.

"Phew! These shoes are killer on my corns. So, Hollie, we're all checked in and Ernie is scrolling through the upper channels—if you know what I mean," she jabs a conspiratorial elbow into my side and snorts, "so I thought I'd come down and we can sit poolside and talk wedding plans!" Lucy squeals again. Now that she's standing in our midst, we all get to witness the glory of the melted tattoo that was probably once a bleeding, pierced heart, inked right atop the bulging boob that covers where her own heart allegedly rests.

My four remaining adventures slink closer to the ficus tree in the corner. I wish I could join them.

"Lucy, right now is not the best time—I'm working and sort of in the middle of something."

Melody Senior's eyes widen as she takes in Lucy's outfit, the unfortunate human cocktail of years of tanning and shoddy personal landscaping of vital areas and contradictory prints as offensive to humanity and animal kingdom as they were when she arrived two hours ago. "This—this is your mother?" she says, her smirk so vicious, I'd pretty much agree to donate a kidney if I could just knock the look off her Botox'd face.

Ryan's giant frame moves between us. "Miss Hollie, please take these junior adventurers to the kitchen for their snack, *okay?*" His green eyes flash.

"Yes, Mr. Fielding. Whatever you require, sir." I curtsy.

"Oh, snack time! I love snacks! Can I come along?" Lucy Collins says.

I spin, ignoring her, and gather my remaining adventurers while Ryan tries to douse the overprivileged flames of outrage snapping and cracking behind me.

In the kitchen, I stop the littles at the stainless steel sink just inside the swinging door and one by one, they take turns washing with soap and water before Chef Joseph, a giant Samoan of a man, helps me escort them to stools set up at one of the prep tables. Waiting for them are paper napkins printed with cartoons of our local beasts—sea stars, cougars, bears, eagles, deer, and yes, otters! This is my favorite part of the tour not only because it's almost over but because Joseph has two of his own kids at home in Nanaimo so he's awesome at keeping these buggers in line with his crazy stories and impromptu sing-alongs with the ukulele stashed atop the fridge.

"Who wants cookies?" he sings. My four remaining adventures—all gluten and peanut safe—cheer like Slurpee-high tweens at a Bieber concert.

"So, when are we going to have girl time to talk about our weddings?" God, for a blissful second, I forgot she was here. She leans across the silver countertop, tits to her chin, and throws a gross wink at Joseph as she helps herself to a stack of cookies. "We can stay a lot longer if you and your hunky fiancé can get us the family rate. By the way, nice catch, Hollie. That Ryan is a total stud. Is he good in the sack? Is it true what they say about hockey players?" She thrusts her hips grotesquely.

The record screeches; all the children stop midbite and stare at the lunatic in the tiger bathing suit.

"Miss Hollie will be right back, okay?" I throw a desperate look at Joseph. He nods in understanding and reaches for the ukulele. Arm looped through Lucy's, I drag her out of the kitchen before she has her balance. Cookies go flying just as Joseph launches into an upbeat version of "Somewhere Over the Rainbow."

I'd like to go over the rainbow. Any rainbow. Right this second.

"You wasted perfectly good cookies!" Lucy screeches.

I push her against the wall in the servers' hallway just outside the kitchen door. "You need to leave. You need to get your boyfriend or husband or whatever he is and you need to take the next scheduled boat or plane home, to the mainland or to Whitehorse or Siberia or wherever you want to go next in this giant world, but you cannot stay here."

Lucy Collins pushes her lower lip out. "You don't mean that. We're family."

"No, you are my biological mother, and that is where it ends. You deserted the idea of family when I was five weeks old. You showed up once when I was a kid to give me an otter toy. I'm now a grown woman and I can say for certain that we are *not* family."

She reaches for my wrist and pushes up my sleeve. "You really like otters, don't you ..." Her smile looks so proud, as if she's taking all the credit for something that is very precious to me.

I yank away. "Lucy, I work here. This is not playtime. Right now, I'm in charge of other people's children. When I'm done with that, I have my regular workload to tend to. I don't have time to sit and talk about old times we never had together. You should go."

Her eyes look like they're welling with tears but through the spider-leg mascara job, I can't quite tell. Until a black sludge trail trickles down her cheek. "I thought this could be a new beginning for us. I wanted to be there for you, I did—and I know you must be really mad at me, but this isn't all my fault, you know. Your father, he didn't make things easier—"

I put my hand up. "Stop. Right there."

She smears the goopy eye makeup across her cheek and snorts her sinuses like a trucker.

"It would be so great to have a double wedding. You know, like a fresh start for both of us. For us to share our big days and then we could be in each other's lives from today on."

"I have to go," I say, turning to go back into the kitchen.

"Hollie, wait." I stop but keep eyes forward. "I have a bad heart. Bum ticker. The doctor says I could die any day. Drop dead, just like that. We should really put the past behind us and cherish whatever time I have left."

Shiiiiiiiiiiiit.

Hand against the wall, I drop my head to my arm. I really need to talk to Dad. And Ryan. I cannot trust anything this woman says.

Slowly, I turn. Her eyes are hopeful, despite the smear of black and blue cosmetics that makes her look like she's been assaulted by Crayolas on a bender. A quick glance down at her ridiculously melodramatic tattoo and I can see pretty clearly the name etched in the cliché banner across the heart's front: *Hollie*. It looks way fresher than everything else. Which means it's probably new.

Which means this is a con.

"I will meet you after I get done working. Five o'clock, in the dining room. Come alone. Leave Enrique in your room. This is none of his business."

"It's Ernesto, and he's going to be your stepfather. He has a right to know about—"

"No. No, he does not. You either come alone and we can talk, or I can make sure you find space on the next transport to the Lower Mainland. Your call."

She sniffs and wipes her snotty face against the leopard-print sleeve.

"Five o'clock?"

"Yes. And dress appropriately. This is a family establishment."

I leave her in the hallway, the swinging kitchen door whooshing closed behind me as I walk head-on into a rousing chorus of Raffi's "Baby Beluga," a song my dad used to sing to me during bath time or on long car rides or when I had to have my teeth cleaned or just about any opportunity where he wanted to make me feel better, to remind me that I'm never alone, that we were the Dynamic Duo.

I didn't need Lucy Collins back then, and I sure as shit don't need her now.

9

Caipirinha Coupons for All!

If I weren't on the clock, I'd go hide behind the bar and finish the remains of whatever bottle had less than three fingers in it. I don't want to tempt fate with asking if this day could get any worse ... but it sorta feels like it couldn't.

Fate, if you're listening, just leave today alone. It's enough. I get that I've had a good year of blissful happiness that maybe I don't deserve, and you brought me a man who so far hasn't kicked me out of bed for eating crackers (or snoring or talking in my sleep or farting occasionally—YES, it happens, especially when Joseph makes those incredible burritos) and I've been working on being less cynical and on that whole more vegetables/less whisky thing and I'm really trying hard to not freak out when my junior adventurers eat their boogers or sneeze on me or even when they don't listen and I want to duct tape them to the flagpole down on the boat dock. Is this about me letting those little boys pee behind the trees earlier? I'm so sorry about that. They really had to go, though.

Honestly, Fate, between you and me—I don't see how Lucy Collins reappearing in my life at this late stage can do anything but signal the end of times. Right? Haven't I been okay for the last twenty-six years without her? Nurse Bob and I did okay. Didn't we?

Plus, I am a responsible adult these days, working to make other people's lives happy and pleasant, hoping to instill the next generation with the same love of nature that has kept me afloat since I was old enough to understand I couldn't have an orca living in my bathtub.

Why now? And me without my flask?

Upon redelivering the remaining kids to their families, I had to come clean about the peeing-in-the-woods situation. Thankfully, these parents got a good chuckle out of the whole thing, especially when Easton and Jack mimed a reenactment.

I sneak around to the rear deck to call my dad. I could really use my daddy right now.

"Hi, this is Bob Porter. Hope I did this right. Leave me a message. <Now what? Do I hit end or the pound sign?> Beeeeeep." He's either working or asleep from working. Or he's out throwing his homemade flies around the end of his fishing pole.

"Dad, call me as soon as you get this message. Lucy Collins showed up at the Cove. I really could use your advice. Love you." I stuff my phone into my ass pocket, hoping Dad will figure out how to access his voicemail without having to call me at the front desk so Ryan or I can walk him through it. Again.

"Hey! I've been looking for you. Didn't you get my text?" Tabby, mermaid hair draped over her shoulder as she leans out the opened glass and wood door, wiggles her cell in her hand but doesn't give me a moment to answer. "Dude, you have to come with me *right now*." She steps forward and pulls me inside by the wrist.

"Where's the fire?"

She drags me into the air-conditioned lobby and we sneak to the spa entrance that sits behind and to the left, hiding just out of sight of the main desk. We can see it, but it can't see us. "What are you—"

"Sshhh. Look." She positions my head forward, peeking through the branches of yet another indoor potted ficus tree, so I can see the check-in counter. A tall, very put-together blond woman, brown Vuitton luggage at her feet, stands next to a ginormous smiling man—he has to be a hockey player with that physique, which means these people must be Ryan's cronies. And likely I will be summoned for introductions. This often makes me uncomfortable, dressed as I am in my amazingly androgynous uniform, when many of Ryan's pals are fresh-off-the-runway stunners.

But my phone doesn't buzz as it sometimes does when Ryan's friends arrive, folks he wants me to meet. Other couples, some old, some younger, shuffle through the front entrance, eyes alight with delight at the lodge's impressive interior—the float plane has newly arrived, which means Lucy and Loverboy must've come on the earlier charter boat.

Ryan's not at his concierge desk, and that hunky specimen and his arm candy are still smiling and nodding, so that must mean Ryan is behind the counter alongside his mom and the other front-end clerk.

"I should go help," I say, stepping from behind the tree.

"Hollie—wait." Tabby won't let go of my wrist.

"Why? They probably need extra hands so no one gets pissy about having to wait their turn."

"Miss Betty and Ryan have got this. You stay here with me for a second."

"You're acting so weird. What is going on?" Just as the question finishes, Ryan appears in my line of sight offering a manly, one-shoulder hug to the guy and then a gentler, two-armed hug to the woman. A third party—a younger woman with onyx hair pulled in a tight ponytail and a squirming toddler in her arms—is summoned. The nanny? Ryan manages to get a high-five out of the littlest human who squees and giggles at his giant new friend.

"Who are they? Should I know 'em?"

The woman rests a hand against Ryan's damaged left arm, her expression one of concern.

And then with her next bright smile it dawns on me—I know that face. I saw it last in a photograph right before I ran into the woods and brought doom upon Ryan and myself outside Tanner's cabin last year.

I look at Tabby. "Alyssa. Isn't it ..."

Tabby's eyes look worried for a beat, and then harden as she wraps her arm around my waist. "Don't you worry, Hollie-Berry. Ryan adores you. She could've come through that door in nothing more than pasties and a G-string carrying the Stanley Cup and he'd still only have eyes for you."

"Why are they here?"

"Her husband is a friend of Ryan's. They played together on one team or another. Drew something. I can't keep hockey players straight. His team must've been eliminated, though, if the guy's here and not playing. Plus, no beard," she says. Ryan's is still firmly in place. "My stepfather says I'm a terrible Canadian because I hate hockey."

"Your stepfather? Who likes curling? What does that sport even *mean*?"

"No accounting for some people's taste?" she says.

I know Tabby's trying to help, but Alyssa, standing there in smiling flesh and blood in an off-white pants suit, the red soles of her heels proof enough that they cost more than I earn in a month ... I feel about three inches tall in my sloppy ponytail and super-sexy khaki cargo pants with crusty sea slime dried on my shirt from the day's earlier adventures.

"Remember, she left him. She doesn't want him anymore, Hollie, just like you don't want your old paramedic nerd."

"This is different. Keith never looked that good. She could be a model."

"She was. A model, I mean."

"Not helping."

"Pretty on the outside, vapid on the inside. Rumor had it that she cheated on him before they'd decided to split up, so ..."

And now this is just weird that we're standing here spying and talking about my *fiancé*. I fiddle with the heavy white gold band that still feels out of place on my left ring finger. But before I can push Tabitha back into the spa so we can pretend we're earning our paychecks, Ryan's head turns. And he sees me.

Followed by his hand waving me over.

Ah, shit.

"Good luck," Tabby says. "Come see me later and we'll play supermodel. Oh! We can practice wedding makeup!" Makeovers are what Tabby does when I'm not feeling great for whatever reason—she throws me into her chair and works her insane magic on my face. Her earlier plans to disappear to Hollywood sort of fizzled when she didn't get a bite from the zillion jobs she applied for down south. "No one wants to take a chance on a Canadian without a work permit, I guess." Her loss is my gain, and the gain of Revelation Cove's spa guests.

But as of this minute, I have on essence of makeup and I'm not feeling super confident but Ryan is still grinning at me and this introduction is going to have to happen one way or another so I should just get it over with.

I watch the patterns in the shiny hardwood floor, counting the reflections of the overhead light fixtures with each step forward.

"Babe," Ryan says, extending his arm and pulling me

into his side, "this is Alyssa, my buddy Drew, and their little fella, Theo." I smile and shake everyone's hands, including little Theo, feeling a bit sorry for the left-out nanny.

Social protocol be damned, I offer her my hand. "Hollie Porter. Nice to meet you," I say. She smiles quietly and offers me just her fingertips. I'm trying so hard not to check out Alyssa, stealing glances where it's not too obvious, but this woman was once engaged to the man I love—she was his before I was. She's seen his penis too. Oh god, she's done unholy things to his lovely body. I hope I'm better at being unholy than she was.

I'm sorry if these thoughts make me juvenile and petty.

I am not good at adulting, obviously, stewing in my vat-o-small-minded angst.

"So, Hollie, congratulations! Ryan tells us you two are getting hitched!" Alyssa says, her voice a notch too high. Maybe she's trying to hide her own stewing pot.

"Yes, that's the rumor," I say, leaning harder into Ryan, squeezing around his middle so it is very clear that we are super in love, like, more in love than any humans have ever been on the whole planet, in the history of humans and even in the history of those hairy, heavy-jawed creatures that came before humans who just woke up one day with a boner and boom! The first love affair was born.

"Have you set a date yet?" Drew asks, lifting an eyebrow at Ryan.

"Not yet. Still working out the details," Ryan says. Miss Betty leans into the conversation.

"Sooner is better, hey, Drew? Tell your old pal Ryan here to make me a grandmother."

Wow. Okay. That blush starts from my toes and moves clear through my split ends.

"Well, Hollie, if I were you, I'd marry this boy in a hot minute before someone else tries to get her claws in him. Ha! No pun intended," Alyssa says, growls once, followed by a limp-wristed tap to my shoulder. She looks down at my engagement hand, hoists it gently, and gawks at the hardware. "Wow, Ry, you went all out, didn't you?"

Folks, that little change in attitude brought to you by Envy.

As she lets go of my hand, I tighten my grip on Ryan's side until he flinches. As if in reassurance, he leans over and kisses the top of my head.

"Thanks for the advice, Alyssa." I smile tightly. "Well, awesome to meet you both. I have work to do. And please, do let us know if there's anything we can do to make your stay more pleasant."

"See, I just think that it's amazing that you work here too—you're a better woman than I am. What exactly do you do, Hollie?" I guess Alyssa didn't recognize the social cue that suggested I was about to leave.

"I'm a wildlife experience educator. I also help the photographers when they need it and pretty much help out wherever Ryan needs me."

Her smile diminishes just a click but brightens again. "Awww, so it really is a family-run business now, isn't it, Ry?"

Ryan shoves his right hand in his butt pocket, his tell that he's annoyed. He says that when he was a kid, his mom would make her fighting boys shove their hands in their back pockets so they couldn't punch the crap out of each other.

I love that he maybe wants to give Alyssa a little nudge.

Also, I now know why he cringes when folks call him "Ry."

"Yeah, Alyssa, it truly is. Tanner's running the charters, and he and Sarah are about to have their first baby, Mom loves it here, and now I've got my Hollie."

"But don't you guys get on each other's nerves, being around one another all the time?"

Ryan and I look at one another, the smile on his face melting all the frost off my heart. "No. Not really. I mean, she's not the greatest cook," Ryan says, flinching as I smack his stomach, "but with Hollie Porter around, there's never a dull moment."

"You should add that to your website," Alyssa says. Snidely. And then her flawless grin loses what's left of its sheen. I almost feel sorry for her. *Almost.*

Ryan pinches my ass, and then he and Alyssa's husband slide over to the counter to finish the check-in process. I will now head off somewhere safer, somewhere without my fiancé's ex-fiancée chewing me up with her eyeballs—

"Alyssa? Alyssa Burchfield? Oh my goodness, it IS you!" Enter Melody Senior, stage right.

"Itsy-Bitsy? No way. Wow, look at you!"

Melody Senior's name is *Itsy–Bitsy*? No. That's not real.

It falls out of my mouth before the censors catch it. "Your name is Itsy-Bitsy?"

Oooooh, that stare could refreeze the Arctic.

Alyssa turns to me, the women holding hands like first graders walking to the bathroom together, and lowers her voice. I guess she doesn't sense the death rays coming out of Melody Senior's laser-guided vision. "Oh, we used to call her that in college because she dated this guy who had a very tiny—well, you know …" Alyssa laughs. Melody Senior is not laughing.

I, however, am. Just a little.

"How fun that we can reconnect! How long are you here?" Alyssa says, turning to Miss Bitsy.

"Well, Jarrod and I were planning on staying through the weekend, but—"

"You married Jarrod? But—he … he was the one with the …" Alyssa holds up a hand, index finger and thumb demonstrating what is probably the tiny penis of the man Miss Bitsy dated, and evidently, married.

Melody Senior blushes a hue new to the color palette. "He had a surgical procedure," she says under her voice, a tight smile that means to end the conversation.

"Wow, modern science is so incredible, isn't it?" Alyssa says, looking at Melody Senior and then at me, as if I'm part of this conversation. I can't wipe the shit-eating grin off my face.

My phone buzzes. "Alyssa, nice to meet you finally. Enjoy your stay. And you and Itsy-Bitsy should stop by the lounge." I pull free-drink coupons out of a pocket of my cargo pants—everyone on staff has these to keep the guests happy. Plastered guests usually complain less. "Have a drink on the house."

I turn to move away, smile still in place. If glaring were an Olympic sport, Itsy-Bitsy would take home gold.

Tabby has texted: "Hol, come quick. Tiff gave some woman named Lucy a Brazilian and there's blood. She's threatening to sue."

Aw, fuck it. I'm out of cuss words.

10

Only Cake Can Save This Day

The raised voices reach me before my hand is on the spa's glass door. What I'm not expecting to see—and something I will never be able to unsee—is Lucy Collins standing with her spa robe open, boobs spilling out of her bra (this one a zebra print) and two ice packs shoved on her groin. Despite the apparent agony she claims to be in, she's doing a fine job berating Tabby and poor Tiffany, the waxing esthetician.

"Ladies, let's take this into one of the rooms, shall we?" I don't give Lucy Collins an opportunity to object. Arm draped over her shoulders, I steer her into the room farthest down the hall, away from the other customers having massages and treatments that are meant to be relaxing.

Once the door is closed, the tirade starts anew. "This girl

is the devil! She tore my skin! Do you know how sensitive that skin is down there? Do you?"

"Hollie, I swear to you, I followed protocol. It's just that Ms. Collins is very, *very*, um, hairy—"

"I am not!"

Tiffany looks at me like she might burst into tears. "Lucy, I can assure you that Tiffany is not the devil, and she certainly didn't intend to tear your skin, but sometimes with hairier regions on skin that is a little looser—"

"Oh, puhleez. She's inept. She doesn't know what she's doing!"

"Lucy, have you ever had a Brazilian wax before?"

Lucy Collins looks bewildered. "I heard about them on *Real Housewives*. I wanted to get one to make Ernesto happy." And she goes from scorned customer to weeping victim in less than a heartbeat. "I just want to make the people I love happy before my heart gives out. Is that too much to ask?"

I nod at Tabby, a motion that says *bring wine STAT*, and she's off like a shot.

"Lucy, I understand wanting to make your partner happy—"

"Do you have a Brazilian? Did you wax all your parts to make your Ryan happy?"

Deep breath in. "We're going to get you a little something to calm your nerves, and then we'll have a look at what's going on, okay?"

"I can't believe you hired a *sadist* to work in your spa," she says, sniffing in Tiffany's direction.

"Our employees are not sadists, Lucy."

"And why do you keep calling me Lucy? You should be calling me 'mom.'"

Tiffany's eyes widen—I meet her surprised glance and shake my head. "Tiff, I got this. You go ahead. Tabby and I can finish with Ms. Collins."

"Here we go! One wine spritzer with complimentary cheese plate!" Tabby breezes through the door.

Lucy sniffs at the hors d'oeuvres. "I shouldn't eat Brie. It makes me gassy." But she eats it anyway, washing it down with the wine spritzer in one long pull. I guess moderation isn't her specialty.

Once the wine glass is emptied, Tabby and I help Lucy onto the massage table. When the baggies of ice are removed, my eyes are assaulted with images no human should see on another, never mind a child seeing it on her mother.

Raw meat. Remnants of hair—a lot of hair. Lucy Collins makes my panty tarantula look like a daddy long-legs. Hers is serious Venezuelan jungle spider action. And the loosened skin and the—oh god, I do not want to look at this.

"I'll need a washcloth," I say quietly, slapping on the latex-free treatment gloves Tabby has handed over.

"I knew it. Is it hemorrhaging? Should we call 911? Am I going to bleed to death?"

Like a surgeon's assistant, Tabby is quick with the washcloth. I drape it atop her terrifying female anatomy. "Lucy, I can assure you that you are not going to bleed to death." And even though I handled the blood last year with the cougar run-in, it doesn't mean I'm over my fear of crimson oozing from body parts better left untouched. "I'm going to use Bactine to wash this off—it might sting—and then I will trim some of this remaining hair. When I'm done, I'll coat the injured areas with Neosporin and light bandages."

"Does this mean I can't have sex tonight?"

I swallow the bile riding the wave up my throat.

"And Ernesto just found a good channel. He wants to reenact some of—"

"Gonna have to stop you right there, Lucy. Let's keep the private talk *private*, shall we?"

"What? You don't want to hear that your mother has a healthy sex life? Your father raised you to be too uptight. Sex is a natural part of a happy life and marriage, you know." I yank a piece of leftover wax a little harder than necessary. "Oww!"

"Probably best if you lie still and be quiet."

Tiffany pops her head in with another wine spritzer—thank Jesus—and Lucy sits up long enough to gulp it down. It's not enough alcohol to get her to shut up but at least she's not yelling anymore. She rambles on about how her pre-honeymoon is ruined while Tabby and I strap on paper facemasks and use tiny scissors to mitigate the damage. The skin looks like a latex balloon deflated and then coated itself in raw hamburger because it was feeling sad and forgotten.

This is hands down the grossest thing I've ever had to do. Even grosser than pulling shreds of Ryan's flesh and muscle and tendon together with strips of denim. The difference? I loved him, even then. I would've done anything for him; I would do anything for him today. Which is why I'm torturing myself fixing a botched Brazilian on one of his resort guests who coincidentally happens to be the woman who gave birth to me.

When we're finally done, Lucy Collins asks for a wheelchair.

The front desk is quiet, all the new check-ins sorted, but as I yank the chair out of the office closet, Ryan stops me. "Do I want to know?"

When I look at his ruggedly beautiful face, the sting of frustration chokes off my voice. "It's fine. Later," I whisper. I push the folded wheelchair out of the office, to the spa where Tabby and I help Lucy Collins get situated. A flask has materialized from her enormous purse. She offers it to me. "Still working, Lucy." Even though I very much want the flask.

No way she can wheel herself to her room, so that joy falls to me. "Ernesto is going to be very unhappy when he sees what happened to me down there," Lucy says, taking a long swig.

"I'll talk to Ryan about giving you an extra night's stay, on the house. Will that make Ernesto less unhappy?"

"And free dinner. Four courses. That will keep him off TripAdvisor for a few days." She hiccups.

Their room is on the third floor, in the direction opposite our apartment. *Thank you, Ryan. So much thank you.*

As soon as the door is opened, Lucy Collins launches into a renewed performance of the "terror" she experienced in the spa. Ernesto, who pauses the Playboy Channel long enough to look at the damage, shrugs and makes some comment about how her mouth still works.

Ew. Ew. Ew. Ew. *I need an acid shower.*

"But my Hollie says we're going to get a free night and some free meals out of it," (meals plural?), "so she's doing everything to make it right, Ernie, don't you worry." She musses his hair, pushing it forward. So the hair plugs do go all the way to the back.

He slaps her hand out of the way and fixes his plume.

I help her out of the wheelchair and onto the bed, making a note on my mental to-do list to burn this duvet set when they check out.

"Is there any way you can just sit with me so we can talk about our weddings?"

"No. Sorry. I'm still on the clock, remember?"

Lucy points at the knitted throw nestled atop the sofa near the window. "I'm cold. Be a dear, would you?" She has to be talking to me because Ernesto has crouched in front of the open minifridge, pulling out whatever little bottles are left, which aren't many.

He looks over his shoulder at me but my attention is fixed on the very long, very hairy second toe poking through the sizable hole in his sock. Pretty sure that's nail fungus. "Maybe you can send up a bottle of Glenfiddich? With ice? You know, on account of her injuries sustained while in your care," he adds.

"Absolutely. I will have a bottle sent up right away." I pull out my phone as a show of good faith. Text Ryan: *Please send Glenfiddich to Lucy Collins' room. The whole bottle. And ice. Send one to our room too. Also rat poison or a time machine. Thx.*

"Okay, room service will get that right up to you. In the meantime, I need to get back to work so just take it easy and, um, you know, lie still for a little bit and try to relax. Do you have any Advil? If it hurts, take some Advil. Maybe read a book or watch a movie or something." I don't know what to say to this woman. Or her—whatever he is.

"But aren't we still going to meet for dinner? Mother and daughter time?"

Shit. I was hoping she'd forget. "You know, it's probably best you get some rest. I can have dinner sent up to you. Whatever you guys want," I step over to the small wooden vanity and extract the room service menu from the drawer, "it's on the house tonight."

"Did you hear that, Ernie? I told you they'd take care of us here."

Ernie grunts, kicks the minifridge closed with his fungus foot, farts, and slams the bathroom door behind him. Lucy laughs. "You might wanna clear out before he gets done in there. He's got some serious gut rot," she says, howling, waving a hand in front of her face.

We're going to have to decommission this room when these people leave.

"Show me how the remote works, would you? Ernie has hogged it. And this here is fancier than the one we have at home." She pats the bed next to her, inviting me to sit down. I pretend to have not seen it and instead stand next to the bed, the egg timer in my head counting down the minutes until Ernie is done in that bathroom and I could be facing death by fumes.

"Um, this button turns the cable box on and off. This one is the cable guide that tells you what channels we have—"

"You got movie channels?"

"Yes. HBO Canada. Another one is called Movie Central. Then there are Canadian channels that play sci-fi shows, sports, home and garden—"

"Any *Real Housewives*? I just love that show. I could handle being someone's trophy wife. Don't you just love that show?"

I respond with a tight smile. I don't need to watch *Real Housewives*. Working here is its own reality show with the likes of Alyssa and Itsy-Bitsy on the property. "This is the Discovery network, and higher up is Animal Planet."

She laughs and snorts. "Higher up is porn. Ernie found that already."

"Yes. Yes, you have mentioned that. Several times now."

A knock befalls the main door, not a moment too soon. I need to get out of here. "I'll get that!" Upon opening, I almost kiss Crispin the bellhop. "THANK YOU," I say quietly, taking the ice and bottle of single malt from his tray.

"Just put it over there and Ernie can fix me a drink when he gets done in the shitter."

Lovely.

I make sure she has access to the room service menu and then grab another pillow for behind her. Pillow plumped and stuffed, I'm about to make my clean getaway when she stops me with her hand on my wrist.

"We should talk, Hollie."

"Lucy, right now is not the appropriate time. I already told you, I'm working."

"Your boyfriend owns this place. He's rich. Why are you working like a dog if he's rich? You should be planning your wedding! Tell him you need some time off so we can sit and figure out what we're going to do. We need girl time! And me and Ernie, we can't stay here forever at these room rates, so it would be good if we could talk wedding stuff. Think about the headlines a double wedding would make with your fancy boyfriend and a long-lost mother/daughter reunion."

I stop short of yanking my arm free but stand far enough away so she can't touch me anymore. "Lucy, while I appreciate your enthusiasm, I respectfully have to decline. We are not having a double wedding."

"But don't you think it would be so—"

"No. We're not having some magical reunion where everything is suddenly okay. It's not. You left. You chose a different life. Dad and I had to get on without you, and we did. We did very well. Whatever amazing, fairy-tale plans you had about how this was going to go, I'm telling you that it's impossible. Ryan and I will get married when we choose to get married, and not a day sooner based on your desires or the desire of any other person on the planet."

"But my heart—my cardiologist says—"

"Are you medicated?" The anger hums from my heels to

the top of my head. I hate confrontation, but worse than that, I hate being manipulated.

"Yes." She hands me a bottle.

"This is aspirin."

"Yeah. The doctor said I have to take one pill every day with breakfast." Aspirin, eighty-one milligrams, is preventive only. Per training in my former life, I know this dose isn't indicative of a real heart problem. "Are you on anything stronger?"

She doesn't answer.

"If the doctor has you on aspirin only, it does not mean you have a heart condition serious enough to drop dead at any moment." I return the bottle to her.

"Well, he said I *could* develop a heart condition serious enough to drop dead if I don't take this." She shakes the pills at me.

"Lucy, your death is not imminent." *Unless it is at my hands.* "I am sorry that you are experiencing minor health problems but I will not be coerced."

"But I want to be a part of your wedding!" Her eyes well with tears. Again.

The toilet flushes.

Oh god. This is a DEFCON moment. I need to get out before I am assaulted with the remnants of Ernie's intestinal evacuation.

"I—I need to go. Please look over the menu and order whenever you're ready."

Just as I'm passing the bathroom door, it swings open. The blast that hits me sends whatever was leftover in my stomach from whatever meal I ate last bubbling right into the back of my mouth.

"Jesus, Ernie, light a damn match or something!" Lucy hollers. Before she can say another word to me or to Ernesto, I hold whatever breath I have left, slam the main room door behind me, and run down the hall to the nearest outdoor exit.

On the exterior third floor landing that overlooks the pool deck and sprawling golf course, I inhale the refreshing British Columbia air in desperate gulps, trying not to lose whatever marbles I have left pinging around in my sorry head.

At first, I don't recognize the buzzing in my pants pocket as anything other than a physiological reaction from sustaining an emotional trauma, but it's not my muscle vibrating. It's my phone.

"Hello …"

"Babe, where are you?"

"Why? Do you have more awesome news for me? Did my former best friend and all my old high school boyfriends just check in so they could remind me what a dick I am?"

"Awww, someone needs a hug," Ryan says. "Or is that what the whisky was for?"

"Ryan … this day has been the worst. What am I going to do?" I plop down onto the top step, head in my hand. "This crazy woman who says she's my mother—which, by the way, I have no real proof that she is who she claims to be—has, within mere hours, slammed into what is supposed to be the happiest time of my life and smeared it with her ickiness. And then after the bullshit with that demon child this morning, Alyssa checks in? Seriously? Why didn't you tell me they were coming? And why didn't you tell me she was a model?"

"Because I knew if I told you they were checking in, you'd work yourself into a lather. And you never asked what she did for a living."

"Yeah because that's one of those questions I should've put on my New Boyfriend Interview form—*Is your former fiancée a supermodel?*—right after *Do you fart in your sleep?* and *Do you like Yorkies?*"

"She wasn't a supermodel. Just a plain model."

"Oh, right. Yeah, that's so much better."

"But she never ate carbs."

"Someone give her a trophy."

"And she didn't like cake."

"Bloody hero."

"Not a hero. *She* never saved my life, Porter."

"So I get extra points because I saved your life?"

"Absolutely. You get all the points." I can hear his smile through the phone. "Babe, I'd love to sit here and wax poetic about how you have nothing to worry about, that you have your talons so deep into my heart that I fear it will stop beating, but I need you to stop by the office. If you're done doing whatever you're doing."

"We're going to have to call hazmat to deal with 330 after Lucy and her loverboy check out."

"I do not even want to know what that means. Just ... come downstairs, yeah?"

"Fiiiiiine." I stand from the top step and wipe dust off my butt. "Is this more bad news?"

The phone clicks off before he answers. Not a good sign.

Wednesday, I hate you.

11

Letter of the Law

"What does this even mean? Are they not renewing my work permit? Do I have to leave the Cove?" I scan the printed email from Ryan's lawyer looking for evidence that they're going to boot me out of the country.

"It means that Employment and Social Development Canada is requiring an assessment of your job before they will approve you staying another year. Means they want to make sure the job shouldn't be filled by a Canadian citizen instead of an American."

"But ... but this is *my* job. We're all from the same continent. I'm a good person. I filed my Canadian taxes. Don't the work permit people know that I am a positive addition to this country?"

"Keep reading."

I scan but my eyes are burning again because I am really tired and I just want to go find some cookies and maybe take a bubble bath and I am probably PMS'ing but I don't want to move back to Portland, not without Ryan. I thrust the email into his hands. I can't see anything with all these stupid tears clogging my eyeballs.

The corner of his mouth pulls into an understanding smile and he reads aloud. "'One simple and certain way to avoid this detailed assessment process, Mr. Fielding, would be to expedite your impending nuptials. Because Ms. Porter is in the country under a temporary work permit, once you're married, she can apply for permanent residence and the application process is often simplified if the candidate is married to either a permanent resident or Canadian citizen. As you were recently granted your Canadian citizenship, it will make it much easier for Ms. Porter to continue working in Canada without the hassle of constant renewal and possible denial of future work permit applications.'"

"Expedite the impending nuptials. So we should get married sooner rather than later."

"We don't have to rush into anything." Ryan sets the email down on the desk, and then closes the space between us. His long arms wrap around me and I fold into his chest. "There's no pressure, Porter. If you want to wait and they deny your work permit, we'll figure something else out. That's why we have an immigration attorney."

Still in his arms, I lean so I can fidget with the buttons on his shirt. "It's not that—I absolutely want to marry you, more than anything." He bends over and kisses me.

"But..."

"But we've been engaged for, like, eight days, and now

Lucy Collins is here, and she wants to be a part of our wedding and I would rather eat a casserole of broccoli and broken glass and I really just want this wedding to be about you and me, and not about everyone else and whatever *they* want. You know what I mean?"

He nods. "Whenever it happens, it will be about you and me, babe. I promise you."

"Can we talk about this later? I didn't even get one of Joseph's adventurer cookies this morning because dumb Lucy ruined everything, and I'm hungry."

"About that—what happened in the spa?"

I tell him. In graphic detail, at least until he begs me to stop. And then like a true fella, he goes to the antique icebox, atop which Miss Betty keeps some of her teacup collection, and pulls out a stashed bottle of bourbon from behind the first-aid kit. He doesn't ask; he pours about an inch into two flowered porcelain cups and offers me one.

"You're the best boss ever," I say, sipping. He downs his, sets the cup aside, and moves in, hands on my hips as he pulls me against him.

"I've never had an employee who is so ... accommodating." Ryan nibbles my ear, bringing on the giggles, his hand untucking my shirt.

"Stop! Your mom is going to walk in on us!"

"I'm the boss. I'll tell her to go dust something."

"I like your management style, Fielding." And as he kisses me, our comingled breath laced with the hint of aged bourbon, I am again reminded of one of the reasons I love this man so much: he makes everything better. Even ball-busting stuff like absent mothers reappearing with their creepy boyfriends and shitty, snobby resort guests with obnoxious children and supermodel ex-fiancées with perfect butts and shampoo-commercial hair.

The door opens. Ryan has one hand up the front of my shirt.

"When I said I wanted another grandchild, I was thinking the hanky-panky would happen in your own bedroom," Miss Betty says, pushing past us to grab whatever she came in for. Ryan maintains his hold on my boob.

"Mom, you know I will do whatever I can to please the women I love most."

She shuffles past and smacks her son on the ass. "Then set a date," she says, "and come deal with the people at concierge who want to book a whale-watching cruise." The door clicks closed behind her.

"That's your cue," I say, biting his lower lip. He groans, disengages his boob hand, and helps me stand straight, both of us fixing our uniforms so we pass muster. One final kiss and then I gather the teacups to rinse them in the office's kitchenette.

"Porter ... just in case," Ryan says before moving to exit. From his pocket he pulls out a folded Post-It note. "Available dates. Some soon, some not soon. Think about it." He winks and is out the door, the heartbreaking smile that made me fall head over heels pasted wide across his face.

I plop onto the sea-foam green chaise and look at the dates. The nearest one is in three weeks, then two months give or take a few days, then two more in November and then we're into next year. Five options? That's all I get?

This is one of those moments where Nurse Bob would shine brightest in my growing-up years. "Hollie Cat, make a list of pros and cons. Weigh each against one another, risks versus benefits, good versus bad," he says in my head.

What's the rush to get married in three weeks? Well, Hollie, according to the immigration attorney, your work permit is going to expire in August and there's a bunch of dumb administrative maneuvering that could see your job as wildlife experience educator go to a Canadian. Then no work permit means you're only allowed to stay in the country for six months, and then it's back to Nurse Bob's house—and Mangala the Demon Goat who still isn't dead despite efforts to the contrary. Living in the boonies outside Portland, with a demon goat, my dad's not-quite-ex-wife's primal-scream-therapy Thursdays, and without Ryan?

Never. Never times infinity.

Or, go ahead and marry the man of your dreams without a ridiculously long engagement that will only allow people to fuss and fester, apply for permanent residence, and then wait and see what happens with the work permit situation.

Three weeks from now makes a compelling argument.

Then again, only three weeks away means Lucy Collins might hang around and insist on being a part of everything, whereas if we set it a year from now, she might disappear again. Maybe there are more unpaid parking tickets she can be jailed for.

STOP. Am I really going to let this woman determine

the course of my happiness? Of my future with the person I want to spend the rest of my life with?

Man, this chaise is so comfortable.

And this throw blanket is heady with the scent of Miss Betty's wonderful lavender and citrus laundry soap.

I love that laundry soap.

I really love Miss Betty.

And I really love it here. I don't want to move back to Portland. I love my dad, but Ryan is here, and he is my future now.

I drape the blankie over my upper half and bury my face in the soft fibers. It smells so fresh, so much like what has become home.

Could we really pull a wedding together in three weeks? Shit, how would I even find a dress that quickly?

If I close my eyes for just a few minutes, I can meditate on it. Just for a little bit on this very agreeable chaise and the warm drop of bourbon in my tummy and no one knows where I am …

12

Save the Date

When I wake up, it's obvious someone has found me because my body is fully covered with the cozy blanket and the only remaining light comes from the stained glass lamp on the old Victrola cabinet in the corner.

A Post-It note on the pillow next to me: "You've had a hard day so we let you nap," in Miss Betty's characteristic cursive. See? That is what a mom is supposed to be like. She's not supposed to assault the viewing public with her scary fashion sense and freakish, unnatural body hair that makes her look as if she were exposed to nuclear radiation. She's not supposed to barge into your life and stomp on your plans—or hijack your wedding, for Pete's sake.

I know what I need to do; the nap is just what I needed. Clarity sits perched on my shoulder like a cream-drunk cat.

I check my phone—after eight—my growling stomach none too pleased with the day's shoddy nutritional values.

I refold the blanket and splash a little cold water on my face, swish with mouthwash from one of the tiny complimentary hotel bottles, fix my haphazard ponytail, just in case someone is out at the front desk. Upon nudging the door open, it's just Amber, the sweet but skittish night clerk who jumps if you say her name too loudly. I smile and ask gently if she's seen Ryan.

"He was heading out to the pool deck with a book just after dinner," she says, quiet as a mouse. "We wanted to let you sleep."

"Thanks. It was a weird day."

"Oh, Hollie, before you go, the woman in room 330 has called about ten times looking for you. She says she's your mother?" She hands me a stack of messages, the time stamps about twenty minutes apart.

"Like I said, it's been a weird day." I quickly scan the "very urgent" messages from Lucy Collins and dump them in the trash. She has given my customer service muscle enough of a workout for Wednesday.

Before I go out to the pool deck—Ryan likes to bundle up and sneak out there to read at night, especially if Miss Betty and Sarah and I are watching chick flicks—I must make a quick stop in the kitchen. See what Joseph left behind that I might be able to steal.

Shining at me from the middle shelf of the massive side-by-side stainless steel fridge is a plate with my name scribbled across the foil. Vegetarian lasagna and garlic focaccia bread still warm from serving, my watering mouth threatens to spill its banks.

I heat it up and stuff a Diet Coke in my cargo-pants pocket. Ryan Fielding may want to read his book in peace, but we need to talk weddings.

Moving down the long hallway that leads to the pool area, I smile to myself when I see the framed sports jerseys decorating the walls. A year ago, I wouldn't have been able to tell you what these weird shirts were hanging in expensive frames. My education commenced quickly, however, as soon as Revelation Cove's pesky concierge argued that I would not be allowed to remain in this great country if I didn't learn about the beloved national sport.

Now I can tell you most of the teams just by logo recognition, about the Original Six and which team has won the most Stanley Cups, about the ongoing restructuring efforts underway by the Vancouver Canucks (even though they keep trading away my favorite players) and how the only year the Stanley Cup wasn't awarded was 1919, the Seattle Metropolitans versus the Montreal Canadiens, when the Spanish flu ravaged the globe and took the life of Canadiens' defensemen Joe Hall.

I didn't sit and listen to Ryan go on about hockey so that I could earn his affections or appear to be a good girlfriend. I did it because I love watching people talk about the things that make their hearts thrum. I'd listen to someone talk about the stock market if they told the story with a fire in their eyes. And like I said before, for every hockey fact, Ryan gets an otter or related sea life fact, and as doting boyfriends are wont to do, he remembers them. Because he knows it's important to me.

A hockey expert I am not, but I've learned a lot.

I'm at the wood and glass door that leads to a short landing and steps down to the pool deck, dinner plate in hand.

I don't push the door open.

Because while Ryan's bundled up on his customary lounge chair along the deck's far side, long legs stretched in front of him, hiking boots in place to keep warm on a nippy May evening, he's not alone. Alyssa is leaning over him, her long hair pushed to one side so I can see her face, her boobs not exactly concealed in a shirt that is way too thin with a neckline that is way too low for this time of year in this part of the world.

Oh my god, what do I do?

Do I barge out there and dump my dinner over her head and push her into the water?

Do I open the door and scream at her to get away from my man, that she had her chance and screwed it up?

Or do I slink back to the apartment and wait for Ryan to come in and see if he has something he needs to tell me?

I'm frozen with uncertainty. No one else is on the pool deck; no guests are in the hot tub, but why would they be because so many of the rooms have private soaker tubs.

Alyssa and my boyfriend are out there alone, and oh my god, she is moving—no longer leaning over him—now she's straddling him. Across his lap. Her girly bits aren't far from his boy bits and she's leaning forward, flipping her hair, and I can only guess that his view is boobs, boobs, boobs.

I can't see their faces. It doesn't look like they're kissing.

I have to dump my plate—somewhere, anywhere—so I

can go out and nix the shit out of whatever is going on. But once my hands are free, they do nothing but rest on the varnished driftwood door handle, my legs like concrete pillars, my chest feeling full of foam with no room for breathable air and my head screaming that this isn't happening. Ryan doesn't want her anymore. He told me so. Tabby told me so.

Right?

And then movement—Ryan's hands are on her upper arms, pushing her away. Pushing her off. Not caring if she falls onto the ground. Standing above her, saying words I can't hear because this confounded double-pane glass is too thick but his face doesn't look pleased, and her cowering on the pool deck doesn't last very long because she's up on her feet, her arms flailing like she's got a litany of Very Important Things to screech at him.

Oh, he's pointing at her. The mean finger. I've only seen that once when he and his brother were having a row after a poker game that had been soaked in too much tequila.

And then he's moving around her, but she grabs at him and he yanks free and she loses her balance and *almost* goes into the water but he clamps onto her forearm before she splashes in, and lets go as soon as she is securely upright, her mouth still moving, her face still angry and I think those might even be tears but he's got his hands up, fingers spread, palms out, in front of him, backing away.

Walking away from her, shaking his head, hands into fists, then open, fists, then open. And toward the stairs that lead exactly to where I am.

I'm easing backward down the hallway, one tiny step at a

time, my lasagna plate abandoned on the carpet, the sweating, cold Diet Coke can leeching through the fabric of my cargo pants adding extra oomph to the freaked-out chills cascading up and down my arms and legs. I don't know what else to do and I don't want to be that girlfriend who spies or doesn't trust her partner but what was I supposed to do when I saw her sitting on his lap like she wanted to do a vagina dance there in front of all the trees and stars and owls and any hotel guests who might be peeking out their windows at that exact moment?

The door swings open; Ryan's head is down. I stop. He looks up, his jaw set, eyes wide—almost with guilt. His lips part, as if to say something. Mine are trembling.

He rushes at me, his hands on each side of my face as he dips down and our lips meet. I choke on a sob as he pulls away.

"You saw."

I nod.

"Do you ... are you having second thoughts?" I whisper.

He lifts my ring hand and kisses my adorned finger.

"I'm going to show you how much I am *not* having second thoughts."

Without saying another word, he pulls me into his side. We walk down to the apartment. Inside, I stand against the marble kitchen island/counter hybrid and watch him move from our bedroom to the kitchen. Then the bathroom. Then he's in the kitchen, pulling two bottles of champagne from the fridge. He stops at the hall closet and grabs heavier coats, one for each of us.

"Put this on, Porter," he says. Then he hoists the heavy flannel quilt off the couch and throws it over his shoulder. He hands me the duffel he has magically prepared, his last motion to snag the boat keys hanging on the hook by the door.

I don't have to ask. I know where we're going.

We pause long enough to knock on Miss Betty's door. When she answers, Ryan tells her we're going out for a nighttime cruise and we'll be back for morning checkouts. I wave to Tanner stretched on his mom's sectional, his pregnant wife dozing against his chest, his hand resting protectively across her stretched abdomen.

"Don't do anything I wouldn't do," Miss Betty teases.

And then we're off, our fingers laced together like we're stitched that way, down the residence hallway and then through the wider guest-room hallway and through the quiet lobby. A head nod to quiet Amber and we're out the front double doors, inhaling the fresh smell of wet grass from the soaker sprinklers keeping our lawns green and the tang of seawater and under a cloudless night sky that is absolutely bursting with stars and distant galaxies given the lack of light pollution, serenaded by our footsteps and the distant hoot of an owl who is probably getting ready to murder some rodents.

We're quiet as we move down the concrete path, then along the wooden dock, the water so black between the LED lampposts. The water at night still scares me, no matter how often I go near it after the sun has gone down.

It doesn't take long to get the family's older cabin cruiser untied—the same boat he used last year to rescue me the night I had my thunderous rowboat-and-orca adventure. Gliding away from the dock, the rumble of the motor is little more than a frothy gurgle under the boat's rear end. Inside the cozy cabin, I stand at the helm, Ryan's long arms wrapped around me as he steers, my back curled against his chest, feeling his heart beat against my shoulder blade, us breathing the same air but not privy to each other's thoughts because it feels okay to be quiet for a bit.

We move about a half hour south of the resort and tuck the boat next to a narrow beach in water protected from any potential winds by a rocky outcropping. As Ryan drops anchor, I throw our bag into the forward cabin sleeping area, although with any luck, there won't be a lot of sleeping tonight.

When I emerge, he's sitting on the built-in couch, legs stretched in front of him, his face serious. I sit next to but facing him, one leg under me, my hand atop his that he quickly buries with his other hand. We're quiet for a revolution of the clock's ticking secondhand, just looking at one another, me trying not to get lost in the stormy depths of his green eyes. And then I have to know.

"She wants you back," I say.

"She's unhappy. And seeing me happy makes her crazy."

"That's shitty."

"That's Alyssa."

"And they have that little baby. Is her husband a dick or something? Is he a cheater?"

"Drew? God no. He's so smitten with her. Whatever

Alyssa wants, Alyssa gets. But that's the problem—he's not much of a challenge because he's so eager to please."

"And she takes advantage."

"Alyssa's all about the conquest. She likes drama and strife."

"Did she get that with you?"

"We were younger and wilder. I didn't want to get married and she did, so it became a power struggle."

"But you were engaged."

"Only because she kept threatening to leave me if I didn't propose."

"Would that have been so bad? Her leaving you?"

He laughs under his breath. "I didn't know what I wanted. My career was bouncing me all over the place. We'd break up and get back together, and then break up and get back together. She couldn't stand not being a future hockey wife, but she wouldn't give up on what she thought was going to work out well for her."

"But there are other hockey players she could've chased."

"She chased a few."

"And she kept coming back to you."

"It was not a healthy relationship, Hollie."

"Then what was tonight all about? She's a hockey wife. She has the big house and the handsome husband and what looks like the perfect life."

"Like I said, she relishes a challenge. Drew's not a fighter. He's a monster on the ice, but at home, he's a teddy bear."

"And Alyssa needs someone to box with."

"Pretty much." Ryan exhales, a tired sound.

My voice is smaller than I mean it to be. "Does any part of you miss her?" I think of how she was straddled across his lap. Her beautiful body, touching him so intimately, clearly an invitation. How could any man resist?

Ryan sits up straighter and grabs my upper arms, almost painfully. "Hollie Porter, I need you to hear me when I say this: there is no such thing as perfect, but if there were, you are my perfect. There is nothing more in this world that I want than a future with you. Whatever that means. Whether we're married or we just live together until our hair falls out or whether we have babies or whether we adopt an army of sea creatures. There is just you."

He cups my face, a soft thumb brushing across my cheek, his eyes fixed on my lips.

"But she's so beautiful. Everything about her—her body, her hair—"

"Porter, really? Are you being serious right now?"

I pull back a little. "Yes, Ryan, I am. It's hard to compete with someone like that."

"Right, because you're so hideous and your personality is so revolting," he teases, the mischief in his eyes reflecting a lightening of the mood.

"That's not what I mean," I say. I don't want this to turn into me swimming in my insecurities.

"Everything you think she has? It's fake. It's a ruse." He moves onto his knees and wedges himself between mine, adjusting my legs around him, leaning me into the stiff-foam couch cushion. "Everything you have ...," he says, unzipping my coat, sliding his hands under the layers and atop my shoulders, sliding my coat down my arms until it's shed behind me, "is everything I want."

He untucks my black Revelation Cove polo and eases it over my head, loosening my ponytail so he can fan my hair over my shoulders.

I return the favor and remove his coat and shirt, goosebumps rising on our skin from the contrast of chill in the boat's cabin and the fire burning from our respective fingertips. I can't help but run a gentle hand down his damaged arm, the texture of the healing scars squeezing my heart in constant reminder of that day.

He kisses me, and I return with equal fervor, his hands buried in my hair, my head supported by the impressive diameter of his palm as he pushes me into him, kissing me so hard that it feels like he will fall into me and we will never be separated.

Ryan straightens, breaking our connection, breath short in our chests, his voice low. "Last year when I found your scrawny ass under that tipped-over boat, inches away from being eaten by a hungry pack of raccoons, I wanted you. Right then and there. You with your sore ankle and your little black dress dripping all over the carpet, your smart-ass mouth asking for whisky despite the obvious hypothermia. I wanted you right there. I wanted to tear that dress off and mark my territory like any self-respecting caveman." The harnessed power of this man's smile could bring an end to our reliance on fossil fuels. Groan all you want, but it makes me want to lick him.

"A gaze."

His head tilts like a confused puppy.

"A group of raccoons isn't a pack. It's called a gaze. Or a nursery."

"You are such a nerd," he says.

I kiss the bridge of his crooked nose and bite his lip, talking against his mouth. "And last year during your rescue endeavor, if you'd given me the whisky like I'd asked instead of being all chivalrous and gentlemanly, I would've taken the dress off for you."

"I'll bet you say that to all the boys." He kisses my neck, a deft hand unclasping the bra hooks.

"No, just the boys who come out on their boats late at night dressed in yellow slickers like salty seamen."

He chuckles. "You said seamen."

And then he's up, his excitement obvious against his pants, eyebrows waggling.

"You're pretty impressed with yourself, aren't you," I say.

He tugs me to my feet, tosses me over his shoulder, and slaps my ass. With the curtain divider pushed aside, he tosses me onto the wall-to-wall mattress in the forward cabin and then takes his time removing my shoes and socks, and finally my pants, until I am in nothing more than panties. With the speed of a man who knows he's going to get what he wants, he strips down to his boxer briefs and slow-crawls up the bed until our lips are again aligned.

"Wait—" I put a hand against his chest. He lowers himself closer to me so I can feel that certain parts of his anatomy are not interested in waiting. "Ryan, wait." He pushes onto his right side without untangling our legs. "When I saw you guys ... I was on my way out to talk to you about a wedding date."

"And?"

"Your Post-It note listed five options."

His lips press together.

"I picked an option of your five," I say.

"Anything you want, Porter." He groans and leans into me again, nuzzling my neck, biting at my jaw. I nudge him away for another beat.

"Three weeks."

His eyes pop open. "Really?"

"Let's just do it. I don't want a huge wedding, and we have pretty much everything we need—a venue, Joseph and his team can bake the cake, unless my non-sister freaks out and wants to do it, we can find a photographer easy enough through the resort's contacts. Really all that leaves is making sure your family can get here, and finding a dress and a tux."

"You've been thinking hard this afternoon," he says, kissing one side of my mouth, and then the other.

"I don't want to be without you, ever. And I don't want to drag this out so it becomes some stressful thing that takes over every waking moment. I want to move on to the part where we plan whatever grand adventures are coming to us next. And if that means we step on the gas and just do it, then I'm in."

Ryan answers with his hands, removing the remaining

pieces of clothing from our bodies and pinning my arms above my head, me giggling as he bites my collarbone.

"Three weeks it is," he whispers. "Here's to the future Mrs. Ryan Fielding."

There are no more words after that.

13

Embrace Thy Enemy—Because Drowning Them Is Illegal

We sneak into the resort early enough that Miss Betty won't notice that I'm walking funny or that her son looks like the cat who ate the canary—beak and all.

Ryan crouches in the shower so I can wash his hair but also so I can do a few range of motion exercises the physical therapist gave us for when he "overuses the arm." Last night's activities might qualify as overuse.

He winces with one revolution of the shoulder joint. I stop. "No, it's good. All worth it," he says, blowing a raspberry on my naked belly.

"Do you think your mom will be okay with June 14?"

"Are you kidding?"

"Shit—Ryan—wait—when's Sarah's baby due?"

He stands. "Right around then, I think? But if she gets any bigger, she's gonna blow."

I rinse my hair, talking through the water streaming over my face. "Should we wait? Let's talk to Tanner and Sarah before we tell your mom. I don't want to make this about us when it's supposed to be their special moment with the new baby."

"Tanner's going to tell us to go for it."

Water off, Ryan hands me a fluffy towel. One of the perks of living in a hotel: nice towels, always fresh, always laundered. Gone are the days of stacks of dirty towels in the crappy bathroom in our tiny Portland apartment that the Yorkies sometimes used as a litter box. How did I ever live like that?

Ryan, half dressed, wastes no time in texting his brother. By the time a fresh uniform is slapped onto my body and my hair is tightened into a French braid, Tanner has texted back.

My soon-to-be husband leans against the bathroom doorjamb, evidence of our shower still trickling down his chest. I have no control over my hands when Ryan has no shirt on. "Tan says we do it. Not to worry about the baby."

"But did he ask Sarah?"

Ryan looks at his phone and reads the text: "'*Sarah agrees but says if she goes into labor on the same day, you have to have the wedding in her hospital room.*'"

"Wouldn't that be something ..."

I lead Ryan over to the dining room table and sit him in the chair so I can rub sunscreen and vitamin E oil into his damaged arm. The last surgery reduced some of the scarring but the plastic surgeon told us to keep the sunscreen and vitamin E regimen up until the scarring had settled. Or at least until the next surgery.

My phone must feel lonely that Ryan's is getting all the attention. It jingles its little tune. And then another. And another. One text jingle can't even finish before another one interrupts it.

I'm afraid to look.

"Shit, how did she get this number?" The lingering happy feelings that Ryan gifted to me last night are now cowering in the corner as their bigger, meaner cousin—Anger—lopes into the room. "I gotta go. Lucy Collins is in the dining room freaking out because they made her eggs wrong."

"Don't let her get to you, babe." Ryan stands, thanks me for my expert lotioning skills, and kisses my temple. "We'll talk to Mom after morning checkouts are done, yeah?"

I give him a thumbs up and grab my card key off the hook before leaving the apartment, but what I don't say is that I'd love to tell his mother about our marriage plans, as long as I'm not busy filling Lucy Collins's boots with concrete and throwing her off the island's edge.

~ ~ ~

If you've ever read *Titus Andronicus*—a scandalous high school teacher broke the school's ban on this play and let us read it in twelfth grade English lit—there's a scene at the end in which Titus hosts a dinner party where he exacts his revenge on the evil Tamora, Queen of the Goths and later Empress of Rome, by serving her a meat pie made of her own (rapist) sons, Chiron and Demetrius. Titus also then kills his own daughter, Lavinia, out of mercy as she was horribly victimized by Tamora's sons, and then Titus kills Tamora and is in turn murdered by another dinner guest, Emperor Saturnius, who is then killed by Lucius, Titus's son. In one short scene, there are five murders. Bottom line: it's a bloodbath—with pie.

The dining room at Revelation Cove sort of looks like that right now, guests dining, minus the blood, plus the shrieking harpy in the corner. Lucy Collins is dramatically berating the table hostess and chef and anyone else who works in the kitchen for screwing up her breakfast—quiche, no less—and it dawns on me that baking her into a pie might prove an interesting culinary undertaking. You know, if I were into murder. And baking.

When I've heard enough, I excuse the hostess who is seconds from tears. With both hands on Lucy's shoulders, I force her down into the wheelchair she apparently still needs, and then lean over her. "Listen to me very carefully. Are you listening?"

"Have you seen what they did to this quiche? It looks like snot!" she yells, flicking the plate sitting in front of her, which, by the way, looks totally edible and very un-snotlike.

"I'm going to say this one time, for the benefit of you

both." I look at Ernesto who doesn't seem to give two shits about what's going on. "This place here?" I wave my hand around in front of me. "It belongs to Ryan and his family and his business partners. It does not belong to me, nor to you. You do not get special privileges here simply because we have common DNA. It does not mean, on any level, on any day, that you are allowed to abuse the staff who work here, whether it be in the spa or the kitchen or the person who comes in to clean the crap splatter out of your toilet."

"But—"

"This is your last warning. One more outburst from you, and I will drag you out of this resort by your hair and ferry you back to the US border myself. Do you understand me?"

Lucy looks at me with spit and fire in her eyes, but two can play that game. And she's on my turf. "I wouldn't be so edgy if I weren't gravely injured from your sadist spa girl. Or if you'd stop ignoring me. I came here to see you. I came here so we could talk about our weddings, but you're just too busy to make time for your mother."

I pull a chair over from an adjacent empty table. Maybe if I talk really slowly … "Lucy, I appreciate that you've traveled this long distance to see me, however suspect your motives may be. But you've had twenty-six years to 'spend time with me.' And I want you to understand that I do not now, or ever, want to have a double wedding. I thought I made that perfectly clear, but I'm repeating it for you now. If the two of you would like to have a small ceremony here at Revelation Cove, we can arrange for the local marriage commissioner to come on over and get it done, and then you can stay for a week, go home, and move on with your lives."

"Why are you so opposed to having a double wedding? I am your mother! What greater expression of our mother-daughter love could there be but to get hitched on the same day?"

This woman cannot be related to me. There has to be some mistake.

My phone vibrates in my hand. My dad. I have to talk to him. I put my finger up to truncate Lucy's diarrhea of the mouth. "Heyyyyy, can I call you in five minutes?"

Call disconnected, Lucy glares at me. "Was that your father?"

I don't answer her.

"He is so rude. I've tried calling him, you know. Over the last year while I was trying to find out where you were living."

"Leave it alone, Luce, for Christ's sake. You found your kid. Stop nagging on your ex-geezer," Ernesto says with a mouthful of eggs Benedict. "I almost feel sorry for the guy." A blob of Hollandaise falls off his lip and onto the table linen.

And then the sugar tap is back on, thick like sap coming out of a Quebec maple, and Lucy conjures tears as she leans across and drapes her hand on my wrist, her fingers nicely painted a coral pink—guessing her spa visit yesterday wasn't a total waste. "I just want to get to know you. I had to work very hard to save the money to afford this trip."

Ernesto's laugh gives the world an unpleasant view of another half-chewed bite of his breakfast.

"Well, I'm sure your employer is anxious to have you back, rested and ready for action," I say.

"Her employer? Stop! You're killing me," Ernesto says, slapping the tabletop. "Did she tell you where she works?"

Lucy glares across the table. He stuffs more food in his mouth, head shaking in amusement. "Anyway," she hisses, "I just want to be a part of your life, Hollie. Can you give me a little of your time?"

I'm not interested in her being a part of my life. And I have to get to work. I slide my hand free and sit straight against my chair. "How are you feeling today? Down ... there?"

"It's very tender. But you giving us a few free nights here at the hotel is really making it feel better." Tears magically vaporized, her cheesy smile reveals lipstick on her teeth.

I open my mouth to protest—I agreed to no such thing. I said free dinner, maybe a discounted room rate. I never said anything about *multiple* free nights. Whatever. I'll tell Ryan to take it out of my next check. It's so not worth arguing over.

"I have work to do. Please, stop harassing people. Be nice. Remember—final warning."

As I stand, she looks up at me with melodramatic longing. "Say hi to Bob for me."

I have Dad's number queued before I've made it down the three steps leading out of the bright dining area.

"Hollie Cat, what's going on?"

"Dad, oh my god, the last twenty-four hours have been the absolute worst." Well, except for the eight hours Ryan and I spent on the boat that were the absolute best but my dad doesn't need to know that part. I push open the front door and wander down the path a ways so I'm out of earshot of guests and staff alike.

And then I sort of go off, explaining everything that has happened but most notably the explosion of Lucy Collins into my otherwise serene life. He lets me rage as I tell him about her plans for us to have a double wedding, about the spa incident, how she just freaked out in the dining room and made a total scene and now she's thinking that I'm going to just give her a blank check so she can stay at the resort until she decides she's ready to go.

"You have to get her out of there, kid. That woman is trouble."

"I'm half tempted to call Keith and see if he can get one of our Bureau friends to run her for outstanding warrants."

"That's not a bad idea, Hol."

"And then what? The RCMP aren't going to come up and get her unless it's something really bad, something extraditable like murder or assaulting an aesthetician with her felonious grooming habits."

"I don't think murder is her speed."

"You wouldn't say that if you saw her wardrobe."

Dad snorts. "Just don't let her get to you. You and Ryan focus on yourselves right now. It's a special time in your lives, and you don't need Lucy Collins mucking it up."

"She's high if she thinks I'd ever agree to a double wedding."

Bob laughs, hearty and strong, a sound I've missed lately. I ask about work, his friends, how the fishing is going, if he's taking his cholesterol medication. But Dad doesn't want to talk about his blood work. "You and Ryan talked any more about a date?"

I chuckle. "Et tu, Brute?"

"Miss Betty's probably asking enough for both of us."

"Let me guess: you guys are working in collusion. If we pester the kids long enough, they will tire and set a date."

"You and Ryan were the ones who introduced her to the magic of text messaging, so you have no one to blame but yourselves."

"As a matter of fact," I say, speaking slowly so the suspense builds, "we did decide on a date that might work."

"Yeah?"

"No one else knows, though. We only decided about ten hours ago."

"Drum roll, please ..."

"But before I tell you, you should know that my work permit situation could get sorta wonky so the immigration attorney has told us to maybe move things along a little."

"And?"

"Three weeks. June 14. It's a Sunday. Can you get that weekend off?"

"Whoa, three weeks from now? But I wanted to lose a few pounds to fit into my gown," he teases. "Damn, kid, when you set your mind to something ..."

"Nah, it's not that—like I said, the immigration lawyer said it would be easier if we just got married and then we could move forward with a permanent residence thing. Plus, you know me—I don't need a long engagement. I don't want anything too fancy. We had about five open spots to choose from, and so we chose this one."

"I think that's terrific, Hollie Cat," he says, his voice cracking. He clears his throat, and I hear him breathing on the other end of the line, trying to be strong dad and not the dad who cries when his little girl does big stuff. Even though he is that dad. When I graduated from high school, I thought he was going to need an oxygen mask. "I can't wait, kid," he finally manages.

"But you need to come up a few days before. I'll need some pancakes to celebrate."

"I'll make 'em for the whole place."

"Deal," he says.

"Hollie!" Someone is calling my name—Sarah, waddling down the path toward me. "You set a date?" she shrieks, her swollen hands waving above her head like she's flagging down Superman.

"Daddy, I have to go. When can I call you again?"

"Working 7 p.m. to 7 a.m. this week. You remember Manjit?"

"You tried to set me up with her cardiologist son."

"Yeah, yeah. But he's engaged and they're in Mumbai to meet her family, so I'm covering Manjit's shifts."

"Tell her mazel tov."

"Wrong religion, little heathen, but I'll pass along your greetings. Say hi to the gang for me."

Dad hangs up just in time for Sarah to throw her arms around and squeeze me tight enough that I'm pretty sure her baby kicks my spleen. "We have a date!" She steps back, her eyes already glossing over with that thing she does when she goes into planning mode. "When are we dress shopping?"

"Um, soon? I guess?"

"A wedding in three weeks means we're going dress shopping immediately."

"You're not upset that we're hijacking your due date?"

"Not in the slightest. Although I am a little miffed that I won't get a cute bridesmaid's dress. These tits wouldn't fit into a hot-air balloon right now," she says, giving her ample bust a good juggle.

I tuck my arm in hers and rub her belly, but not too long because the alien inside might kick my hand and that freaks me out. I turn us so we're walking back into the resort—I need coffee and probably some electrolytes and Advil to replenish and repair last night's sporting fun.

"Less is more, Sarah. You wear whatever you want. But you have to be my maid of honor."

"Matron. I'm old and married. And really? Little old me?"

"Will you? You're the closest thing I have to a sister."

"We're gonna be real sisters soon enough. I promise to share my Barbies but stay away from my shoes."

"Deal." We shake on it. "But you don't need anything

fancy. You have some cute maternity dresses—one of those will be perfect."

"Ah, hell no. I'm getting something new, even if we have to steal Barnum's tent."

I hold open the main door for Sarah to pass through first, both of us met with the usual morning crowd checking out. Miss Betty and another front-end clerk finalize room bills and collect card keys while Ryan, being generally beautiful and charming as per usual, makes small talk with his adoring guests.

"You guys are so cute. I remember when I used to look at Tanner that way," Sarah says. "Now I just pray he doesn't leave me for someone who can still see her own feet."

"Oh, you mean Tanner Fielding who looks at you like his next breath can't happen unless you smile? Yeah, I can see how you'd be worried," I say. I pause, almost telling her what happened last night with Ryan and Alyssa on the pool deck, but it feels wrong to share. That's Ryan's business, and he handled it, and then he proved to me that I'm his one-and-only. Multiple times, actually.

How did I get so lucky?

My phone buzzes with a text message—from my dad: *Any chance you can come to Pdx to look for a dress? Is it weird that I want to be a part of that? Do dads do that?*

I respond: *Absolutely. It wouldn't be the same without you. xoxo*

Sarah and I squeeze through to the office and I make tea while we wait for the buzz to settle at the front counter.

When Miss Betty flies through the doorway, I know her son has put the "we have news" bug in her ear.

"What? What? What?" she says, her thin, red-painted lips disappearing with the force of her grin.

"I'll wait for Ryan," I say, handing her a full teacup.

As I say his name, he ducks through the open doorway. "Wait for Ryan for what?"

"To tell her we've decided to wait five years to get married."

Miss Betty's face drops.

"No, no, I'm just kidding," I say, laughing. Ryan wraps an arm around his mother's shoulders and she punches his gut, her tea sloshing over the side of her dainty cup.

"So?"

Ryan looks at me. I nod. "June 14."

"*This* June 14?" she says, eyes twinkling.

"Is that soon enough for you?"

She thrusts her teacup at Sarah and hugs her boy so hard, his face reddens. When she opens her arms and motions for me to join the group hug, tears are already trickling down her cheeks. And then she stops bouncing and pushes away. "We have so much to do!" Turns to the laminated calendar taped on the floral wallpapered wall. "That's, what—three weeks?"

"We should go dress shopping. This weekend," Sarah says, looking at Ryan hopefully. "Tan can fly us wherever Hollie wants to go, right?" Weekends are best because most guests stay through until Monday morning and we have front-office staff and a second concierge to deal with the needs of the weekend crowd.

"Whatever you guys want to do, I'm sure we can work it out," Ryan answers. "Just give me a list of what you need from me." He pulls me into his side and whispers in my ear, "I like being bossed around."

I elbow nudge him, my gut butterflies stirring as I think about last night and just how much he enjoys it when I tell him what to do.

"I have to tend to my duties, ladies, so let's reconvene later and you can fill me in?" He kisses me, his beard scratchy but who cares because his lips are giving it a little more oomph than perhaps is necessary given present company. But the mood feels celebratory, what with Sarah and Miss Betty talking a thousand miles a minute about everything we need to get done in the next twenty-one days.

Twenty-one days.

Wow.

I can do this.

Can I do this?

Maybe I should sit down.

Revelation Cove sees a lot of weddings, so the planning on this end is an everyday occurrence. We even have worksheets we send to brides and grooms so they know what they need to bring with and what we can provide on site. Which also means it takes all of four minutes for Sarah and Miss Betty to grab said worksheets and start plunking out emails to Smitty, the retired investment banker-slash-general store owner who also happens to be our local marriage commissioner, and to four of our go-to photographers to see if they can squeeze us in because, as Miss Betty says, "I'm sure Hollie could take beautiful pictures herself but that's just silly because she's the bride!" She's so cute when she gets excited.

"You find a cake you want, and Joseph will make it happen," Miss Betty says. "You started that pinning website, right?"

"Pinterest."

"Take me to it so I can see what you've picked."

I lean over her shoulder and log in to the account so she can peruse the cakes I've pinned so far. This leads to more clucking and oohing and aahing—and outright giggling when they see the one with the ocean theme topped by two otters, one with a veil and the other with a bowtie.

"Those otters holding hands—that's a raft, isn't it?" Miss Betty says, winking. "See, I have been listening to all those nature shows."

"We're definitely going to have to have more samples of these. Oh god, is that red velvet?" Sarah says. I swear she wipes drool off her chin. "My blood sugar is spiking just looking at these pictures. Oh, and Hollie, I emailed you that list of bridal boutiques, from Victoria to Vancouver to New Westminster to Seattle and down to Portland. Where would you like to start?"

I pull out my phone and show her the text from my dad.

"Portland it is!"

"Oh! I have to call Hailey and Brody! I do hope they can get out here in time," Miss Betty says, more to herself than either of us. I have a feeling that Ryan's other two siblings and their families will probably drop everything to come out here for the wedding of their terminal-bachelor brother—if Miss Betty has her way.

While I'd love nothing more than to sit in this cozy office and plan my future nuptials alongside my new family, it's almost ten. I have a wildlife cruise to tend to. Yay because I get to spend time on the bigger cruising boat with Ryan, boo because I have to argue with people who think orca are fish. I say a quick prayer to the boat gods that no one will get seasick today.

And then the voice in my head reminds me: Even if someone barfs or argues with you that there are no sharks in BC waters, it's a thousand percent better than people dying over the phone or listening to Polyester Patty extol the virtues of the party planning committee.

My cell phone alarm chimes. "They're playing my song," I say, kissing Sarah's cheek and then Miss Betty's. "If there are more cake samples to be had this day, you'd better save me some."

I step through the main door, buoyant that a decision has been made but mostly because I love seeing Ryan's mother so happy. She truly is the most genuine, caring woman I've ever met, fiercely protective of her children and the people those children choose to love. I saw her face when Alyssa and Drew checked in—though she was full of smiles for their baby, a subtle chill underwrote the greeting granted her almost-daughter-in-law. Brrrrrr.

And speak of the devil. With the assistance of two other

Cove employees, the crowd assembled at the concierge counter tries on and zips up life jackets taken from the wheeled PVC rack—and it includes Alyssa and Drew. Seeing her in broad daylight after what I witnessed last night takes my breath for a second, but she's smiling and chatting as if nothing happened, which means that's what I have to do. Even if I will have to resist the urge to pull her perfect hair or peel back her gel manicure, which would likely see me on Jerry Springer, or worse, YouTube. Have I not learned my lesson?

Her husband is easy on the eyes. Nice strong jaw, big hands, wide shoulders, hazel eyes that smile with his whole face, a healing cut and bruise along one cheek that must be hockey related, dark blond hair long enough to tuck behind his ears, and at least as tall as Ryan. Drew is actually kind of pretty, and the way he's watching his wife confirms what Ryan said about him—he's smitten. Poor guy. If only he knew.

Deep breath in, shoulders straight, avoiding eye contact with duplicitous Alyssa. "Good morning, everyone," I say, gathering the group's attention. "It's Cove policy that we outfit everyone with a life jacket for our water-related adventures. Once you have a life jacket picked out, we can move down the dock to the boat. Concierge Ryan will be our captain today."

And then like the Red Sea parting, Lucy Collins shuffles out from behind the rack of life vests. "Hollie, none of these will fit over my boobs."

Seriously? Wasn't she just whining about quiche?

It takes us ten minutes to find one she will wear—we actually find several that will fit but one is a bright orange "that clashes with my pants." I want to tell her that it will make it easier for the sharks to find her.

Lucy Collins finally handled, my crowd of twelve follows me out the door, down the pathway and docks, and to the waiting boat. Ryan and another young employee named Jonah help get everyone settled as I adjust the mic and small amp that will serve as my voice box for the next sixty minutes. I go through our standard safety procedures, including location of extra flotation devices, the back-up inflatable boats should our main vessel be compromised, the instruction that this is not the *Titanic* and everyone has to share space on the rescue vessels. I point out where the small bathroom is, offer access to the boat's galley for refill of water bottles and remind passengers that hands stay in the boat and absolutely no garbage is to go into the water. You'd think this stuff would be common sense—but you'd be thinking wrong. It is a miracle that humanity hasn't eaten itself alive yet.

As we pass by the rocky outcroppings and islands south of the Cove, I list the birds that make this part of the world home—crows, Canada geese, different varieties of ducks, several cormorant species, gulls, pigeon guillemots, the alcids, which are web-footed diving birds that include auklets, murrelets, and puffins, as well as oyster catchers and of course, birds of prey—bald and golden eagles, hawks, falcons, osprey, kestrels, harriers, and owls. Everyone loves the raptors.

I explain that the biodiversity of British Columbia and its coast is among the richest on the planet, and with ongoing planetary warming, scientists expect that we will see even greater influx of non-native species, including the aggressive Humboldt squid, which can grow more than six feet long and weigh more than a hundred pounds. And if California's coastal waters continue to warm, the great white, not unheard of off BC's coast, might make more frequent trips north to cool off.

Ryan motors along narrow beaches, slowing so I can point out the huge nests where eagles are rearing their eaglets, talk about the fluctuating salmon populations and how seeing Pacific white-sided dolphins in BC waters is always a fun treat—they love to play in boat wakes. This bit always makes people turn around or look over the boat's side to see if we have any water-bound friends following along.

I'm just about to move into my favorite portion of the trip—talking about *Enhydra lutris*, the sea otter, and *Lontra canadensis*, the river otter, when a screechy voice interrupts. "Do you have anything on board to eat?"

"When we stop midcruise, we will provide healthy, litter-free snacks for everyone," I say, trying to ignore Lucy Collins. She has taken up more than her fair share on one of the side benches, even without Ernesto tagging along.

"How long will that be? I'm worried about my blood sugar."

Considering where I am in my spiel, we're about ten minutes from stopping and turning north toward the cove.

I cover the mic and ask Jonah if he will please get Lucy a bottle of orange juice—if she really is having a blood sugar moment, I don't need her to lose her shit out here in the open water with all these onlookers.

Jonah hands her a bottle but instead of thanking him, she whines that it's warm. The other guests look at one another and then me, a few throwing irritated stares at Lucy, as happens when one amongst a crowd is obnoxious. "We're going to stop here in a little bit, and then when we return to the resort, the dining room will be happy to make sure you have all the cold orange juice you need."

"I shouldn't drink orange juice. I might have an ulcer."

Now I know she's full of shit because if she has an ulcer, her doctor wouldn't have given her aspirin.

Ryan coughs behind me, from his position at the wheel.

"Moving on, as we round the next series of small islands, if we're lucky, we'll be able to see a local population of northern sea otters basking in the morning sun, tethered either to one another in gender-specific groupings called rafts, or entangled in the kelp so they don't float away with the current."

I explain the status of the sea otter populations along the West Coast, stretching from Monterey, California, to Alaska, and how these amazing creatures were almost hunted to extinction, prized for their dense pelts, the thickest fur of any land or sea mammal.

Ryan kills the engine, and for a brief moment, the sun shining down on us in a near cloudless sky, I close my eyes and listen. Water lapping the side of the boat, the distant call of seabirds, the wind whispering through some of the leafier trees along the cliff edges and the seagrasses along the rock-and-sand strips of beach—and Lucy Collins belching.

"Where are the otters?" she asks, loudly enough that if there is any wildlife nearby, it's going to turn tail and run. And while I'm disappointed the otters aren't here in what we've informally dubbed "Otter Beach," I'm glad she doesn't get to see them. Otters are special. Lucy Collins is not.

Ryan's fingers press into my upper arm. He takes the mic, charm oozing through those pearly whites. "Some of you who've been to Revelation Cove know that it's a family business, that my brother Tanner is among the pilots who flies the charters to and from Victoria and the Lower Mainland. Last year, Hollie and I had stopped by his cabin a few kilometers from here, and while we were there, we ran into a cougar."

A murmur of acknowledgement vibrates through the passengers. "She was not a happy kitty and she got a good nip out of my left arm," he says to soft laughs, "but what is interesting about the behavior of these cats is that they will swim long distances between these islands in search of prey."

"What—the cougar come out of the woods in Daisy Dukes and stilettos, asking for a cigarette?" Drew asks. A few people laugh. "Ever had any at the resort's island?"

"No, seems she was waiting for me to come to her."

"Typical woman," Drew teases. Alyssa ignores her husband, eyes fixed on Ryan. And my eyes fixed on her.

"But another thing these cougars will do—if they're swimming and a fishing boat is nearby, the cats have been known to swim toward the boats, as if they're looking for a spot to rest."

The passengers look around the vessel again, over the edges and along the nearby shore.

"Cougars can't swim," Lucy says, flopping a limp hand at us.

"Actually, they're quite good swimmers," Ryan says. "They also will eat a human if the cat is sick or malnourished. I guess we mammals will eat anything if we get desperate enough."

"I don't buy it."

Please don't let me smack her please don't let me smack her.

"Female cougars are also excellent mothers, usually staying with their kittens until the young reach eighteen to twenty-four months of age." He looks directly at Lucy as he speaks. "They don't abandon their young to the wild, although if the mother is killed, an immature cougar can survive on its own from about six months old."

It's like one of those cartoons where the steam whistles out of the bad guy's ears.

Lucy Collins purses her lips together and looks away.

"S'pose it's good to know your enemy, hey, Fielding?" Drew says.

"Awww, poor cougar wasn't the enemy. She was just hungry and my flesh apparently looked rather delectable that day." Ryan kisses the side of my head and returns the mic to me before resuming his post at the wheel. I turn around so only he can see my face and mouth *thank you*.

It probably seems like a low blow, the underhanded comparison of a cougar's mothering habits with my own deadbeat incubator, but if it shuts her up for the remainder of our voyage ...

As promised, we break for snacks and water or juice, answering questions from guests with a keen interest in British Columbia's wild coast. A few guests inquire about fishing opportunities, and Jonah helps me pass out binoculars from those wanting to spy on the surrounding island's trees.

She moves pretty fast for a woman with a severe Brazilian wax injury. Before I can protest, she has the mic in hand, the on button flicked. "Hello, everyone. I know you're looking at the birds, but I wanted to say a few words because I'm Hollie's mother. I came to Revelation Cove with my beau to celebrate the engagement of my baby girl to her knight in shining armor. There's even talk that we might have a double wedding! Wouldn't that be fantastic?"

People stare at her, confused, looking amongst Ryan and me and Jonah and then to Lucy, wondering what the hell is going on. I try to take the mic but she holds me aside with her other arm. "Are there any mothers on board? Any of you?"

A few of the women nod, including Alyssa, a smug smile stretched across her lips.

"Well, I don't have to tell you the love we mothers feel for our babies." Nods and murmurs of agreement.

Oh, spare me.

"Sometimes life makes us do things we're not proud of, but we always want what's best for our darling children, no matter what, just like that cougar who will take care of her little kitty-cats. Am I right?"

"Lucy, that's enough. Give me the microphone."

She yanks away. "Now, this is just an informal poll amongst you folks, but how many of you think a double wedding would make headlines? Mother and daughter, wedding their One True Loves? Bring some great publicity to the resort Ryan has worked so hard to build?"

A few tentative hands go up.

"Hey, Ry, that's a wonderful idea," Alyssa says, giving Lucy a tepid once-over. "Any publicity is good publicity, right? Resort owner marries the help? It's a real rags-to-riches story, isn't it."

"Yes!" Lucy squawks. "See? That pretty little gal has the right—"

That's it. I grab Lucy's wrist and take the microphone, leaning in so she can hear me loud and clear. "Sit your ass down on that bench or I swear, I will throw you overboard."

She pats my cheek and snickers. "Think about it. You heard the woman—any publicity is good publicity."

"I'll show you publicity when I feed you to the orca," I whisper.

Lucy Collins smiles, takes another bottle of juice from Jonah, and shuffles back to her bench seat.

An hour later as we pull alongside the dock at the resort, I stow the amp and mic, and help tie off. The guests disembark, chatting about getting lunch or going for a swim or hitting the spa. Lucy Collins lingers behind, scuttling like an injured bird.

"Hollie! Wait for me."

I ignore her and pick up the pace, cutting around the crowd so I can handle life jacket returns and move on with the rest of the day, which will likely include calling in sick and hiding in our apartment. I cannot handle this woman. What was that bullshit about mothers wanting the best for their babies? And doing the best for our children? And seriously, it's a good damn thing Alyssa sat facing the water for the return trip. *Oh yes, Ry, why don't you? Any publicity is good publicity* ... Me maiming her modelesque face in front of a crowd of onlookers would qualify as "any publicity" too but I kept my talons sheathed like a good green-eyed monster.

Sarah sneaks behind me as I'm hanging up life jackets, a stack of papers in her hand. "Hey, Hol, is Ryan still on the boat?"

"Yeah. You need him?"

"Just to sign payroll," she says, resting a hand on her belly. "What's wrong?"

My mouth is opening to answer when Lucy stomps through the front door, yanking on the snagged zipper of her life jacket, cussing up a storm about how it's a piece of shit. Sarah doesn't have to ask again about the murderous look on my face.

"I cannot get this damn thing off! Can someone please help me?" Lucy stops in front of the concierge desk, looking disgusted. Sarah sets her papers down on the desk and moves to the stubborn zipper.

"Sometimes these things are a little tricky," she says, her voice soothing. "Just have to pull the fabric out of the way of the zipper pull ... and there!"

"Finally someone with some respect for the elderly," Lucy mumbles, handing Sarah the discarded life jacket. "You look like you're about to pop. When's that kid gonna fall out of you?"

Sarah's face registers that she has answered this question a zillion times but customer service is always priority one. "Soon. In a few weeks, probably."

"Jesus, a few weeks? You look like you don't have more than a few hours, sweetheart." Lucy touches Sarah's belly without invitation. "I'll bet it's a boy. You're huge."

"Nice. Real classy, Lucy. Every pregnant woman wants to hear how huge she is," I say, pushing the wheeled cart into the closet.

"It's true, though. Boys are always bigger. I hope one of these days, Hollie decides to pop out a few pups. I could use a few grandchildren."

Sure, Lucy. Grandchildren you can abandon? Reason 412 why I should not reproduce.

Ryan walks in and drops his keys on the concierge desk, a polite smile on his face. "Hey, handsome, when are you going to impregnate my daughter? She'd look good walking around all fat and pregnant like this, don't you think?"

"Oh, for god's sake, woman, give it a rest, why don't you!" I holler. I cannot take another moment of this idiot windbag blowing her bile all over my life. "What are you doing? Do you ever shut up? Did you ever stop to think that not everyone wants to know what the hell you think?"

I slam the storage closet door and take off down the hall.

Ryan finds me an hour later. "Hollie, come on, open the door."

"Go away." I pull my knees tighter to my chest. The bathroom's tile floor is cold under my ass. I should've just drawn a bath and soaked—alone and quiet—instead of sitting here balled up festering in my anger.

"Open the door for a minute. If you don't like what I have to say, then you can close it again until you're ready to come out."

"Is she gone?"

Ryan doesn't answer. Which tells me she's still here. Causing trouble. Screwing everything up. Of course she hasn't left. There are no shuttles or flights until tomorrow morning.

I uncurl my stiff legs and stretch to unlock the door. Ryan steps in and sits on the closed toilet lid. "Why is she here doing this?" No risk of tears—I'm too angry to cry.

"I talked to her for a few minutes. She just wants to be a part of your life, Hollie."

"She should've thought of that twenty-six years ago, then, shouldn't she?"

He leans forward on his elbows. "I have no context for this. When my dad left, it was because he died. And I was still angry, for a long time, because he died for selfish reasons. I was angry that—"

"Ryan, sorry, not trying to be a dick, but it's totally not the same thing."

He sighs. "I know. I'm trying to put myself in your position. All I can recommend is that you give a little. Let her be a part of the wedding planning—not a double wedding, but just the preliminary stuff while she's here. And then she will get her fill of you and leave. The room they're in is only theirs for a week, and then the hotel is fully booked. They're going to have to leave here eventually."

"Try telling her that."

"I did. I told her that she and Edward could stay until next Wednesday, and then they have to leave. No extensions."

"Ernesto. His name is Ernesto."

"Whatever."

"And she agreed to this? To one week?"

"She doesn't have a choice. I'm not afraid to call the RCMP to send someone up to forcibly remove them from the premises."

"Do it. Call them now. I'll dial."

He chuckles. "No. Lucy and I made a deal."

"A deal? You realize you made a deal with Satan, right?"

"Really? Satan?"

"I am so not going to like this."

"I told her she can fly down to the city with us to go dress shopping on Saturday—"

"Ryan! Jesus! What did you do that for?"

"—but she is responsible for her own accommodations

while we're down there and she is absolutely not to steal the spotlight from you. This is your day, to shop for a dress."

"Get out." I thrust a finger at the open bathroom door.

"Porter, come on. You need to handle this like a grown-up."

I glare at him. "You have no idea what you're talking about. Everything that comes out of that woman's mouth is a lie. This isn't about redemption, about me being a 'grown-up' and giving Poor Old Mommy a second chance. She screwed up. She's had two and a half decades to fix it. She didn't. She's a fame-seeking pit viper who is only here because she thinks you're rich. Is that grown-up enough for you?"

"You don't believe in second chances?"

"With her? Are you kidding me?"

Ryan stands and straightens his work cargos. "I didn't invite her along to hurt you, Hol. I swear. I'm only trying to make you happy and keep the peace." And he steps over my outstretched leg, out of the bathroom, the main apartment door whooshing closed behind him.

The least he could've done is slam it.

14

Silk, Organza, and Satin—Oh My!

I'll spare you the details of what happens on the floatplane Saturday morning. If you imagined Lucy Collins demanding a window seat and then whining the whole time about how bumpy it is and making more fat-lady comments to Sarah and extolling the horrors and agony of childbirth, including detailed assessment of hemorrhoids, shitting on the birthing table, and your vagina splitting in two so you will never have satisfactory sex ever again, congratulations. You imagined correctly.

Once all the blood in Ryan's and Tanner's faces has drained into their shoes, Miss Betty tries to argue that she had four children and all of those side effects are manageable, and that she and her husband had a fine sex life *thank you very much*, which, naturally, made everyone related to her by blood and marriage and engagement wither into our hollow selves even more than we already had.

By the time we get to the rental car place, I think if I had a roll of duct tape and a tarp in my bag, my cohorts would gladly risk the jail time. Miss Betty has developed a strange tic in her eyebrow, and Sarah keeps clearing her throat and sighing heavily, like her abdomen is filled with a rage ball and not a baby. The look of relief on the Fielding sons' faces that they get to go do manly bonding things while we traipse through the city with Lucy Collins in tow ... a little too gleeful for my sour mood.

I'm the one searching for a wedding dress, a day that is supposed to be filled with excitement and giggles, but all I want to do is follow Ryan to a pub and binge-eat chicken wings and gulp cheap beer. Although we're in Portland. So it would have to be craft beer. Probably one brewed in a tree trunk with organic hops and hipster, Birkenstock-wearing beer fairies arguing over who has the nicest Subaru.

"You gonna be okay?" Ryan asks. I'm still pissed that he invited her along. We're inside the rental car place, picking up two vehicles for both weekend days, while the remainder of our crew waits outside in the stunning May sunshine.

"Fine."

"Have you texted your dad?"

"He's meeting us at the first bridal boutique and then we'll carry on from there. Until a dress is found or until I commit matricide."

"I'm going to miss you today," he says, pinching my ass when the clerk is turned away. I might miss him too, a little bit—we've been nearly inseparable for the better part of a year—but I'm not giving him the satisfaction. Just like I didn't give him the satisfaction Thursday or Friday nights. Hey, you make your bed, you lie in it with your blue balls.

The clerk hands us the keys—oh joy, I get a minivan—and explains the insurance procedures should we have any mishaps. Before we rejoin our party in progress, we agree to meet at the Spaghetti Factory on the Willamette River at seven. Then to the hotel, then another day of shopping tomorrow if today isn't fruitful, and home to the Cove tomorrow night.

It feels like a million years away.

"I love you, Porter. Try to enjoy the day. Remember what you're doing this for, yeah?"

I kiss him on the cheek and push the door open, the warm outside air raising goosebumps on my air-conditioner-chilled skin. "Shall we?"

Locked and loaded, we head into the heart of the city. Thankfully, Sarah knew that the bridal salons usually require appointments—I did not know this—so she called in a few favors to get us seen on short notice. Perks of working for a resort where we do more weddings than a serial polygamist.

"You do know that the chances of you finding a dress on such short notice is slim to none," Lucy squawks. "These things take time. Alterations, fittings, size adjustments—especially if you get knocked up before the big day. Although my best girlfriend was huge like this one over here," she hikes a thumb at Sarah, "and she had one of those dresses where the fabric was cut out—so her baby belly was on full display. She was a stripper back then so she had great tits and legs, but that was a wedding to remember."

"Sounds charming."

"Plus you're pretty much gonna have to stop eating so you can fit into whatever dress you find."

"I'm sure Hollie will pick something wonderful. And I deal with a lot of brides in my job at the Cove," Sarah says. "Finding something right off the rack is not unheard of."

"I'm sure Ryan's got the cash to make sure she gets what she wants, hey, Hollie?" Lucy smacks the back of the driver's seat. I grit my teeth.

"I brought my iPad, so we can log into your thumbtack account and show the boutique girls what you're looking for," Miss Betty says from the front seat and pulls the device from her bag.

"Pinterest, Mom," Sarah corrects.

"Right, right. Pinterest. What's your password again?" I tell her and she brings up the page, cooing about the gowns I've selected, showing it over her shoulder to Sarah in the captain's chair behind. In the rearview mirror, I see Lucy angle forward so she can have a look too, her displeasure with my choices registering in the curl of her lip.

"Why do you want something with flowers on it? Bring on the bling!" she says.

"I don't want a lot of bling on a gown. I like flowers."

"Why no bling? Rhinestones and sequins are so sparkly! Like a party on your dress! And you should definitely have a big ball gown with at least two petticoats to really fluff it up."

"I don't want something fluffed up."

"Phhht. You don't know what you want. You haven't even seen a gown yet."

"I do know what I want, and it's not rhinestones or sequins or petticoats."

Lucy leans back in her seat, pooh-poohing that I'm clueless, that I will want bling as soon as I see myself in a few dresses. Miss Betty's kind hand on my upper arm reminds me to not take out my frustration on the steering wheel or my poor white knuckles.

We find parking for the first place on Yamhill and my stomach is a mess. Maybe I don't know what I'm looking for. Maybe Lucy is right and I won't be able to find a dress today. Maybe I will have to get married in cargo pants and a Revelation Cove polo.

As we round the corner, my dad is already there waiting, ratcheting up my anxieties as I realize Nurse Bob and Lucy Collins will be in the same space for the first time this millennium.

Oh dear lord, let the next few hours pass without bloodshed.

Sarah moves slowly secondary to a child kickboxing her kidneys, and Lucy continues to walk like a lame seagull, reminding us about her tragic spa accident. I run ahead, so relieved to see a smiling, nonconfrontational face.

"Hey, Dad," I say, squeezing him until he squeaks. "No scrubs today? You should wear civilian clothes more often."

"Work hard, play hard. How ya holding up, Hollie Cat?"

"Dad, promise me you will keep her from ruining everything today."

He looks over my shoulder, his eyes widening. "Wow. Some of us haven't aged well."

"Hard liquor and a life of crime tends to do that to a person," I mumble, just as they reach us. Miss Betty is generous with her hugs; Bob slips into nurse mode for a brief second, asking Sarah about gestational diabetes and swelling of feet and ankles and fundus measurements; and then he pockets his hands and nods at my mother.

"Lucy."

"Bob. You have less hair than I remember."

"Apparently you do too." He quirks an eyebrow and looks in the direction of her groin. "Shall we, ladies?" he says, smiling and holding the door open.

Inside looks like a cake, all whites and creams and taupe, serenaded by soft music, accented with cushy furniture and gorgeous gowns on svelte mannequins. A quiver runs from head to toe.

We're greeted by a young woman named Felicia—also pregnant, though not nearly as swollen as Sarah—who, after indulging in a few moments of Miss Betty and Sarah chattering about upcoming babies, checks us in and escorts us to our own private bridal suite outfitted with plush couches and modern glass-and-chrome accent tables, a ginormous wall-to-wall mirror, and a secluded, curtained change area. And champagne!

Once we're seated, Felicia, clipboard in hand, questions

me about what I'm looking for in a gown—color, budget (I whisper this part because it's ridiculous to spend multiple thousands of dollars on a dress I will wear for a few hours, right?), shape, width, length, specific designers. She takes notes as we speak, and I show her my Pinterest page. She nods and smiles as she scrolls through—I hope that's a good sign.

"I want to see her in something with a lot of bling," Lucy chimes in.

I shake my head at Felicia. "No bling. Thank you."

"Felicity, tell her that bling is all the rage. And she needs something that will make her tits look bigger. Grooms want their brides to have big knockers."

Felicia blushes.

"Her name is Felicia. Now please be quiet," I growl, returning my pasted-on smile to our attendant.

"So, when is your wedding?"

I laugh nervously and lean forward so maybe Lucy can't hear me. I haven't quite told her when the wedding is, in the hope that she will disappear before then. "Three weeks."

"Wow, okay."

"What? Did you just say three weeks? Jesus, Hollie, are you knocked up? Oh man, there's no way you're gettin' a dress now."

I close my eyes, lips pressed together for a calming beat. Felicia's hand rests atop mine. "Three weeks is no problem. You're about a size eight?"

"About an eight. Depending on the cut. I don't know. I've never tried on wedding gowns before."

"We can take some quick measurements, but you look about an eight to me," Felicia says, smiling.

"I was a four when I married your father," Lucy says. "Too much good eating for you at that resort."

"Well, you're not a four now, so let's listen in on what Felicia has to say about Hollie's choosing a dress." Dad to the rescue!

"We have a lot of options in stock—some girls find their gowns right off the rack—or we can see about rush orders with minor alterations. Don't panic, okay?"

"Hollie Cat, if you find one you want to order, have it shipped to the house so Ryan doesn't see it. I can always bring it up with me," Dad says.

"Oh, I see, your father gets an invite to the wedding but I don't?"

As if Lucy hadn't spoken, Felicia continues. "We'll get you squared away, and if we can't find one, we are never shy about recommending other boutiques. We just want you to be happy."

I want to hug Felicia, especially as she tops up the champagne I've already managed to slurp to less than halfway.

Once she has an idea for what I'm after, she invites me to join her at the gown racks. Lucy is on her feet to accompany us. "Oh, we like to take the bride in first so she can look at her options without any outside pressure," Felicia says.

"I'm her mother. I should be able to see what she's looking at."

"Maybe let's let Hollie have a look on her own first, hey, Lucy?" Miss Betty says.

"She doesn't know what she wants. And I wouldn't mind seeing what they've got in my size too. Hollie isn't the only blushing bride around these parts—"

"Lucy, sit down," Bob commands. She opens her mouth to protest. "Sit down, or I will sit you down."

"You can't boss me around anymore. I'm not your wife."

"Thank the good lord for that but I can kindly ask Felicia here to have you removed from the premises for being disruptive, so keep it up."

She snorts at Bob and glares at Felicia, who looks a bit fierce all of a sudden. Me likey.

I knew Lucy would do this. The woman doesn't even give you an opportunity to find a redeeming quality because she is always so busy being a selfish asshole.

Felicia hugs her clipboard above her bulging belly and then looks right at me, nodding. "Let's go find you a dress, Hollie." Her white smile and tumbling brown waves and lovely powder-blue maternity-shaped suit make me all warm and fuzzy inside. "Enjoy the champagne," she says over her shoulder. "Oh, and I will have one of the girls bring our little momma some sparkling cider."

I follow Felicia out of our private suite to a wide, open-ended, chandeliered room with so many dresses tucked into alcoves—white, cream, lace, silk, satin, organza, taffeta, chiffon, velvet, and enough tulle to smother a country—and sample bridesmaid dresses in every imaginable color and length. Right away, I see the alcove with a number of floral-inspired gowns, some with embroidery directly on the bodices and skirts, some with flowers in the overlaid netting, and a couple particularly bright dresses in brilliant fabrics.

Felicia pulls a few different options free from the bar and asks more searching questions about fabric choices, necklines, and dress cuts.

"Is it okay if we just try on a few different shapes? I've never really given any serious thought to a wedding gown until very recently."

"Absolutely. Let's see what fits your body best. Often you'll see a gown online or in a magazine that you love, but then when you see it on your body, it's just not the right shape at all. I'm going to check the storeroom for a few new floral motif gowns that have just come in. Be right back."

I thumb through the remaining gowns, pulling the "possibles" sideways on the bar so I don't forget about them, totally second-guessing myself when I see how beautiful all of these dresses are. I wish Ryan were here to help me. I didn't even ask him what he wanted. Maybe he hates ball gowns, or maybe he doesn't like strapless or ruching, or maybe he prefers A-line or Empire waist or the tight mermaid style ...

I pull out my phone. *Preferences? Anything you hate in wedding dress fashion? Seriously so many choices. Freaking out.*

Felicia returns with several gowns hanging from her fingers. "Now one of these has a more subtle flower motif embroidered into the organza in peach, which is a nice contrast to the rest of the gown in cream silk ..." As she presents the different dresses on their hangers, panic nibbles at me. These dresses are so incredible, I'm afraid to touch them.

"This one is by Amsale—a sweetheart neckline ball gown with a natural waist in white silk with floral embellishment ... Lazaro has an old Hollywood feel with a lot of hand embroidery but we may not be able to find the profile you're looking for ... I know Oscar de la Renta did a lot of floral designs last year but we don't carry his line in-store so this one has a similar feel ... A less-expensive designer, for sure, but still beautiful with the floral accents you like is the Sophia Tolli. This one is an A-line with sweetheart neckline and a chapel-length train with floral embellished beading in tulle over cream satin ... This one is a Monique Lhuillier, absolutely gorgeous gown ... This cream-colored number is CB Couture—not sure if you're comfortable with strapless but this is a ball gown with a natural waist and modified sweetheart neckline with embroidered floral appliques on tulle. The bodice also features inverted ruching and there is the option of adding 'bling' if you want a Swarovski crystal belt—"

"Okay. I am getting very confused."

Felicia smiles. "Let's take what we have here and go play dress-up, shall we?"

In our suite, Dad, Miss Betty, and Sarah are where we left them, sipping from sparkly crystal flutes. "Where's Lucy?" I ask.

"She had to use the bathroom," Miss Betty says, putting her drink down. "What did you find?"

"We're going to work through each gown so Hollie can narrow down shape and cut, and then when she's ready to show you all, she'll pop out. Sound good?"

"Can't wait!" Miss Betty says, sitting on the edge of her seat, knees bouncing.

"Pick a good one, Hol," Sarah adds just as the heavy gray curtain closes behind us. She had advised me to wear a strapless bra, which thankfully, I owned. I even remembered matching panties, which doesn't happen often. I know, *très chic, non?*

I will never admit this out loud, but Lucy was sort of right. I am clueless. Once I saw gowns on my body, I realized that my broader shoulders looked nice in the mermaid and trumpet styles, but the way my hips and thicker thighs pooched out did not please me. The sheath felt too informal, like I was going out for dinner or to the symphony, not getting married. The first gown I showed my party was an Empire waist ball gown with a colorful floral pattern.

"The Empire cut looks beautiful on you, kiddo, but that looks more like a prom dress to me," Dad says. I laugh. Since when did my father become a wedding dress aficionado? He looks at the four women smiling at him. "What? I've been reading up."

He's right. And there are too many colors. It's a wedding dress, not an Impressionist painting.

"Dad, where is Lucy?" I ask, realizing she's been in the bathroom for a hell of a long time.

"Don't worry about her. Focus on you," he says, although I know that look on his face. He knows that Lucy Collins is not in the bathroom and is likely stirring shit up somewhere else. Whatever. It's refreshing to not have her sitting here bullying her way through the conversation. Even Miss Betty looks more visibly relaxed.

I try on the CB Couture ball gown but it's too much dress. Good for a huge church wedding but maybe not appropriate for the Cove. "I like the floral embroidery and beading on this one, though," I say. The crowd agrees.

Felicia unbuttons me out of the latest "no." "How long does it take brides to find dresses? Am I screwing myself, thinking I'm going to find The Dress with so little time?"

When she has the gown replaced on its hanger, Felicia puts a soft, warm hand on my bare shoulder. "Not while I'm on the job," she says. "Don't despair. That's only a few dresses down. We have lots more to go through."

"Are you married? Have you tried on a zillion dresses and found The One?" I ask, noting a single diamond solitaire on her left hand but looking for anecdotal encouragement.

"Maybe after the baby. Engaged for now," she says, touching her tummy affectionately. "But sweetie, I've worked in bridal for years, and I can tell you that miracles happen in these rooms every single day."

I try on dress after dress, none of us reaching a consensus about what works. One dress will have the right neckline but the wrong profile, or the right profile but the wrong neckline. I'm not too excited about strapless simply because I don't have awesome boobs. If you think talking about your cleavage, or lack thereof, would be embarrassing in front of your dad, you'd think wrong. Apparently all body talk is fair game today.

In the middle of swooshing about in a too-fitted, trumpet Lazaro (phenomenal beading but way too sophisticated for me), shuffles and grumbles filter in from the hallway.

And poof, standing in our doorway is another boutique clerk and a security guard as they present Lucy Collins—no longer wearing her clothes but rather her ample body shoved into the gaudiest, most blinged-out wedding dress I have ever seen.

"Are you kidding me?" Dad says. Miss Betty hides her mouth behind her hand to conceal the smile but Sarah laughs loudly enough for all of us. I, however, am not laughing. Instead I'm actively dying of embarrassment.

I disappear into the change room with Felicia while my dad handles Lucy, though I peek through the break in the heavy curtain to hear what's going on. They won't kick her out of the store if she sits with us and agrees to stay out of the storeroom where the dresses are. She also has to pay for cleaning to remove the lipstick on three other dresses besides the one she's wearing. Lucy cusses and hisses enough to make the meanest tomcat slink away in fear, but my dad handles her with a startling finesse.

"Tell Hollie I'll be right back," he says to Miss Betty and then follows Lucy and collected staff out.

Felicia hands me a silk cover-up, our eyes meeting, her noticing the tears welling in mine. She smiles sweetly and steps out briefly to refill my champagne, returning to hand me the bubbling flute. "I have another dress I want you to try. It's strapless, and I know you're nervous about that neckline, but we can look at adding spaghetti straps if you like it. It's a little pricey but it was inspired by gowns you might find by Marchesa or Carolina Herrera. Do you want to see it?"

A little pricey? How pricey? I smile and nod. The choke in my throat doesn't want me to make words yet.

"Stay here and relax for a second," she says, tiptoeing through the curtain.

I check my phone to see if Ryan's texted me. *"Whatever you choose will be perfect. I wear cargo pants for a living."* Wow. Super helpful, Ryan. I consider texting for reassurance about the price, but his parting words from this morning replay in my head: *Find what you want. Don't worry about the cost.*

But I will worry because spending five or more grand on a dress is ridiculous and wasteful. I'd rather donate that money. Think of all the baby otters we could feed!

Felicia returns in a heartbeat, zipped white garment bag in hand. "Okay, I want you to close your eyes until I get this one on you." I pivot away from the mirror. "This gown is from a local designer. Done in white silk, it has a corset top and strapless sweetheart neckline with white floral accents along the bust. The modified A-line is overlaid with a fuller embroidered organza skirting, fully decorated with hand-stitched white flowers and a matching satin ribbon at the waist. If you want a fuller gown, we can easily add a petticoat, which will make it feel more like a ball gown, or if you prefer the narrower profile, the gown is perfect that way too," she says. "Eyes still closed?" I nod as she moves to zip me up. "My favorite part about this dress is how true the sizing is—not even kidding, this is an eight and other than a little room in the bust, I don't have to clamp it—and of course, the train. I know you were worried about a train being too formal but this floral-accented organza, chapel-length train is so feminine and soft ..."

She again helps me into the loaner shoes and then turns me around slowly. "Okay, so if this one doesn't work, don't give up yet. We can always break for lunch and try some more this afternoon." I nod, hands fisted, eyes still squeezed closed. "Open your eyes."

I guess when she hands me a tissue, we might have found The One.

"Shall we show them?" Felicia pushes the curtain aside and pokes her head out. "Everyone close their eyes until I say."

"Is my dad back yet?"

"Not yet. Do you want to wait another minute?"

"No. No, it's fine."

"Let's get you set up on the pedestal and then I'll go find him." This girl is doing everything to earn the biggest tip ever. I sort of want to pet her flowing chocolate-brown hair or ask her to be my BFF.

Deep breath in, I step through the parted curtains. Miss Betty and Sarah both have their eyes closed, grins plastered across their faces. Felicia helps me up onto the pedestal and then fans the dress around me. The train on full spread is breathtaking. The three-dimensional, hand-stitched flowers make the dress look like it's blooming.

"Open your eyes!" I say to my party guests.

And then it's all gushing and clapping and oohing and ahhing, just like those ridiculous wedding-dress shows and the moment is almost perfect … I keep looking toward the door, hoping Dad is on his way in. Felicia meets my eye and steps out.

"Ryan is going to love this," Miss Betty says, dabbing at her eyes with her monogrammed hankie. "You look absolutely beautiful."

"This is it, Hollie. This is so it," Sarah says. She can't stop shaking her head and walking around me. My arms feel as if they have balloons attached at the wrists, my body so giddy and weightless. I never knew I could feel so … *pretty*.

"Hollie Cat," my dad says, stopping in the doorway, his hand clutched over his heart. And then he can't talk anymore, even when Lucy Collins pushes her way through and plops onto the couch. I don't even care that she's here, or that she grumbles, "Yeah, that one's nice but there's no bling." In that moment Nurse Bob and me smiling at one another through the tears, I know this moment couldn't be any more blissfully superb.

Dad walks to me and does a three-sixty around the dress. "This is the one. Like it was made for you." Felicia looks elated, our excitement reflected in her eyes. She notes that we might have to have a quick modification at the bust but if this is THE dress, we can come back after lunch and I can meet with the seamstress.

"We can have the gown done for you in a week," she says.

Only one worry remains: how pricey is pricey?

While Dad and Sarah and Miss Betty pull out their phones for photos—with strict promises that there is no sending shots to Ryan—and Lucy Collins pouts because she doesn't get to try on any more dresses, I whisper into Felicia's ear.

"How much ...?"

"The nice thing about shopping in Oregon? No tax."

Ouch. This is going to sting.

"Seven thousand," she says. I cough. Seven thousand dollars for a dress? That I will wear once? I could buy a car for seven thousand dollars. I could help fund an otter research team for seven thousand. We could buy hockey equipment for an entire team of needy little kids with seven thousand.

I'm lightheaded.

"Can I ... ?" I point to the change room. "Just for a second." I have to call Ryan. Before I perspire on and ruin this seven-thousand-dollar dress.

He answers after three rings, chaos in the background of wherever they are. "Are you guys having fun?" I ask, my voice small. They're at Portland International Raceway with one of Tanner's friends. Guy is the pit crew chief for a Formula 1 team and today is a qualifying event. It sounds really loud.

"Crazy as hell out here. I want one of these cars," Ryan says. The roar dulls; he must've stepped into a quieter space. "How are you doing? Are you enjoying yourself? Is Lucy behaving?"

"I ... think I found the dress."

"Porter, that's great! And you were so worried! Is it gorgeous? Will I want to ravage you the second I see you walking down the aisle?"

I smile and regard my reflection in the change-room mirror, twisting this way and that. No need to beat around the bush. "Ryan, it's seven thousand dollars."

"And?"

"And, seven thousand dollars is a lot of money. Think of all the good we could do with seven thousand dollars."

He snickers. "Hollie, we do plenty of good. It's okay to spend money on this."

"But it seems ... wasteful."

"Well, your option is to find a cheaper dress that doesn't make you feel wonderful, but you save the money and feel less than perfect on your wedding day."

"Yeah ..."

"I'm telling you—buy the one you want. We're only doing this once. Right? And think of all the money we're saving on venue and everything else."

He's right. We're basically paying wholesale, and paying the business Ryan and his partners own. In the bigger picture, we're almost getting this wedding for free.

"You still there?"

"Yeah."

"Buy the dress, Hollie. And in three short weeks, I'm going to fall in love with you all over again. And then I'm going to tear it off you—"

"No tearing. It's gorgeous. You may unzip it carefully."

He laughs. "And then I will unzip it carefully and make

you the happiest woman in the world for that night, and every night after."

You already have, you big jerk.

15

My Uterus Has Left the Building

We spend another hour deciding on simple dresses for my bridal party of two—swollen Sarah and tiny Tabitha—a process made easier by the fact that there are three options available for a pregnant matron of honor: light lavender off-the-shoulder, midcalf-length sundresses in polished cotton it is. A fortuitous benefit of working with a pregnant saleswoman? She understands what Sarah is going through, and how comfort is priority one.

Felicia invites me into a private office to make an afternoon appointment with Antoinette the seamstress, to place the order for the bridesmaids' dresses, and to handle the financial details. My dad tries to insist on paying for my gown, but I tell him that Ryan and I have got it handled, and we can talk later if he wants to contribute. If he really wants to do something nice, he can buy Lucy Collins a one-way ticket to a remote island in the Pacific Ocean filled with cannibals. That's insensitive, isn't it ... those poor cannibals won't know what hit 'em. Okay, sorry, cannibals. I'll send her to the Sentinelese, that tribe in the Bay of Bengal who makes archery practice of anyone who tries to step foot on their island. I'll probably be given some sort of humanitarian award—my second of the year after I rid the world of the plague known as Mangala. I could probably wear this seven-thousand-dollar dress to the grand ball scheduled for after the humanitarian award ceremony.

Because the damage Lucy Collins did to those dresses she smeared? Yeah, like, four hundred dollars' worth. She tries to get out of paying until they threaten to call the police. I've never seen someone pull that much money out of her bra before.

As we're walking out of the office toward the front of the boutique where my entourage awaits, I stop cold. Ahead, at the front counter, stands Keith. In uniform, stethoscope around his neck as per usual. He looks surprisingly ... good. Like, happy.

"You okay?" Felicia asks.

"What? Yeah. Fine. Sorry." We continue forward, and when Keith sees me, his face lights up. Only he looks away from me, takes a step forward to meet us, and kisses Felicia on the cheek.

Wait. What?

"Keith, what are you doing here?" I ask. Felicia turns so she's the bridge between my ex-boyfriend and me.

"Babe! That proposal I showed you? The one at the Moda Center where the soon-to-be bride threw up and passed out? It was Hollie!"

Felicia's eyes widen. "*You* are that Hollie? Oh wow! You're Keith's ex! You're marrying the hockey player! I cannot believe I didn't put two and two together. I am so embarrassed!"

"Are you—are you guys a couple?" I ask Keith.

"Isn't this the craziest thing?" Keith says, placing a protective hand over Felicia's protruding belly. Her smile never wavers, doesn't hint at jealously or suspicion that might otherwise accompany meeting your boyfriend's former squeeze. Certainly not how I behaved when I saw Alyssa the other day at the resort. *Alyssa*, my brain growls.

"Wow. Just ... wow. Congratulations! Keith, this is ..."

"Incredible, isn't it? Oh, Hol, I gotta say thank you a million times over for dumping me. You were so right. It honestly was the best thing for both of us." He says hi to my dad, Dad congratulates them heartily, and once we're all up to speed with what is really going on here—Felicia is the sister of one of Keith's longtime EMT buddies, a total sleazebag we in dispatch called "Mushroom Cap Joe," but Felicia is amazing so she obviously got all the cool genes in her family. I do not say this out loud.

"And my Felicia is helping you find a dress? When's the big day?"

"Three weeks," Lucy snipes from across the sitting area.

"What she said."

"Seriously? That's so soon. You sure you don't got a bun

in the oven after all, Hol?" He doesn't let me answer. "I can't even tell you how excited we are about this little nipper. Did Felicia tell you it's a boy? I'm gonna be a dad!" he says, throwing his arms around me in a near-strangle hug. "I was gonna tell you the that night at the game but your dad kept kicking me out of the room, and then it didn't seem appropriate, you know, 'cuz you had vomit coming out of your nose and stuff—"

"Yeah. I remember it. Thanks."

"Yeah! So, when are you guys gonna start popping out some little Ryans? I'll bet he's jonesing to start his own hockey team, huh? Is he here, by the way? I'd love to say hello."

"No. He's ... he's in town but he's with his brother."

"Oh, right. Superstition, can't see the dress and all that, which is sorta weird because you're already living together. Tell me, Fel, did she pick a white gown, or did the angels scream when she tried it on?"

Ha ha ha.

"Wow. Three weeks till the wedding?" He drapes his arm around Felicia again. "Cupcake, that's what we should do. Just say screw it and get married."

Felicia smiles and kisses his cheek before removing herself from his embrace and stepping behind the front counter, her smile still intact. As it should be. The commission on a seven-thousand-dollar dress can't be too shabby. Which is probably why she has such enviable hair.

"I'm sure you guys are starving, so grab some lunch and then Antoinette will be here waiting for you at two. Oh, and

Hollie," she says, leaning closer to me, "don't eat too much before the fitting. I tell all my brides that."

"Hollie, it is so good seeing you again. And you too, Bob," Keith says, pumping my dad's hand.

All of a sudden, Lucy Collins is right there. "You're Hollie's ex?"

"I am. And you are?"

"I'm her mother. Although you wouldn't know it by the way she treats me. Probably not even invited to the wedding." She points a finger at Felicia. "You're gonna practically die through thirty hours of labor for that baby, but it's only the beginning of the suffering, believe you me."

Miss Betty links her arm through Lucy's and drags her toward the front door. Her head tilts close to Lucy's but I have no idea what she's saying. Something threatening, I hope.

"So, hey, that was weird," Keith says, "but seriously, Hol, tell Ryan that you guys should hurry up and have a baby so our kids are close in age. They can be, like, pen pals or something, and when you come visit your dad, we can have play dates."

I need to leave.

"Great. Okay, thank you so much, Felicia. See you at two."

Dad and I walk with Sarah in between us, our arms looped together so we take up most of the sidewalk, Miss Betty and Lucy still up ahead. Dad and Sarah take turns near-whispering to me about letting it go, that the Lucy situation is temporary. Just before we're seated in a quaint Italian joint around the block, Dad reminds me again that once Lucy gets bored, she'll move on. "It's what she does, kid. Try not to let her get to you."

But it's not Lucy I'm thinking about as I stare blankly at the menu. Well, I am thinking about Lucy, but not a hundred percent.

Keith is having a baby. A real live baby. We never talked about having kids because we couldn't get past the part where he treated his Yorkies better than me. Not even kidding. Our last Christmas together, I got a superhero T-shirt and a set of fuzzy handcuffs from the mall novelty shop. The dogs got to go to a doggie spa and have the full treatment—the two girl Yorkies even had their toenails painted.

Then why do I give a shit that Keith is happy? I don't. It's been a year since we parted ways. He deserves to be happy. It makes me feel less shitty about dumping him so abruptly. And there isn't a single cell that pines for him or my former life. Are you kidding? Look at what I've got. *Look at who I'm marrying.*

But ... babies. Why does it always come back to babies?

"Hollie Cat? Are you going to order?"

"I'll just have a salad. Bleu cheese on the side. Extra tomatoes. And a Perrier."

"You're gonna have to eat like that for the next three weeks or you won't fit into that dress. I've heard of brides turning into total fatties before their weddings because they can't manage the stress. With what you just paid for that piece of fabric, you'd better not go fatty," Lucy says, the impatient waitress tapping her order pad. Lucy then proceeds to order the four-cheese lasagna, an extra serving of garlic bread, an Italian soda with whole milk, and tiramisu. Pretty sure that distant scream is her arteries begging for mercy.

Dad and Miss Betty manage the lunch conversation, thank baby Jesus, and by the time Dad has paid the tab, Lucy has withdrawn into a food coma, practically snoring on her feet.

"Sarah, you know how to get to the hotel from here?" Dad asks. "Why don't you ladies go check in, maybe take a rest." He lowers his voice. "Give yourself some space from certain company." He throws a subtle thumb in Lucy's direction. "When Hollie's done here, I'll bring her by and you folks can go about your evening. Sound good?"

Sarah looks so relieved I swear she might cry. Which wouldn't be totally out of character for her.

"You picked the perfect dress," she says in my ear as she hugs me. "I'll see you in a few hours."

And then they're off. Dad sits in the waiting room upstairs during my appointment with Antoinette, an adorably compact Russian woman who used to be a dancer before she moved here from Moscow. She asks me a hundred questions about Canada, and then teases me about what I ate for lunch. When she helps me into the dress again, my love swells for this "piece of fabric." I absolutely made the right choice. And then Antoinette pokes and prods around my boobs so we can get the best fit, discussing options of silicone bra inserts stitched into the corset or going with those stick-on bra cups. We decide that I do need a little lift, so silicone it is. Hey, Ryan knows what's underneath. No false advertising here.

"You are veddy lucky to find de perfect dress. Not every girl has dat happen," she says. "It ees like it was made for you! Only have to fix de bosom!" she says, the skin of her fifty-something throat jiggling when she giggles.

Upstairs, we meet again with Felicia—who is still genuinely nice—where we arrange for Dad to pick up the finished dress in a week. He can keep it for me until the weekend of the wedding. Because nothing on heaven or earth will keep him from being there, he promises.

Walking out of the boutique, I'm exhilarated and exhausted. Dad wraps his arm around my shoulders but we don't talk for a few blocks, instead taking in the late-afternoon sun painting cool shadows as the light bounces between the tall buildings. The sky is nearly cloudless, a deep turquoise, and the occasional breeze reminds you that it's May in Portland. Global warming will scorch this pavement in a month's time, but right now, the urban trees are proud of their soft green foliage, and newly planted color bursts in pots and planters along the storefronts scream springtime. I love this time of year.

I let Dad lead me to a coffee shop, just like old times when we would hang out on Sunday mornings, post-pancakes, pre-his work shift, him reading the newspaper, me reading whatever novel or nature guide had caught my fancy. Only today we aren't talking about current events or dietary habits of sea otters.

Cups in hand, we find two unoccupied overstuffed chairs by the dormant fireplace.

"You okay, kiddo?"

"Yeah ... just tired."

"Today was a lot. I can't believe you found a dress after one store. I thought we'd be driving all over the place this weekend."

I smile. "I'm sort of in shock myself."

"Hey ..." He nudges my foot with his. "I'm sorry about your mother."

"Nah. Why are you sorry? You had nothing to do with it."

"I know, but I'm sorry she tried to crap on your day."

"Now you can see why I'm not super excited about inviting her to the wedding."

"Totally understandable." He sips his coffee.

"Did I tell you she wanted to have a double wedding? I cannot believe she was trying on dresses."

"I can. Lucy has always been like that. That's why she left, you know."

"Meaning ..."

"Meaning she hated that you, the baby, were getting all the attention from family and friends. She loved being pregnant because she was the center of attention for a few months, but when you were born, that ended and it became all about you."

"Is that a bad thing? Isn't that what's supposed to happen?"

"Well, *I* think so. Babies are a miracle. But they're also

a lot of work and some people just aren't cut out to be parents." I nod but the voice in my head is screaming *Like you Hollie you shouldn't breed because you will end up just like her.* "I see the wheels turning, kid. You are nothing like her."

"How do you know, though?"

Dad tips his head. "Really? I raised you. I know you better than you know yourself."

"I'm freaked out because it seems like everyone is having babies—Jesus, even Keith!"

"Yeah, that came out of left field."

"And he didn't mention it that night after the Moda disaster?"

Dad laughs. "No, he was too busy showing everyone the video of you barfing."

"Nice. Awesome."

"Just feel sorry for his kid, Hollie Cat. And be glad you didn't reproduce with *him*."

"Amen to that." I swirl the stir stick to melt the raw sugar along the cup's bottom. "But ... what if I don't want to reproduce at all? Why is that everyone expects that as soon as you get married, you'll start squeezing out mutant life forms?"

"Society, kid. That's just what people do."

"But what if I don't *want* that?"

"Have you and Ryan talked about it?"

"He loves kids. He wants a whole bunch of them."

"Do you see this becoming a problem?"

"No. At least not yet ... he says he wants whatever I want. He's a little older than I am, so maybe he's closer to being ready, but twenty-six still feels really young to be a mom. I'm still trying to get my own shit together. How can I possibly be responsible for someone else?"

"You never know, Hollie. I see how you are with animals and how caring you can be. I've seen you with the kids on those nature walks. I think you might surprise yourself—the maternal instinct is in you. It's just dormant right now."

"Dad, taking care of an injured bird or letting other people's kids pee in the woods for fun is a lot different from taking care of a baby twenty-four/seven."

"Where you're living, it's the perfect opportunity for you to test drive a baby. Sarah and Tanner are going to have their little one, and you'll get to be the doting auntie. That's exactly what both you and Ryan need. And when—if—the time is right, you'll make it happen."

"But won't you be disappointed if I don't have grandbabies for you to spoil?"

"Truth? Of course. But it's not about me, is it. Just like this wedding—and even this day, today—was not about Lucy Collins. You'll know when it's right, Hollie. You and Ryan are a team. You guys will call the shots."

I drain the rest of my cup and drag the stick through the sugary residue. "I'm getting married."

"That's the rumor."

"It is a pretty awesome dress, isn't it," I say, a satisfied smile pulling at my lip.

"You done good, kid. All around." Dad sets his cup on the table and pulls me to my feet. "And I'm guessing your knight in shining armor would like you to join him for dinner."

"You want to come too?"

"No," he pulls his wallet out and stuffs a hundred-dollar bill into my hand, "because I want you and Ryan to order room service and shut yourselves away from the madness that is your mother. She's not staying with any of you, is she?"

"Oh god, no. She had strict instructions that she had to find her own accommodations. Although she is going back to the Cove with us tomorrow ..." I just want it to be over.

"How much longer?"

"We only have room for them until Wednesday."

"Four more days. You can do four more days." Dad pushes the coffee shop door open for me and we retrace our steps to his car.

"What am I going to do about inviting her to the wedding?"

"That's totally your call. If you don't invite her, she may crash it."

"That's what I'm afraid of."

"So maybe invite her, but tell her she can only stay for that night and then she has to go home. Just because Ryan is the boss doesn't mean he doesn't have partners to answer to."

"That's what I told her." I wait for the car door to unlock and slide in. "How did you ever marry someone like Lucy, Dad?"

He laughs as he pays the parking attendant standing at

his window. "She was a different person then. We both were." When the lot gate lifts, Dad pulls onto the street and heads toward the Marriott where I hope my Ryan is waiting for me. With champagne. And chocolate. Or maybe chocolate champagne. Do they make that? My brain is so tired ...

"I know you can't see it now, Hollie Cat, but your mother wasn't always the person you're seeing today. She got lost. There was a lot of hurt in her childhood. I know that's no excuse for her behavior, and I'm not asking you to cut her any slack—that's the worst thing you can do because she smells it and will take advantage. But don't look for her flaws in yourself. You had a completely different life than she did. You know right from wrong. You can make the choices for a better future, for yourself, and for your new life with Ryan." He chokes up a little. "I'm really proud of you, kid." He reaches a hand over and squeezes my shoulder.

"Thanks, Daddy. For being awesome." I hold onto him until he pulls into the hotel's parking garage.

"Oh—wait, before you get out." He puts the car in park and leans into the rear seat for a shoebox. "Some flies for Ryan and Tanner. My latest creations. They can catch some fish for the wedding banquet."

"That they will ... thanks, Dad. See you in a few weeks?"

"Wouldn't miss it, kid. And keep me in the loop with the dress—I'm not working next Friday or Saturday, so whenever it's ready, I'll go get it."

The funniest thing happens as I wave goodbye, a box of fancy fishing hooks in hand, watching my dad circle around the parking garage to the exit. It's like whatever was left of my childhood, of not quite being a grown-up, is buckled into my spot, twisted in her seat and waving at me from the rear window.

16

Fire ... and Fizzle

Never underestimate the superpowers of a man in love.

I'm at the door, fussing with a card key that evidently thinks I'm lying and won't grant me access to our hotel room, praying that Lucy Collins is not on this same floor and she doesn't smell that I've returned and then attack with claws and fangs exposed, when the door flies open. Before me stands a hunky, curly-haired fiancé in nothing more than a towel.

"That took forever," he says, pulling me into the room, taking Nurse Bob's shoebox from me, peeling off my clothes. "Close your eyes."

"What are you doing? Tell me there's food in here. Oh—wait—Dad gave me a hundred bucks for dinner."

"Room service has come and gone. No peeking."

"But you're making me nekked."

"As you should be."

"But I need the foods."

"All in good time, Porter."

He turns me by the shoulders and leads me into what must be the bathroom. "Ryan, I smell fire."

"'Tis only the smell of my burning desire." I reach behind to see if I can find his burning desire under his bath towel but he smacks my hand away. "You cannot have dessert yet, missy." The smell of flame is overridden by that of ... flowers?

"Can I open my eyes yet?"

His fingers drop from covering my face. What a sight to be greeted with. Candles—hence, the smell of fire—and bubbles and so many flowers in crystal vases surrounding the giant soaker tub and food on a sprawling cart and champagne and fluffy robes hanging on a warming rack.

"After you, Miss Porter," he says, offering a steady arm to help me into the fantastically warm water.

It shouldn't be this much fun—we have a soaker tub in our apartment at the Cove—but this is a new place. A hotel that we don't have to clean up after we splash water all over the tile floor or carry our own towels to the laundry or load our own dishes into the dishwasher. Decadence that you don't have to tidy is the highest level of luxury.

We take turns feeding each other from the spread he had delivered, laughing when an errant chunk of butter chicken and a very stubborn grape tomato disappear under the bubble-topped water. We drain the first bottle of champagne and pull our bodies out to lean against the tub sides to take care of coupling business that proves hilariously challenging when attempted under the suds. Also, I don't want a bladder infection. Too much bubble bath can do that, ladies. Pissing superheated urine tinged with blood where the nearest doctor is three islands away and probably short on antibiotics? Not awesome. Lesson learned.

Breathless and drunk on booze and one other, we slither back into the tub. Ryan stretches to the cart so he can dip strawberry and pineapple chunks into a fondue pot gurgling over a tiny flame, both of us laughing like idiots when the chocolate goes from polite dipping to full-on body paint. For the record: fondue chocolate can be rather warm on bare skin (although, I will admit, nothing like Sriracha).

Ryan refills our glasses and lifts his to mine. "To the future Mrs. Ryan Fielding. And to the miracle of finding a DRESS!"

Clink and drink, baby.

I immerse to my chin against my end of the tub, legs stretched, propping my foot on Ryan's bent, hockey-scarred knee. "Did Sarah tell you what Lucy Collins did?"

He finishes his champagne, puts the glass aside, and sets to rubbing my foot. "Four more days, and she'll go home."

"You sound like Dad. Oh, he sent some flies for you and Tan, by the way." I flinch when he hits a sore spot in my arch. "Today was awesome, but bizarre." I fill him in on seeing Keith, how Felicia helped us and then turns out she's his girlfriend and they're having a baby ...

"Was that weird? Seeing that he's having a baby?"

"A little. I never imagined he'd have a human child."

"As opposed to an alien child?"

"As opposed to a Yorkie child."

Ryan snickers. "Look at you, though. A year ago, did you think you'd be marrying someone as dashing and charming as *moi*?"

I splash the few remaining bubbles at him. He's quiet for a beat, his smile shrinking into something that looks like nostalgia.

"Alyssa was pregnant."

Whoa.

"What?"

"She was about three months' pregnant when I hit the boards and blew out my knee."

I pull my foot away and sit straighter against the tub. "Why haven't you told me this before?"

"It didn't seem relevant."

I'm not sure how to react. I guess it's not relevant ... there was no baby. I panic for a brief second thinking about little Theo but the timing is totally wrong. And that's ridiculous—if Ryan were Theo's father, he'd still be with Alyssa. No way Miss Betty would let her grandchild get away from her, nor would Ryan ever shirk being a dad.

"What happened?" I ask quietly.

"She had an abortion." He gathers straggling bubbles into a bigger clump in front of him. "We'd already started talking about names and everything but then she just came home one day, not feeling well, and fessed up. Said she wasn't ready to be a mom."

"Wow. Jesus, Ryan ... She didn't even talk to you about it?"

He shakes his head no. "That was the worst part, you know? I get that it's her body and she had the ultimate choice, but we were engaged—it was my baby too. And she just took it into her own hands and didn't give me any say."

"But you guys stayed together after that?"

"For a little while. On and off. I knew, though, even then, I'd never marry her. I couldn't spend my life with someone who had such little regard for my feelings. And my mom ... she was devastated. You know how much she loves her grandkids."

"Shit, Miss Betty knew?"

"Yeah. That was really hard."

I need to reassure him. "Ryan ... I would never do that to you. I'm not going to lie—it feels like the entire world is pregnant right now, and I am so not ready to be a mom, and everyone keeps asking me and it's freaking me out a little and it could be years before I'm ready to take that next step, but if we *did* get pregnant, we'd have the baby. I wouldn't go behind your back like that."

His smile is sad, but genuine. "I know, Porter."

"What names did you have picked out?"

"For a girl, Clara—after my grandmother. It means 'bright.'"

"And a boy?"

"After my dad."

"Patrick ..."

Ryan reaches for my foot again and resumes kneading the sole. "Seeing Alyssa the other day with little Theo—that was strange. So I get what you might be feeling about Keith having a baby on the way."

"Well, sort of. Keith's kid isn't mine. Thank heavens." He snorts and nods in agreement. "I'm sorry that happened to you, Ryan."

"Hey, everything happens the way it's supposed to. Like my mom said at the time—if we'd had the baby, we probably still would've broken up because I couldn't give Alyssa the fantasy she wanted, so what kind of a life would that have been for the kid, split between his or her mom's house and the Cove?"

I pull my foot away and move across the tub to straddle him, cupping his bearded face in my hands. "I promise you, no matter what, I will never do anything to betray your trust."

He squeezes my buns. "I know. That's why I picked you."

"Oh, it is, huh? I thought it was because of my beautiful round breasts." I shove them in his face. He kisses each one accordingly.

"Those too."

"And my mad skills in the sack."

He hefts me out of the water and onto his lap atop the ledge again. "Absolutely that."

There was something else he picked me for, but I can't remember what. Because the time for words is not right now. Not until we've almost fallen off the ledge and we're cackling like idiots and he's carrying me, our bodies still connected, to the bed where he finishes the job in a crescendo of flaming, skin-on-skin fireworks.

As he covers us with the sheet and curls me against his tired chest, I can say with confidence that accepting this concierge's proposal was definitely the best choice I've made this month.

~ ~ ~

Knock knock knock.

Knock knock knock knock.

"Ryan ... someone's at the door," I slur into the pillow.

"Whaaaa?"

KNOCK KNOCK KNOCK.

I sit up. "Babe, someone's at the door. You're the man. You go."

"Shit ... yeah ... okay." He rolls over and scrabbles around for pants.

"What time is it?"

He drags a finger against his phone's surface. "One thirty." And then he's up, moving through the cozy, dark bedroom, lamplight from the living room spilling through the open door. The main door's slide lock opens, followed by voices.

One of which, more than anything, I do not want to hear.

Groaning, I jump out from under the sheet, grab the hotel robe, and move to see what the hell is going on.

"There she is. Tha's my daughter. She'll take care a' me now so let GO," Lucy says, trying and failing to yank herself away from two burly hotel security guards clad in black. A scrawnier manager type stands to the side, a worried look on his ruddy face.

"I'm so sorry, Mr. Fielding, but we were trying to close the bar and she wouldn't leave. She said you're her family, and that she was staying with you."

"Does she not have a room?"

"No, sir. Not here, at least."

"Why do I need ta get a room when you got tons a' space in here? It's a suite! Look at all tha' space! I'm already payin' for a room at your stoopid hotel. Some of us ain't made a' money, ya know, *Ryyyyan*."

I move into the frame. "And you're drunk?"

"It was just a few drinks."

"She, uh ... she left an unpaid tab," the manager says, his cheeks aflame. His copper-penny-red hair is parted funny, like he's been in a scuffle with someone. Probably someone named Lucy Collins.

"How much?" Ryan asks.

"Uh, $230, sir."

"Jesus, Lucy! Who drinks two hundred dollars' worth of booze in one night?" I say.

"Mr. Fielding, we can call the police, if you don't want to take her in. This seems like an awkward—"

Lucy drops to her drunken knees, the security guards hanging onto her limp-noodle arms. "Please don't let 'em call the cops, Hollie. Lemme crash on your couch. I promise ta be good. I promise ta shut up and jus' go ta sleep."

"Un-fucking-real," I say under my breath. "Hang on a second." I find the jeans Ryan peeled off me just a few blissful hours ago and dig out the money from my dad. I then stretch to hand it to the manager. "For her bar tab. I'll take care of the rest in the morning when we check out. I'm so sorry about this."

"So ... should we leave her with you?" the manager asks, his face almost begging us to relieve him of whatever nightmares Lucy Collins has wreaked in the past few hours.

Ryan and I look at each other, and then he instructs the security guards to help her into the suite and onto the couch. The manager leaves me with Lucy's overnight bag, the one full of her own stuff that she should've used to stay in her own damn room.

Once the hotel staff has departed, though not without more apologies from the manager to Ryan, I pull a spare blanket and pillow from the bedroom closet and throw them at Lucy.

"You were told that you could come with us if you had your own accommodations."

"Well, I woulda had my own acc—acc—accodations if I din't have to pay so much at the dress store. I din't damage those dresses. They lied 'bout the whole thing jus' to get cash from me."

"I saw you in the dress. You damaged their property. They were within their legal rights to charge you for the damage."

"No way. Four hundred smackers worth a' damage? You kiddin' me? D'you know how long it takes someone like me to earn four hundred bucks?" She flaps her arms helplessly, trying to spread the blanket across her legs. Her face is a cosmetics nightmare, smeared eye shadow and mascara and lipstick that was likely applied on a drunk face by a drunk hand in a funhouse mirror. "You got anythin' to drink in here?"

"Water."

"Tha's it?"

Ryan offers a bottled water over my shoulder.

"Well, Mr. Fancy Pants, I hope after ya bought a dress worth seven grand tha' water isn' too much for ya."

Ryan is better at ignoring intoxicated people—occupational hazard—but I want to throw her out the window. Luckily for Lucy, the windows on the fifteenth floor don't open wide enough to cram a body through.

"Oh, come on, li'l girl, don' look so mad. What have ya got ta be mad about? Livin' in the lap a' luxury?"

"Shut up, Lucy. Lie down and go to sleep, and not another effing word or else I will call the police."

"You wouldn't."

Ryan speaks from the doorway to our bedroom. "She would. And if she doesn't, I will."

She cackles. "They'd probably be happy ta see me ag'in."

"Are the police looking for you, Lucy?" I ask. Jesus, is she really on the lam? Am I harboring a wanted person?

Her eyes look momentarily sober. "You gonna call 'em ta find out?"

"You've seen enough action for one day, Ms. Collins," Ryan intercedes. "Go to sleep." Lucy opens her mouth to protest but Ryan beats her to it. "Not another word." He sounds mean. It sort of turns me on. I feel so ... protected. "In the morning, we will get ready, return to Revelation

Cove, and this will be the last incident from you, or else you will never be asked back."

"Even for tha wedding?"

"Especially for the wedding," he says. "Hollie, let's go to bed."

Once the door clicks closed behind us, Ryan is quiet as he tucks me into bed and pets my hair until I finally stop shaking and fall asleep.

17

I Shall Call Her Squishy and She Shall Be Mine

How a person can drink that much and not be making soul-bearing promises to the toilet the next morning is beyond me.

Miraculously, though, Lucy Collins is awake, fresh makeup on, sitting on the couch in what appear to be clean, albeit garishly unmatched clothes. The living room reeks of nail polish as she fans bright red fingernails while gingerly flipping through a glossy magazine about Portland nightlife. She's rather silent. Which is weirdly unsettling. Perhaps she learned her lesson last night? Perhaps when she murmurs a small "thank you" to Ryan as I stand at the front desk paying the balance of her bar tab, she realizes she might have stepped over the line?

And then she departs in the middle of cramming blueberry pancakes into her face in the dining room, disappearing into the ladies' until the bill is long paid and we're all waiting on her in the lobby.

Forget it. I just want to go home.

The original plan was to return to the Cove tonight, but as the dress has been conquered (I so love my dress!), and given the events of the last eight hours, Ryan had an off-camera chat with Tanner et al, and we're leaving this morning. The sooner we get home, the better.

Six hours later, as the pontoons glide across the water just off Revelation Cove's docks, the excitement of being home and away from Lucy's constant whining bubbles in me like that feeling just before the grown-up-sized roller coaster rockets down the steepest incline. Like, so excited, you might pee your pants but you won't because that would be super gross and then the attendant would see it when you get off the coaster and you'd have to walk around the amusement park in wet pants. I will neither confirm nor deny that this is from real-life experience.

Tanner ties off the plane, the boys help us unload, and then Tan and Sarah bid us adieu, en route in their own boat to their cabin for some much-needed peace and quiet. Though Sarah says she's worried about her tomatoes, I think the truth is she's had her fill of The Lucy Show. I almost take her up on the offer to come hang out, but that wouldn't be fair to Ryan or Miss Betty.

Life as resort managers is never dull, so as soon as we're through the door, Ryan and his mom disappear into the office to catch up on the goings-on missed in the last two days.

"Hollie," Miss Betty says, drawing me aside as we watch Lucy Collins sashay down the hall toward her room, "tonight, let's the three of us sit down and finalize some details. Colors, flowers, what have you. I'll cook. Sound good?"

"Sounds perfect."

I drop off our bags in the apartment, grab a heavier pullover from the closet, check my camera for batteries and install a fresh memory card, and pluck the boat keys off the hook by the door. I need some Me Time.

The main kitchen fridge has silver buckets of fresh butter clams, and Joseph is happy to part with a few, reminding me how to use the clam knife so I don't slice the meaty part of my thumb open. Again.

I text Ryan and tell him where I'm going rather than interrupt whatever administrative stuff he's dealing with. But given that it's technically my day off, he knows that if he can't find me curled up on our couch reading or Netflix bingeing, I'm probably out looking for otters. And I'm much better with water safety than I was a year ago, thank you very much. No more lost oars for Hollie. Well, maybe one lost oar. Which is why I take the boat with the engine. See how smart I am now?

The water is a bit choppy in the main inlet with a southerly wind stirring it up but once I steer around the side into the protection of the scattered islands, it calms, giving the afternoon sun a chance to burn through what's left of the morning chill under a mostly blue sky. As happens when moving into a new neighborhood, I've slowly learned the markers that help me find my way—they're not street signs or buildings that serve as landmarks but rather certain shapes in the rock or a series of trees that grow out of the sides of the islands or a giant eagle's nest that expands throughout the season. I'm learning the stars with Ryan's help, depending on how bright they burn, how dark the night is. If I screw that up, GPS will sing me home.

I can independently navigate to Smitty's General Store south of the resort—helpful when I need tampons and chocolate or when Ryan needs beer because I need tampons and chocolate—as well as to Tanner and Sarah's cabin and of course to Otter Beach. Which is where I'm headed, ready to cut the engine and float in quietly to see if my friends are around.

Once the gurgle of the outboard is silenced, I step onto the rear deck and scan for otters. Success! A handful of regulars—all females and their youngsters—float and frolic near the shoreline, chomping on small crabs and urchins. Female otters will often have scarred noses from aggressive mating, although seeing an otter floating with a buoyant fluff of new life on her tummy is all the proof you need that she's a momma. We think there are at least three males who frequent the area—they're much bigger than the females—but they don't often hang out once they hear the boat.

I quietly lower the anchor into the water by hand so the winch doesn't startle them, although I visit often enough that they know the sound of the boat. With the vessel steadied, I break out the butter clams and pop the shells, setting the halved delicacy in tidy rows on the stern's small deck. I step aside, and before long, my first customer arrives. One female in particular, blond head and a pink, scarred nose and always the bravest, makes short work of the chewy clams, scurrying away before I can inch closer for a photo.

Legally, I'm not supposed to be feeding them. It's not healthy for these animals to become habituated to humans. Ryan said once or twice a year should be okay, and only if I'm discreet about it. And we don't do this with the guests—it's between me and the otters, and sometimes a few sharp-witted gulls.

Two other females nearby are definitely onto their sister otter. More clams halved, I again step out of range, kneeling with camera at my eye, so the otters will feel comfortable enough to slide onto what is basically a thick shelf and help themselves. I photograph them through the gap left by the open half-door, and only once did that prove unwise. A big male came all the way onto the deck looking for the stash of clams, but I think we scared the hell out of each other when I stepped forward and shooed him into the water.

Over the gummy, slurping chewing of otters in mollusk heaven, high-pitched squeaks echo off the rock face. Unmistakable—it's a new baby!

I trade the camera for the binoculars from the steering column and tiptoe out to the rear deck, scanning the beach.

Sure enough. Elation! Otter babies are the cutest things in the whole wide world.

Wait, though. There's another baby. Momma has one on her tummy, grooming, licking, tugging, and then she drags this one ashore and switches them out. They are very young twins, judging by the size and fluff, likely only a few days old. The twin not on Mom's tummy squeaks holy hell until she swaps them out.

Twins are a problem for otters. She can only float with one at a time, so that means the stronger one survives while the other one will languish on shore, and usually succumb to whatever predators lurk about. A baby otter is an easy meal for a bird of prey, which is why moms don't leave their babies unattended for very long, and when they do, it's usually in the water, anchored by kelp, or floating in quieter waters such as those found in Elkhorn Slough off the California coast.

I watch Momma for a while, swapping out one baby for the other, each getting a chance to nurse and be groomed and tugged about in the water. Baby otters don't know how to swim when they're born, which is why nature gave them incredibly buoyant bodies coated in thick, fluffy fur. It also means Mom has to teach them to swim, which can look a little violent at times. But I don't think swimming lessons have yet begun for these two—they're still too small.

Camera again in hand, I capture some heart-swelling moments with this extended family, hardly noticing that two hours have gone by and I should probably head home.

Only, I can't. Because when else will I get a chance to see something so amazing? Baby otter twins!

Clams long gone, two young females aren't shy about using the stern's deck to relax, alternately napping and grooming like housecats. I set the camera aside and settle atop one of the built-in side benches, legs pulled to my chest, watching Mom juggle her babies, using the quiet that is pierced only by bird calls and the squeaking baby otters to think about the last few days and how grateful I am to be here, on the water, in this boat, right this second.

But the calm doesn't persist—the baby on the shore is squeaking with pronounced vigor, almost like it's in pain. I don't see anything near it on the beach, so I grab the binocs again and watch. For over an hour, this baby squeals and chirps, its calls like a two-tone whistle, and I keep waiting for Mom to come back for it. Another half hour passes and the mom is nowhere to be seen. Even my sunbathing beauties have slid into the depths and disappeared to wherever they go when the sun shimmies behind the rocky outcroppings.

The radio crackles inside the cabin. Cell reception is dodgy out here so Ryan typically relies on the two-way. "This is Hollie," I answer.

"Hey, you okay?"

"I'm at Otter Beach."

"Coming home soon? Sun is starting to fade."

The otter squeals in the background. "Yeah. I'll be home in a bit. Everything okay there? Is Lucy causing any more trouble?"

"Quiet as a church mouse this afternoon."

"Thank heavens."

"You're sure you're okay out there, Porter?"

"Everything's fine. I'll see you in a little bit."

Only that little bit turns into a long bit. Because the otters are gone, and the baby on shore is alone. When the shadows disappear and dusk wraps itself around us, I pull the portable spot from the work chest, affix it to the deck, and plug it into the boat's main power source. I need to keep light on that baby so that predators stay away.

As my anxiety percolates, stance rigid and eyes on the shore, I have to remember that this is nature's way. She knows what she's doing. Maybe Momma Otter is putting the other one to bed and will come back for this baby. Although the little scientist in my heart knows that's not the case. Both babies in an otter twin birth rarely survive. It's too much for a mother who spends most of her life in the water.

For a beat, I think of my own mother who, in essence, left me on shore. Only she didn't have twins to deal with—just me. What would life have been like had she stayed? Would it have been one long, embarrassing parade? Would it have been twenty-six years of what I went through this weekend? How would life have been different? How would *I* have been different?

Maybe what Dad says is true. That everything happens the way it's supposed to. Maybe I should forgive Lucy Collins a tiny bit. Maybe she did what she had to do to survive, just like this momma otter is doing what she has to do to save at least one of her babies.

Seeing this little one alone onshore, though, I can't just go home and let nature take her away. She's alive, she's viable, and this population is endangered. Should I call someone? Or should I wait a little longer and see if the momma does reappear?

"Little sweetie," I say under the waning sun, "mommas don't always come back. But that's okay. I won't leave you."

While I still have scant daylight, I unload the inflatable dingy and battery-powered pump. If I need to go ashore, I want to be ready. It's not a boat I want to spend a lot of time in, but here to shore isn't far and it's better than swimming in water that darkens in accordance with the sun's fading position in the sky.

Dingy tied off, I sit, serenaded by the otter's urgent squeals, and watch.

And watch.

And watch.

And the sun is definitely gone. It's getting cold, and there are no otters in sight.

Mom's not returning. The baby won't last the night.

The radio crackles again. "Porter, it's getting too dark for you to be out there alone. You on your way home?"

"Yeah. Leaving here soon."

"Soon as in now?"

"Soon as in soon. I'm ... monitoring a situation."

"Hollie ..." Ryan drags out my name.

"Save me some dinner." I put the mic down and ignore

him saying my name a few more times. I'm not ready to leave yet. And if I tell him what's happening, he'll tell me to walk away and let the otter be, to let nature take its course. But I can't let this baby suffer alone on the shore tonight.

I give it another hour, until it's properly dark, only a half moon hanging out with us.

Still no mom. A few curious seagulls have landed near the mewling pup. One even takes a nip until the otter squeals so loud, the bird skitters away.

I check the time. It's been hours since Mom was here. And as the baby's squeals lessen, it's obvious she's wearing out, that she's probably hungry. Plus those damn birds are getting more aggressive.

That's it. I'm going ashore.

Life jacket on, I grab an extra fleece sweatshirt to wrap her in. If nothing else, I'll sit on the shore and wait for a while longer with the baby wrapped up to keep her away from the birds. If Mom pops through the water's surface, I can return her infant, no harm, no foul. While we wait, if I can get a connection, I'll Google the Vancouver Aquarium Marine Mammal Rescue folks and let them know she's here.

I angle the spotlight so that it's squarely on shore to give myself a wider landing spot. In the last year, my hunky concierge has instructed me in proper piloting technique for these smaller boats as we sometimes take our nature-tour guests ashore in small groups if they want to fish from the beaches. Ryan only reminds me every third time I climb aboard a boat of that one fateful night when I took a dip with some orcas ...

With a last pull on the oars, I feel sand under the rubber bottom. I tug the boat onto the beach, and realize I'm shaking—I've never been this close to a wild otter before. The babies have teeth but if I keep my fingers away from her mouth ...

"Shoo, dumb birds. Get away from her." The baby's squeals and squeaks are quieter, but she's still occasionally flapping her wide, webbed feet. "Heyyyyy, little sweetie. Where's your momma? Ohhhh, you are so beautiful ..."

The warning echoes in my head that I've heard from conservationists and the otter pros—"Don't touch a wild otter without a specialist on hand"—but this is an extreme situation. I can't just leave her here! She'll starve!

Right?

I pull out my phone and check for a signal. One bar. Open Google but the screen cycles and cycles and won't connect. If I were Smart Hollie, I'd have their number in my contacts, or better yet, memorized.

But I'm not Smart Hollie, and this baby needs help.

Executive decision time.

Save the otter, or return to the main vessel and hope for the best, hope that she's still here in the morning and not pulled into twelve pieces by the sniping gulls or bigger, meaner birds? Will her cries attract a cougar taking a leisurely swim past the island in search of hors d'oeuvres?

Shudder. No more cougars.

I can't leave her here. I might get a big fat slap on the hand, or worse, a meaty ticket, for wildlife interference but I'm not some newb strolling along a beach. I've trained for these situations, I've been here observing for hours, I'm familiar with this romp of otters, and this baby is in jeopardy, in a population that cannot afford to lose a single member.

I spread the sweatshirt out on the sand, and with the care given to a newborn—because that's what she is—I scoop her up. She's so light! And floppy! Both hands under her body, I hiccup with excitement. Is this real life? She's absolutely the most breathtaking thing I've ever seen. And her little fuzzy brown face, the curled-down whiskers, the marble eyes rimmed in white that suggest she's distressed ... I can't see her clearly for a beat because my own eyeballs are clouded with happy tears.

"Are you cold? Your momma didn't mean to leave you. Mommas do that sometimes. They get busy or have boyfriend problems or sometimes they go to jail for unpaid parking tickets. It's okay. I won't let anything hurt you." I wrap her in the sweatshirt, wishing like hell that I had some of the clams left so I could chunk it up and give it to her. She nuzzles into the sweatshirt fabric, squeaking. She's gotta be hungry. It's been hours since she last ate.

We sit on the shore in the glow of the spotlight, me rocking her in my arms, cooing to her adorable little face, the cold sand freezing my ass through my jeans but I couldn't care less. I scan the water and between her baby otter sounds, I listen for activity in the quiet surf, that maybe Momma Otter has come back for her. My phone vibrates in my pocket, surprising given the shoddy signal, but I can't move. Because I'm very busy right now.

With a pop, the spotlight goes out, a slow fade to black, followed by the shudder and disappearance of the remaining lights on board the cruiser.

Now, that is a darkness I do remember from last year.

Which makes things remarkably more interesting. Well, at least for me. The baby is snoozing, warm and cozy, in my arms. I watch her nose and chest to make sure she is indeed sleeping, and that hunger and exhaustion haven't claimed her.

Carefully, I ease my phone out of my pocket, not surprised to see the battery life is at thirteen percent. It wouldn't be a Day in the Life of Hollie if I didn't do something dumb. A text message has squeaked through: *"You're taking too long. I'm coming out after you."*

Oh man, I hope he has a battery charger on board.

~ ~ ~

Having a concierge-shaped Ryan motor in like some water-bound guardian angel never gets old, I gotta say.

Even when he can't decide what to scold me about first.

"You weren't answering the radio," he says as he stomps ashore through the dark water, long legs clad in hip waders. A new spotlight on his boat lights us up like noon.

"I was busy. And the battery's dead."

He looks over his shoulder at my very quiet, very dark vessel.

"The spotlight. It was on for a few hours," I say.

"That'll do it." Ryan takes the last step out of the water and freezes. "What are you holding?"

I smile at him, a big, goofy, don't-yell-at-me smile. "She needed help."

"Hollie, what is it?"

I try not to grin but I can't help it, even if he's going to be angry. "A baby otter."

"Oh man, what the hell?"

"She's a twin. And her momma has been gone for hours. She's had to leave this one."

"You cannot just pick up a baby otter off the shore! What if her mother does return and the baby's not here?"

"Did you hear what I said? She's a twin. Otter twins rarely survive. Female otters are not physiologically capable of nursing two babies—their bodies can't make enough milk. This little sweetie can't be more than a few days old, but she has about another twenty-four hours of life if we don't *do* something."

"I know you love these animals, Hol, but this is dangerous. Intervening like this."

"No! It's not! It's our obligation as caretakers of this place. I came ashore when the seabirds starting picking at her. I couldn't just sit in the boat and watch them eat her. What if an eagle saw?"

"This is illegal. These animals are protected under federal and international law. I know you mean well ..."

"Ryan, if I had left here earlier without making sure she was safe, I'd never have been able to live with myself. And I tried to look up the Vancouver Aquarium rescue number but I can't get any service. I'm not leaving her here."

"And she's safe now in—in a sweatshirt? With a

human?" He leans over and looks at her little face, and in that brief second, I swear something melts in him.

"Isn't she gorgeous?"

Ryan sighs and scratches at his beard. "What's your plan?"

"Well, I could sit here all night and wait for the momma to reappear, which she probably won't, or ..."

"Or what?"

"Or we take the baby to the Cove with us, get her warm and feed her—"

"What do baby otters eat?"

"Ideally? Their mother's milk. We can't give her cow milk because it's not good for her, and she needs something with a lot more fat in it. The aquariums use a special recipe to emulate fatty marine mammal milk that is super rich in vitamins."

"I'm thinking Joseph might not have that in his kitchen."

"She can have finely chopped clams, crab, and squid for tonight. We should definitely call Fisheries and Oceans Canada or the Vancouver Aquarium."

He's shaking his head again.

"I'm not leaving her out here alone. Seriously, she has an expiry date. These pups are fragile without their mothers."

"Shiiiiiit ..."

"Do you have any food on your boat?"

"Not unless she eats string cheese or energy bars."

"She needs baby-otter food."

Ryan turns away for a second, scanning the darkness,

hand over eyes squinting against the bright artificial light. "Is there ever a dull moment with you, Porter?"

"You should've run while you still had the chance."

Without saying much else other than the mumblings under his breath, Ryan pulls the inflatable dingy into the water to deal with my dead battery. Even though I know he's not super pleased with me, I'm grateful he's here—I had no idea we had a battery charger on board, so I would've spent the entire night shivering in the dark. Well, shivering with a wee fuzzy lass to keep me company.

She's been quiet for too long. Which makes me nervous again. I give the baby a slight shake, and she squeaks awake. And squeaks and squeals for the next fifteen minutes until she wears herself out. By then, Ryan has my boat motor churning, cabin lights on, and is again rowing toward shore.

"She needs food, Ryan."

"Come on, sailor. I'll row you out, and then you follow me home. When we get to the Cove, we're calling Fisheries and Oceans."

Until then, however, I have a baby otter in my arms.

Achievement: unlocked.

18

Love Is Spelled O-T-T-E-R

The gentleman we talk to on the phone at Fisheries and Oceans is not pleased.

However, once I explain my background and training, how I'm not just some crazy otter lady, how I worked at 911 so I understand emergencies, and how I sat with this otter for the better part of eight hours and the mom was definitely gone, he softens.

"Give small bites of clam, squid, crab, urchin, or shrimp, but be careful of its teeth," says Officer Johnson. "Don't give the otter any cow milk. It can dehydrate. Use a tear dropper or medicine syringe to get some water into her, if you can. And do you have any cats?"

"No. No cats."

"Excellent." He's asking because cats can carry toxoplasmosis, lethal to otters.

"Should we call the Vancouver Aquarium rescue people?"

"I'm going to do that now. They'll probably send someone up first thing in the morning." I get to spend a whole night with her! "You can put her in your tub to float but don't leave her unattended, and absolutely dry her off completely when you take her out of the water. Try to collect any feces so they can analyze it. It won't smell pretty."

I chuckle. "No worries here." Who cares what it smells like? I have a baby otter in my apartment!

"Okay, thanks for your help, Hollie. Although I can't say that there won't be some penalty for intervening," he says, his voice hardening to sound like the tough upholder of the law he is. "You should've just called us directly and we could've coordinated the rescue."

"Well, like I said, I couldn't get service out there in the middle of all those islands, and the birds were attacking. I couldn't, in good conscience, leave her alone. I monitor these otters regularly, and twin births are so rare ..."

"Stay close to a landline. Either I'll phone you back, or a member of the Aquarium's Marine Mammal Rescue unit will phone to coordinate a pickup. And ... thank you. I'm sure he or she is a little sweetie."

Miss Betty doesn't quite know what to think when she walks into our bathroom in her robe and slippers long after her son has had to launch another daring midnight rescue. Ryan explains that this is all legit, that we've called the proper authorities and someone will come for the otter in the morning. But this is a baby, and Betty is a mother and a grandmother, so even if this creature is covered in fur and smells kinda funky, it's useless to resist the cute.

"Can I touch it?" I nod, and she uses her knuckles to rub the otter baby's tummy. "Ah! It's so fluffy! And soft!"

"Amazing, huh?"

Ryan steps into the kitchen to finish chopping up the seafood as I explain to Miss Betty the details of recent events—and that I might get slapped with a ticket—but she agrees that I did the right thing, even as her son hitches an uncertain eyebrow upon his return. He hands me the silver bowl full of slimy, raw deliciousness.

"I never understand how those nature photographers or biologists can just walk away when they see an animal in distress," Miss Betty says.

"Law of nature, Mom."

She flaps a hand at him. "Do you know if it's a boy or girl, Hollie?"

"I just checked—didn't find a wiener."

"We should name her," Miss Betty says.

"Mom, no," Ryan scolds. "Don't get attached. She's not a puppy."

In the confines of the bathroom, without the beach noises and natural surroundings to absorb the sound, this little sweetie is *loud*. Like, really loud. The high-pitched squeals and squeaks bounce off the walls, but like any baby, the best way to quiet her down?

Food.

I feed her tiny chunks of clam and crab and shrimp. Hope Joseph doesn't mind that we helped ourselves to more of his stash. I'm sitting on the closed toilet lid, the otter settled on my lap so her webbed feet flap against my stomach. She's not too nimble with her little paws yet, and yes, her teeth are sharp (!), but she's ravenous.

"We did the right thing," I say, pointing to the glass of water and medicine syringe on the counter, just out of my reach. "Look at how much she's eaten already!"

Someone knocks on the door. "Crap, she's being too loud," I say. Ryan slides out to go answer, but when he returns, he's not alone.

"What in the world do you have there?" Lucy asks. "I was hungry and the kitchen's closed, so I thought I'd come see if you had anything to eat. Heard this racket way out in the hallway."

I don't want to share this moment with her. Seems I don't have a choice when she pushes past Ryan and Miss Betty. "Oh wow, now this is something I've never seen. Is that an otter?"

"It is."

"Where the hell did you find it?"

I give her the quick story, hoping she'll grow bored and leave.

Instead, she settles onto the tub's edge. "I'm a sucker for baby animals. When I was eight, I moved into a new foster home out in the country—big house, nice enough people. They had this huge orange tomcat named Tigger who used to knock up all the local female cats. Real player, this guy," she says, touching the baby otter's head with a gentle finger. "One night I heard this yowling outside my window. Just wouldn't stop. So I sneaked out in the pissing rain, and Tigger, mean ol' bastard, had a kitten in his mouth. Not like he wanted to kill it, either. I watched for a second and he dropped this scrawny, black-and-white mess and then started grooming it. The damnedest thing! But then the mewling started up again, and Tigger walked away. I think he knew I'd help it, ya know? So I picked up the baby and brought it inside.

"I stayed up with it all night. Fed it milk from a drinking straw, with my thumb over the end to create suction so I could drip milk into its mouth. Pretty clever for an eight-year-old, huh?" She smiles. "In the morning, my foster mom heard the kitten's cries under my covers."

Lucy pauses.

A foster mom? Shit.

"What happened to the kitten?" I ask.

"The foster mom let me keep it. I named her Flower. Like the skunk from *Bambi*? Thought that was appropriate." Lucy's smile fades. "That cat was something else. I wonder whatever happened to her."

"Did you not stay with that family?"

She shakes her head. "Them's the breaks, kid." She leans forward on her elbows, and for a fleeting second, something softens in her eyes, in her face. "What the hell are you going to do with an otter, though? Not sure you can litter train one of these."

"We've called the wildlife officials," Ryan says. "They'll send up a team tomorrow."

"Solid plan," she says. "You're a good kid, Hollie, rescuing this little beast. Even if it stinks to high heaven."

The four of us spend the next hour feeding the otter baby, offering water from the plastic syringe, Lucy remarkably calm and helpful. Ryan runs a tepid bath and we let the otter float, although that makes her shriek again, and it's after one o'clock in the morning. We don't want to wake up our guests, and even though I'm exhausted, I don't want to waste a second of time with her.

I dry the baby thoroughly, just as Officer Johnson instructed, and then once she's rewrapped in warm towels, we move into the living room. Lucy, once she's raided our fridge, ruins all the good vibes by mentioning that she's gotta go because Ernesto wants to inspect her healing bikini line and can she have this extra can of whipped cream?

"Could've gone a lifetime without hearing that, Lucy. Thanks," I say as the door clicks closed behind her.

Soon after, Miss Betty yawns and excuses herself to bed, pooh-poohing my advance apology because the otter has resumed her noisy shrieks. "If anyone complains, we'll give 'em more drink coupons," she teases.

Once we're alone, Ryan plops down on the sofa next to me and blows out a tired exhale.

"Foster homes? Wow, that explains a lot," I say.

"Yeah, that sucks. It was funny to see her chill out around the otter, though." He points at the bundle in my arms and runs a hand over his head, fingers scratching through his thick beard.

"Detroit's still in, I take it?"

"Yeah. They beat Anaheim last night. Double overtime. On to game four."

As soon as Detroit is eliminated, or wins the Cup, the beard goes. "I like Anaheim."

"You like Anaheim's *players*."

"Do you blame me? Hockey players are hot," I say, smiling. He nudges me with a finger.

"Are you going to sit up with her all night?" he asks.

"Absolutely."

"You look like a little kid at the Wonka factory."

"Oh, she's way better than Everlasting Gobstoppers."

He snorts. "You know we can't keep her."

"I get to keep her until someone shows up to take her to her new home." Ryan smiles and shakes his head at me. "What?"

"You."

"What about me?"

"You get so freaked out about having kids, and then look at you."

"This is hardly the same thing," I say, rubbing the backs of my fingers up the baby's furry belly. Seems to calm her down. "You don't let a newborn baby float in a bathtub or feed her chunked raw clam. Which I will need more of before you retire."

"It is the same thing, though. You don't know it yet, but

someday, maybe, you're going to be a natural at this mom stuff."

"Yes, because I've had such an excellent role model?" I don't want to talk about this. I only want to stare at my new friend and watch her chew on her soft, leathery paw pads.

"Not everyone would do what you did today." He leans forward and chucks my chin with his knuckle.

"Because I'm nuts?"

"Probably. But you're my nut."

"Speaking of nuts ... that woman exhausts me. She tells us this sob story about her pet cat—and I feel like a dick even saying this, but how do we know that's real? Did you see her face when we mentioned the police last night? Like, is she a criminal? What if she's wanted for something really bad, and we're helping her hide?"

"That part's none of our business. She's your mother; she showed up at the resort; she stayed for a visit; and soon she will leave."

"But how are we going to invite her to the wedding? It's all about her, Ryan. Everything always has to be about her. You didn't see her at the bridal shop. It was so embarrassing."

"She's desperate for love. She craves your attention because something is missing in her life. You heard her—raised in a foster home? Something went really wrong somewhere along the way, and now her wiring is askew."

"And that's my problem how?"

"It's not your problem. Except, you're a compassionate person so you will do the right thing, whatever that is for

216

you, in your head. You don't have to invite her. But ... you need to think about if you'll someday regret *not* inviting her. Family and all that."

"She keeps bringing up all these exaggerated medical problems, but she's just manipulating my emotions to get what she wants."

"As long as you know what you're getting yourself into, you can establish boundaries. Go from there."

The otter will have none of this grown-up talk and ratchets up her piercing protests. "More food, chef!" I say. Ryan, his green eyes droopy and hooded from lack of sleep, drags himself into the kitchen to refill the silver bowl.

Once she has more food in her belly, the baby settles, wrapped snugly in a towel against me, nestled in the crook of my left arm. The towel weighs more than she does.

Ryan leans over us, his weight supported on the couch's back, and kisses me, murmuring against my lips. "I'm proud of you, Porter. But I really hope any future babies we rescue don't smell like this one."

I smack his damaged arm and he feigns injury, kissing me again quick before disappearing into our room. But my eyes are pried way open, cataloguing every detail on this little creature's face, not thinking about Lucy Collins and her Flower, smiling so hard my cheeks ache, moving my body only enough to reach my phone on the coffee table so I can text Dad a photo.

He's so not going to believe this.

I can hardly believe it myself.

~ ~ ~

In the subsequent six hours that culminate with the sun again rising, I learn a number of things: dozing in an upright position is hard on a person's neck; tiny otters wrapped in towels on the kitchen counter wiggle much less if you shove every other bite into their mouth as you cut their snack; otter poop is super gross and will stain everything it touches. Including the couch when a particularly fearsome squirt leaks through the towel in the two seconds you've put the baby down to get yet another towel.

If motherhood involves this much poop, I am definitely not ready. God, I hope Sarah knows what she's in for.

Ryan holds on to the otter long enough for me to start a huge pot of coffee and slide into a quick poop-removing shower. All clean, I walk out wrapped in my robe to find him with my phone up to his ear. "One sec, here's Hollie," he says, passing it to me.

The Vancouver Aquarium rescue doc. She asks a million questions about the baby—food, fluid intake, how much she's pooped, if she seems alert—and says they're leaving in an hour to fly up to the Cove. She doesn't scold me, not like Officer Johnson did, but her tone only warms after I again explain how yesterday went down. "A Fisheries and Oceans officer will be along with us and will want to see the beach where you rescued her. No guarantees there won't be some fines levied because of wildlife interference, but I'm glad you did what you did. Every otter is precious," she says. Finally, someone who speaks my language.

Ryan, looking slightly more rested than he did when he went to bed, prepares yet another bowl of seafood goodies before he leaves to deal with Monday morning front-desk chaos. "As soon as they arrive, I'll bring them here, yeah?"

"Probably best. The vet said to keep her away from the guests. Germs and all that."

He pours coffee for me and then scoots out the door. Knowing I have two, three hours tops, before my new friend goes to her new home, I draw another bath and let her squeak and eat to her heart's content, grabbing my camera to take a few photos, though I don't want her to flop over in the water and get stuck face down.

Sarah texts me to make sure she heard Miss Betty correctly: "*You have a baby otter in your apartment? Hollie Porter, defender of animals everywhere!*" My dad doesn't believe it either, calling me instead of texting, laughing that his crazy daughter never ceases to amaze him, though our chat is cut short by the otter's deafening vocalizations. "Dad, I have to cut more clam. I'll call you tonight and let you know what happens."

And then, just like that, our floating time is over when a knock befalls the door and the Aquarium people are here to take her away and yes I'm happy that she will be safe and that the vet is impressed with how well she's doing and yes she is indeed a little girl and I'm over the moon when they open a cooler of fresh baby bottles filled with otter-specific formula and the otter takes to it like me on a freshly frosted cake.

The FOC officer wants the GPS coordinates for Otter Beach as they're going to send some observers over to monitor the population. The vet, Dr. Rosamond Little, scoops floating otter poop from the tub water and explains the important health information they can pull from the sample. And then the Fisheries officer tells me that they're not going to give me a ticket for wildlife interference this time, but if I come across the same situation again, I am absolutely to not enact the rescue myself.

Which I politely agree to but if presented with the same situation again, where I couldn't get a cell signal to call for help, I'd rescue away. No baby otters are going to die on my watch.

Dr. Little lets me hold her one more time before they tuck her into a carrier, although they should just hold her because she's tiny and scared and she likes being held. I probably look like an idiot, tears rolling down my face as I snuggle this tiny fluff and tell her that I will come visit and she has to be a good girl and eat lots and get big, but not everyone gets to have a moment in their life like this. I'm not going to miss a thing, idiot or not.

And then they're gone, my heart reassuring me that the squeaks and squeals bouncing off the long hall walls are because she misses me already.

Before they departed, Dr. Little offered a stain-removal recipe for the poop smear on the couch—two parts hydrogen peroxide to one part blue Dawn dishwashing liquid—but I'm too busy blowing my tear-stuffed nose and looking through the photos taken over the last twelve hours to care about erasing stains.

My phone skitters across the countertop.

"Hello?"

"You okay, otter girl?" Ryan.

"Yeah."

"She squealed holy hell all the way out of the building. Tabby came running out of the spa because she thought we were murdering your mother."

"I wish." I snort.

He chuckles. "You did the right thing."

"I know. Thanks for your help."

He pauses. "Can you come down to the office for a minute?"

"Shit, now what?"

"Just come down. I have Irish coffee ..."

"Tease."

But I hate it when he does that. Hangs up without giving me whatever news he has. The hollow feeling returns, an effective mood darkener that reminds me that Lucy Collins is still on the premises, and twenty-four quiet hours is twenty-three hours too many.

19

High Roads Are Full of Stones

When I walk into the front office, it's clear by the small crowd gathered in the security anteroom that we're not here to talk about cake flavors or floral centerpieces.

"Hey, Tanner," I say, stepping in between him and Ryan as they peer at two of the six security monitors. Tabby in her white spa coat and strappy sandals that make her seem nineteen feet tall, her mermaid hair freshly blue, winks at me, though she looks uneasy.

"You saved a baby otter?" she whispers. "You're the coolest person I know."

Miss Betty has her fingertip on the rewind button on the playback machine; Thomas, our Rock-sized head security guy, stands with bulging arms crossed, watching. Cameras throughout the resort monitor the activity in common areas, the pool, the hallways, the exits, as well as behind the bar in the lounge and anywhere on site that has to do with the exchange of money. We don't monitor inside guest rooms but we do have cameras that track the hallways. All this footage is then recorded in twenty-four-hour chunks and archived onto a hard drive that Thomas maintains, in case of customer complaints.

Such as the complaint that came in this morning: a guest room theft, yesterday during the dinner hour.

Miss Betty hits play and the scene unfolds before us: two people suspiciously in the shape of Ernesto Finklestein and Lucy Collins fiddling with a door that does not belong to room 330, going into said suite once access is gained, and leaving a few moments later, pausing only long enough to wipe clean the stainless steel door handle.

Stomachs don't belong in one's feet. It makes it harder to walk when you realize that someone related to you is a conniving criminal and you have to go punch them in the throat.

"What did they take?" I ask, my voice small.

"Allegedly, a Rolex worth about eight grand, two diamond rings, and some cash," Tanner says.

"How much cash?"

"About $500 US."

"Was this stuff not in the room safe?" I ask.

"Apparently not."

"How would they know what room to hit? Or did they go into multiple rooms?"

Ryan looks at me, his expression angry and worried at

the same time. "The suites are the first places these types will look."

"But how did they get in? How would they jimmy an electronic, card-key-controlled lock?" I ask.

"Amber and I were on the front desk Saturday second shift while you guys were out," Tabby says. "The Ernesto dude was alone, so he got friendly with a young couple and their baby. Bought them drinks and dinner. We didn't think anything of it," Tabby says. "You know how people will make friends with other guests."

"We think maybe one of the victim's card keys were stolen at that time," Thomas says. "We're still reviewing the dining room footage from Saturday night."

A young couple and their baby. Please don't say it. I look right at Tabby. "And the couple—they made the complaint this morning?"

Ryan nods. "Right as I got down here."

Tanner looks at the room registration paper in his hand and reads the names out loud, although I already know. "The suite belongs to Drew and Alyssa Clarke."

It could've been *anyone* except them.

"Ryan ... I am so sorry," I say.

"It's got nothing to do with you, Hollie," Miss Betty says, turning in her chair to pat my forearm.

"But we still need to deal with it," adds Thomas, his Revelation Cove uniform slightly more formal than the rest of ours—he insists that a suit makes him look like he means business.

"This situation is complicated," Ryan says. "Mom, rewind so we can watch it again, just to be sure."

I don't need to watch it again. I know what I saw.

"We have to confront them, immediately, before they can leave," I say. "Because if there's one thing I know about Lucy Collins, she's a pro at sneaking away."

"This is theft of big money," Thomas says. "We should call the RCMP and let them deal with it."

Ryan shakes his head. "I know Drew and Alyssa," he says. "If I can recover their property and offer them some free nights, they'll be cool. You, me, and Tanner will go to Finklestein's room and let them know that we have them on camera entering and exiting the room."

"You honestly think they're going to come clean?" I say.

"They will if we give them an ultimatum," Ryan says. "I don't think either one of them want to get tangled up in the Canadian justice system. Might be better if we just recover Drew and Alyssa's stuff and kick out the thieves."

The thieves. As in my mother and her skeezy boyfriend. I'm not sad to have a reason to get her out of my life. She's been here too long already.

"You're the boss, Ryan. If you want to deal with this quietly, I'm game. Less paperwork that way," Thomas says, adjusting his tie. Ryan nods and steps out of the cramped quarters, already dialing his cell. I squeeze my hands into fists, digging half moons into my palms, aware that it's very likely Alyssa will answer his call and that means he has to talk to her again. Haven't they stayed long enough? It's been almost a week. Why couldn't they have just left when Itsy-

Bitsy and her micropenis husband and their tablet-toting brat shipped back stateside? Did Alyssa think that by staying longer, she'd have more opportunities to reclaim Ryan's affections? That maybe I would—I don't know, be busy rescuing baby otters—so she'd have plenty of time to invite him to see how motherhood has made her boobs so much more tantalizing?

"Hollie ..." Miss Betty reaches to touch my hand. "There's something else you should see." She nods at Tabby.

"Okay, my wax pot calls. Lunch today. You. Me. I have to see the dress. Tell me there are photos. And I have to know how the hell you ended up with a baby otter in your apartment. Find me," she says, air-kissing my cheeks.

She follows the men out of the office. Miss Betty pivots in her chair and grabs a faxed document off the adjoining desk.

"What's this?" I recognize my dad's handwriting on the cover sheet: *"Hey, just a heads-up. Keith called in a favor. Love to all, Dad/Bob."* The second page—a printout from the National Crime Information Center, or NCIC, lists several outstanding warrants as well as the criminal record belonging to one Lucille Alice Collins and her multiple associated aliases. My shoulders fall, and with them, my hope that my mother is not a lost cause. "I knew it."

"Hollie, this isn't your responsibility."

"When did this come in?" I ask.

"Late last night." As in, when I was out sitting on the darkened beach, in seventh heaven, cuddling the baby otter.

Shit shit *shit*.

"Has Ryan seen it?"

"Yes."

"What the hell am I going to do? I don't like the woman, but I don't want to call the cops on her, either. What kind of a daughter am I if I turn in my own mother?" I read through the printout—these are all crimes against property, a few fraud charges, public mischief, and public intoxication.

My stomach hurts.

Miss Betty swivels an empty office chair around and I dissolve into it, head in my hands.

"Why does everything have to be so complicated? Why did she have to show up? Now what am I supposed to do? She's a criminal—how can we trust her here if she stays? Especially now that we've got them ripping off guests?"

"You should talk to Ryan."

"I can't keep her here, Betty. We've seen more than enough proof already that she can't be trusted. What do I do now? And what about the wedding? How do I get out of her being here for that? It's still twenty days away! She can't be here for twenty days! I might kill her!"

Miss Betty chuckles, but it's not a happy-ha-ha laugh. "Family can be madness, my dear. My sister, bless her heart, was a troublemaker. The whole time we were growing up. Didn't have an original thought in her head and was constantly trying to steal my friends and my boyfriends. When our parents died—the kids were just little then—it got really nasty when I was appointed executrix of their estate. She didn't speak to me for a whole year—over some stupid painting."

I love Miss Betty but I'm not exactly seeing her point.

"Family doesn't always come in the shape you want it to. It's messy and sloppy and gossipy and even downright mean sometimes."

"But criminal? So, what? I let her stay? Until after the wedding, even if multiple police agencies want her? How the hell did she even get into Canada?"

"I know you don't have much love for Lucy Collins, but she is your mother, and it sounds like she really wants to be a part of your life."

"I don't buy it. In fact, I'm now positive the only reason she came here was because she thinks Ryan is loaded, and like a shark that gets a whiff of blood in the water, she's smells his money."

"Have you talked to her about this? About why she came up?"

"No. Because everything she says is a lie."

"But speaking from my experience as a mother, maybe she does want to be a part of your life, for real, and even though she hasn't gone about it very well, she's here now. If she spent time in foster care growing up, she's probably had a rough go of it. Maybe she wants to try and fix things with you."

She's had my whole life to do that.

"Miss Betty, just because Lucy told us some sappy cat story that's probably not even true, I don't know why I have to open my heart to her. She's ripped off the Clarkes for thousands of dollars. She's carpet-bombed every possible moment since she stepped onto our dock!"

"Yes, and twenty days is certainly too long to have her here. We won't have a guest room for her anyway, so that's all you have to tell her. But maybe, if they work things out with the Clarkes, you can talk to Lucy about returning for the weekend of the wedding. Without the boyfriend, of course. We can't risk them both being here."

"I just want her to go away."

Miss Betty leans closer, her smooth, warm hands gripping mine, her blue eyes soft but strong. "I think a lot of people have just wanted that woman to go away. Maybe we should give her the benefit of the doubt."

"So she can steal from more guests? Tell us more crap stories? Or so we can flout the law, knowing now that there are active warrants for her arrest?"

"I'm not happy about the warrants, I won't lie, but I think there's more going on here than we can see on the surface. Perhaps, for now, we should take the high road on this one."

I'll take the high road—the one that leads right off the cliff and into the boiling heart of a volcano.

~ ~ ~

Two hours later, Finkelstein stands at the front desk, crummy Samsonite at his feet, flanked by Thomas and Tanner. In exchange for returning the watch, the rings, and the cash he didn't spend at the lounge last night, in addition to his immediate removal from the premises and paying a tidy sum for the damage caused to room 330, the Clarkes agree not to press charges. I bite my tongue as Alyssa coos at Ryan—shamelessly, in front of her husband—about how much she appreciates his concern and quick action.

Oh brother.

Thomas nudges Finklestein's arm.

"Where's Lucy? I ain't leaving without Lucy."

"Today, you are. Let's go," says Thomas, puffing out his chest, his bodybuilder shoulders straining against the overtaxed stitching in his suit coat. Ernesto cusses under his breath and picks up the tattered suitcase, turning one last time to look at me.

"Your mother is crazy as they come. Don't turn your back on her for a second," and then he's slithering toward the front doors, Thomas close behind after agreeing to provide escort on the shuttle boat to the Lower Mainland.

As much as I would like this scene to be over, there is still the matter of dealing with Lucy Collins, who is currently sitting in the office under Miss Betty's watchful eye. Once Ryan has settled the situation with the Clarkes, including booking them on an afternoon flight to Victoria, I pull him across to the storage room behind the concierge desk.

"What do I do about Lucy? You know she has active warrants?"

"I read the fax. And yes, she definitely has to leave. We can't risk more burglaries."

"I'm aware of that," I say, a little too defensively.

"Hollie, I know this is an impossible situation for you." He puts his hands on my upper arms, squeezing gently.

"Everyone here loves and supports you. No one blames you for this. Not even Alyssa and Drew."

"Even though *my* mother stole their stuff."

"We got everything back—almost everything—so they're happy. They know this was an isolated incident."

"I feel like a dick."

He looks me over, head to toe, turns me slightly to ogle my backside. "You don't look like a dick. You look like a Hollie."

"Smart-ass."

"The situation has been handled. Your mom can go wherever she wants, and if you want her to come up for the wedding, fine. If you don't, that's fine too."

"That is, if she doesn't get arrested first. I still cannot work out how she got across the border."

"I'd guess she has at least one fake passport."

"I can't be the one to call the police on her. Even if I joked about it before."

"Yeah, that would be tough."

"And I know theft is bad, but she didn't murder anyone."

"Hey, as long as she's not stealing from my guests, I don't want to get involved any more than we have to."

"Do you think I should invite her to the wedding?" I ask.

"Totally up to you. She can't bring Loverboy with her, but she's your mother. If you want her here when we get married, I understand. If she can stay out of jail between now and then."

"Shit, I wonder if she'll add me to her list of people to

call to bail her out. I think she's only here because she thinks you're rich."

"It happens. People don't know the reality, that everything I have is in this place."

"You mean, you don't have a safe stuffed with bullion and cash hidden somewhere on the island?" I pretend like I'm opening the storage room door. "I'm outta here."

Ryan grabs me around the waist. "There is no escape for you now."

I hug him back. "This is such a mess. And I can't believe we're getting married in twenty days. And I miss my otter. I wish we could invite *her* to the wedding. She could be the flower otter."

Ryan laughs and whispers in my ear. "I should probably punish you for all your misbehavior lately."

"Promise?"

But even as he smacks my ass and kisses my head, I think about the criminal record sitting in the back office. "I can't believe she's my mother."

"She's made some bad choices, but that doesn't define who *you* are. And you can't fix her life for her, Porter." He rubs my back and squeezes me so hard. "The tough bit is you don't want to admit you feel sorry for her because then she'll take advantage."

"Exactly." I hook my fingers around the belt loops on his cargo pants. "I love you, Concierge Ryan. Thank you for putting up with so much of my crap. You're a good man."

He plants a lingering kiss that tells me he's had a lot of coffee this morning but I don't care because he loves me and when his face is squished next to mine, the world feels like it's not so impossible to deal with.

"Off you go," he says, kissing the tip of my nose. "Deal with whatever's waiting for you behind Door Number One."

I guarantee it's not a new car or all-expenses-paid trip to Reno.

~ ~ ~

Inside the front office, Miss Betty has made tea but Lucy Collins sits slumped over in one of the overstuffed chairs, the tea and saucer balanced precariously atop a tiger-print-clad thigh.

Her lips part when she sees me, but I stop her before she speaks.

"That was some interesting reading." I point to the faxed pages sitting on the small round coffee table in front of her.

She straightens and sets the tea down atop her criminal record. "I hardly think my legal problems are any of your business."

"You made 'em my business when you decided to stage a heist. Why couldn't you have just kept your sticky fingers to yourself? Just this one time?"

"Betty says you sent Ernie home without me?"

"You're more than welcome to leave on the next vessel out. Well, not the flight. The people you ripped off will be on that plane, and I'm guessing they don't want to commute home with a kleptomaniac."

Miss Betty clears her throat and nods her head gently, her voice echoing in my head: *Take the high road.*

High roads are so dumb.

"Here's the deal, Lucy. You need to leave the premises. That's part of the agreement for us not calling the RCMP. I don't know how you've managed to not be caught—there are active warrants on this list—but we're not going to get involved."

"How noble of you," she spits.

"Point is, Ryan and I ... if you want to return for the wedding, you can. It's on June 14, a Sunday."

Her eyes perk up. "Really? I'm invited?"

"We'll hold a small guest room for you, Friday to Monday only. But further criminal behavior will not be tolerated. We will not make any more deals. If you steal so much as a shower cap, we will absolutely call the police."

"The stealing ... that's Ernie's thing," she says, adjusting her sleeve. "I hate doing it."

"Your rap sheet says otherwise."

"You don't have a problem judging a book by its cover, do you, kid? Your dad teach you that?"

"Why did you even come up here?"

"I told you. I wanted to get to know you."

"Having a hard time believing you, Lucy. Tell me the truth."

She leans back in the chair and crosses her arms, her cleavage testing the limits of her tired shirt. "Fine. I wanted to see how the other half lived. You've obviously done well for yourself—Ryan has provided everything for you."

"And you wanted a piece of the action?"

She doesn't answer.

"You came up here to rip us off."

Lucy unfolds her arms and sits forward, a true flash of remorse washing across her face, though short-lived. "I saw you in the paper. Ernie thought it would be an easy score. But once we got here, once I saw you in person—none of that garbage meant anything to me."

It takes everything I have to not storm out. "How can I believe a word that comes out of your mouth?"

"You don't have to. I don't blame you for thinking the worst of me," she says. "But Hollie, I swear—once I saw you in the flesh, when I saw how happy you are with Ryan—I really do want to be a part of your life. I won't screw up anymore, cross my ailing heart." She drags a finger across her chest.

"Your heart is not ailing. It's only aspirin."

She laughs at me. "Yeah, yeah. But the ulcer bit is probably real."

"From all those years of clean living?"

"Something like that."

This is impossible. "If you return for the wedding, you cannot bring Ernesto with you."

For a second, she looks like she's considering a protest to my demands, but then she melts into the chair. "Fine. I'll take what I can get. If it doesn't put you out too much," she adds, sarcasm on full salute.

"Lucy, seriously? I didn't even want—"

"It looks as though things have been a little hard for you lately," Miss Betty interrupts. "So we will look forward to welcoming you back to the resort on Friday, June 12. Does that sound reasonable with your schedule?"

Lucy's eyes are fixed on me. "I'm sure my schedule can accommodate that. Even if you don't want me here, someday when I'm dead, you might come to realize that you missed your chance to get to know me." She gulps the rest of her tea. "When is my boat home?"

20

Pretty Corvus

Thank the heavens for small miracles.

The moment Lucy Collins left the island last Monday, my blood pressure returned to normal levels. (It was probably normal all along but given my sterling reputation as a drama queen, let's just say it was a million over twenty the whole time she was here.) Her departure allowed us to resume focus, and my personal bridal warriors and I were finally able to tackle the task at hand: planning an imminent wedding.

Antoinette called Thursday night, and Dad went right over Saturday morning. He called as soon as he got home to let me know—my gorgeous dress (and the dresses for Sarah and Tabby) is in his house, waiting for me! I want to press fast-forward so I can put it on right this second and dance around the hotel like a blushing bride is supposed to. But this won't happen because the wedding is two weeks from today, and Dad won't even be here with the dress until not this coming Friday but the following Friday so I just have to be patient and try not to eat my weight in cake samples. Mmmm, cake.

A rundown of Miss Betty's checklist (I am so glad she makes checklists):

Flowers are sorted. For the bouquets—mine, Sarah's, and Tabby's—deep pink peonies with a light purple double stock, Picasso calla lilies, late tulips in white, dusty-rose Lisianthus, purple anemones, locally sourced lilac, and a few succulents to tie in the Pacific Northwest theme, finished with a ribbon wrap. Succulents and anemones in the boutonnières for Ryan and his two brothers, and Dad. Calla lilies for Miss Betty. And yes, for Lucy Collins. Sheesh.

And wow, how much I never knew about the winsome world of flowers until Miss Betty and Sarah schooled me like the sweet-smelling beasts they are. It was a bridal flower catalogue smackdown in our apartment for three consecutive nights until my eyes were bleeding rose petals and baby's breath.

Choosing the cake proved to be super hard because we had to eat a whole bunch of cake. I know. And then I sneaked some out of the kitchen and smeared it all over Ryan's man body to get his opinion—he preferred the red velvet to my tiramisu—and whoa, that was a sticky mess (wink, wink, nudge, nudge). Seriously, the sacrifices I've made!

The cake's decor will reflect our local environs—trees, grasses, sand, water, birds, you name it, only with frosting and airbrushed food coloring and fondant, not real trees or grass or sand or birds because that would be weird and gross. No stuffy ol' boring white cake for Hollie Porter! Three layered, alternating red velvet with cream cheese frosting and French vanilla cake with chocolate mousse frosting. The guest list isn't huge, not with this short notice, so Sarah and I are already banking on enough cake left over to freeze so we can have at least three movie nights' worth after the fact. We cake eaters like to plan ahead.

Plus Joseph didn't laugh too hard when I said I wanted a cake-topper with otters made of fondant—instead he broke out the ukulele and made up a song titled, "Silly Hollie and Her Baby Otter."

Who, by the way, is doing very well so far in her new life at the Vancouver Aquarium. Dr. Little has been awesome about answering my emails and texts this week, keeping me apprised of what's happening, including information that our baby girl was thinner than she should've been at that age, a good indicator that she was not getting the adequate nutrition likely secondary to the twin situation. Though the vet again reminds me that wildlife interference is not something I should make a habit of (I laugh), she then thanks me for saving the little miss.

Today is Sunday, and the resort is full of guests primped and primed for another couple's wedding. Ryan is run ragged handling the concierge desk in addition to front-end duties—our usual weekend concierge, a sweet, long-haired lad named Albert, went to Squamish midweek to rock climb and instead of climbing said rock, he kissed it with his face and is now at his mom's in Vancouver nursing an arm broken in three places, pending surgery. Which means Ryan is in an extra fun mood.

Knowing this, I do what I'm told. And for this wedding, that involves chasing the photographer around, carrying sandbags and light stands, setting up strobes and flashes, retrieving and charging batteries, chatting up the wedding party and their guests while the photographer gets the shots he needs, and keeping everyone dry from the temperamental spring showers that keep mucking up the day.

We're setting up the bride and groom pre-ceremony for their portion of the photo session—I never understand why a bride and groom take these photos *before* the wedding. It feels like I should be walking around with a giant sign that reads, "Spoiler alert!" Everyone sees her dress, the groom doesn't have that OMG moment when she walks down the aisle toward him in the banquet room or on the beach or the dock or wherever the vows are to happen. And isn't that supremely bad luck for the groom to see his bride before they're hitched?

We are so not doing that.

Ryan has to wait. Photos after we're married. I don't want or need any more bad luck, especially knowing that Lucy Collins is going to be here when we do this. As part of our agreement before she left, I told her she can text me. No calls. It feels easier to talk to her electronically, but it doesn't mean she misses an opportunity to make me feel like crap because I "kicked her out of the resort" or because I "hooked a big fish." Despite her fleeting sincerity last week, I think she forgets that Ryan is a human being and not a walking, bearded dollar sign.

"Hollie!" the photographer hollers at me from across the yard just as the bride screams and trips off the six-inch wooden deck, tumbling over into the grass, petticoat to the sky so we can all see she's commando under that fluffy white organza ball gown.

Apparently the very large daddy crow dive-bombing the almost-newlyweds isn't impressed with them getting so close to his family.

Nice Brazilian, though. The bride, not the crow. Way better than Lucy's.

The groom tries, in vain, to help his bride but he's protecting his own head with one arm and the photographer is shrieking like a first grader in a funhouse and the bride can't seem to right herself and the dress is getting dirty, her veil tangling around her head as she yipes for someone to help her up.

I drop the sandbags and spring across the lawn, flapping my own arms at the crow, the photographer a useless huddle behind another tree. The groom grabs one of his bride's arms while I grip the other and we get her onto her feet so the remaining Revelation Cove guests don't see her finely manicured nether regions.

"My bouquet!" The bride points behind us at the wooden deck. Her lovely, blood-red, tightly packed rose bouquet sits perched on the wooden railing, Daddy Crow making short business of the petals—yank, yank, rip, rip. At least the petals look sorta pretty floating to the ground.

"Shoo! Shoo!" I yell, again flapping my arms like a madwoman to scare the bird, but he's obviously thinking this bouquet and these humans are offensive to his own need to protect his family in the towering fir tree behind us so he carries on, cawing at me, his partner cawing and screeching from above, until the bouquet looks less like a bouquet and more like some stumpy green things held together with fine ribbon.

I try to salvage what's left, one hand protecting my face while the other dares to stretch toward the bird and the flowers, but on my third attempt, Daddy Crow is done with my shit. He flies at me, lands on my head, pecking like a son of a bitch, screeching and yanking my hair and then he repositions and scratches my face and eye and I can't see and then I lose footing and I'm going to hit the ground and not the soft grassy bit but the part where we have sizeable river rocks stacked along the slope that leads down to the pool and patio area and then I fall—

Backward.

Left hand outstretched, jarring my whole left side as I slam into the sloping, masoned rocks with a thud. Pain rockets up my arm and the bird releases my face but I know I'm bleeding because there's blood in my left eye and *Jesus that stings whatever that is* but really, I'm not so worried about the blood.

I'm worried about the fact that my misshapen left index and pinky fingers are pointing in a direction not really appropriate for the human anatomy. My engagement ring is almost touching the top of my hand. I don't think it's supposed to do that.

The bride and groom run over, their wedding party close behind, and help me up, though as soon as my audience sees what's going on with my left hand, they're grossed out and squealing and at least one person has the decency to say, "Someone get help!" But that someone won't be me since first I have to throw up on the bride's dress because, as we've established in prior incidents, I vomit when severe pain rockets through my quaking, adrenaline- and cortisol-soaked body.

Revelation Cove: a full-service destination wedding location. Book your stay today!

~ ~ ~

"Hollie ... Hol ... come around, baby." *Pat pat pat.* Oh, I know this game. This is where Hollie does something stupid and passes out. Again.

I really should get that looked at.

My eyes flicker open and my left hand and my scratched face hurt a whole lot, I immediately remember why I'm on the ground and didn't we *just* go through this with the ankle last year and *Oh hey Ryan I love your face so much* but wait—

"Why is Lucy Collins standing over your shoulder?" I say.

"Wow, you really are an accident waiting to happen," she says, winking.

I close my eyes again.

"Up you go," Ryan says, hoisting me under my arms to standing. "We gotta get you fixed up."

I'm wobbly on my feet, clutching my damaged hand against my chest, but Ryan has a firm hold around my waist as we move through the gathered crowd. I turn my head and see Lucy watching us, stepping into line to follow. Miss Betty and Sarah are toweling off what my stomach deposited on the bride's gown—Miss Betty's jam is not nearly as appetizing the second time around. And it's so purple.

"Why is she here? She can't be here! The wedding isn't for two more weeks!"

"One disaster at a time, yeah?"

The front-desk clerk meets Ryan at the dock with boat keys, his wallet and phone, as well as a clean, barf-free sweatshirt that I absolutely won't put on because if anyone thinks about touching this hand ... And then we're on the boat and I'm in enough pain that it's just better for me to sit completely still. Or maybe lie down. Yes, lying down is nice. Ryan's on the phone, talking to Dr. James three islands up to decide where we should go. Nanaimo it is. South. I'm going to need X-rays and someone to set these bones.

"Can I have whisky?"

"You know better," Ryan says, gunning the engine as we speed away from the resort. "How did you do this?"

"Crow. Big crow. Why is Lucy Collins here?"

He doesn't answer except with the pulsing of his jaw as his eyes are forward on the water, which is fine. I don't want to talk. It's better if I not think about anything important.

Like why my mother, the admitted thief, is walking about the grounds of my new life despite the banishment placed on her just six short days ago. If this were feudal times, we'd throw her into the drink and walk away.

Man, that would've made things so much easier.

21

Full-Service Concierge

Ryan says he's not mad at me, but he's really quiet all the way down to Nanaimo.

It has to be stress. Today was nuts at the resort, and then I did *this* ...

When we get to Nanaimo Regional Hospital—closer than going farther south to Victoria—they take one look at my contorted fingers and bloodied face, and we're escorted past the coughing, groaning members of the crowded waiting room. But then this rush turns into a slow trickle. The nurse gives me something for pain, thank baby Jesus, and I'm not sad when it knocks me out for a bit.

I am sad, however, that they have to cut off my engagement ring. So sad that I cry into Ryan's arm because the ring is so beautiful and it hurts like a mother when they're gnawing at the white-gold band and I don't want it to come off because I've only had it on a short time and if it's not on my finger, that might mean I'm not engaged anymore. The nurse pats my leg and reassures me that of course I'm still engaged, even as I wipe my snotty nose against Ryan's cottony, Revelation Cove shirtsleeve.

Now that's love.

The damaged ring safely in Ryan's pocket, I doze off again as he strokes my hair with one hand and scrolls through his phone with the other—the bride and groom from today's fiasco are already asking about refunds, thanks to the crow, as well as demanding we cover dry cleaning to undo what I did to her dress. Ryan's hand is heavy against my head as he pauses the calming strokes for a beat to wipe his own worried face.

I cross my fingers in my head that whatever news they're delivering from the Cove, none of it has to do with the unexpected reappearance of Lucy Collins.

They wake me up when it's time for X-rays, and then when the doctor analyzes said X-rays and tells me both fingers have clean fractures that don't need surgery but he has to "reduce the bones and reposition the dislocations." That bit might hurt a little.

Liars, all of them. They asked me to stop screaming because I was scaring the shit out of the little girl next to me with the broken elbow who wasn't raising even a tenth of the fuss I was. Maybe her pain tolerance is better than mine.

The doctor also inspects the wound on my face from the bird's claws, asking about my most recent tetanus shot—"Last year when the cougar snagged me"—and then after a rousing retelling of that fun story and inquiry about the progress of Ryan's arm and if his slap shot has returned, the doc chuckles and tells the nurse to just use butterfly closures. No sutures. Another moment to be thankful, considering I'm getting married in two weeks and I'm not super excited about looking like the Bride of Frankenstein.

Wait—I'm getting married in two weeks. What the hell am I going to do about a wedding band?

Once my swollen fingers are again pointing in the appropriate direction, the nurse cleans up my face (more bloody stinging) and they send in a cast tech to do up the fingers and hand. This prompts more tears. (Did you know that in Canada, you have to pay for the cast before you leave the hospital? It's not part of the healthcare coverage. That was a new and weird experience.)

Ryan made sure they used water-resistant material. "Seriously, you have no idea the trouble this one gets into."

I watch the layers go on, covering pretty much my entire hand and extending up my wrist and forearm. "There is no way we can get married now. I can't put a wedding band on a casted finger," I say.

Ryan's smile is tired. "Nice try, Porter."

"I'm not kidding, Ryan. This is serious."

But then it's not serious, and we're both so tired that we're laughing like idiots, although no one really knows why we're laughing like idiots, not even ourselves, except for finding hilarity in the part that feels like if it can go wrong with me, it will.

Ryan, wiping his laughter-wet eyes, hands me the phone when my dad's number pops up.

"Hey, Dad ... Yeah, I broke two fingers. You know me ... No, no surgery needed. No, you don't need to come up ... Not a cougar this time—just a pissed-off crow ... Yeah, the baby otter is doing great ... I'm so glad you got my dress. Thank you for picking it up ... Dad, Lucy showed up at the resort again—oh, but I have to go. The nurse is here with discharge papers. I'll call you in the morning. Love you too."

I hand Ryan his phone. "Dad says he's sorry he raised such a klutz."

Six hours, one cast, two butterfly sutures, two prescriptions, and some questionable hospital-cafeteria sandwiches later, we're back on the boat in the dead of night, navigating our way home.

Ryan has pulled out a beach chair for me to sit next to him while he drives.

"We could anchor along the shore and have crazy sex if you want," I say as he tucks the heavy afghan around my right shoulder and gently rests my newly casted arm on a pillow. He raises an eyebrow. "Orgasms are good pain relievers."

"Let's not. We've spent enough time in ERs lately. No more, please?" he says, repositioning the GPS to steer us north. The moon is fuller tonight, and when the clouds part enough to let it shine through, it does help light the way. Without the glow or noise pollution of a bustling cityscape, the darkness that cloaks the wilderness outside the boat's windows is both beautiful and intimidating. Like when you're little and you know there's nothing under your bed or in your closet, but the thrum of anxiety tickles your chest and only the brave voice in your head telling you it's okay to look will move your eyes toward the darkness.

"Why do you suppose Lucy Collins is back?"

"I don't know, babe," he says, scanning the water through the windscreen.

"What do you want me to do with her?"

"Telling her to leave didn't work very long. What else can we do with her?"

"If she thinks she's going to stay here for the next fourteen days …"

"Maybe she has nowhere else to go, Hol. Probably knows if she goes back to the States, it's jail time. And then she'll miss the wedding," he says. "She might be scared."

"Why does this have to be my problem?"

"Because she's your mother, and she's making it your problem."

"Your mother never makes her problems *your* problem."

He snorts. "You've only known Miss Betty for the last year. She's had her share of causing her children grief. My siblings are no different, either. We take turns torturing each other. Part of being a family."

"But not like this. Lucy is different."

"Sometimes family has to do stuff for each other that isn't comfortable."

"Wow … you are your mother's son," I say, smiling at him. "I'd do anything for my dad. Anything. But that's because he and I, we're a team. I'm finding it a little difficult to be so generous with Lucy, given our history."

"Totally understandable." The two-way crackles to life.

Miss Betty, checking in on our progress and if we're coming home. After he puts the mic down, Ryan leans against the boat's side, one hand on the wheel. "One way we could keep her out of trouble."

"Lock her in the dungeon until the wedding?"

"Dungeon's full." The smile that stole my heart last year again dances across his face. "We could give her a job."

"No. No way."

"Not a real, permanent job—just give her something to do for the next two weeks. That would give everyone a little space to breathe, yeah?"

"What on earth could Lucy Collins possibly be qualified to do? Oh, I know—we could hire her to sit in the bar and get smashed and harass other guests. Or maybe we could hire her to stand outside the spa to warn everyone about the sadists that lurk within. No—wait—we could hire her to clean rooms so she could fill our coffers."

"You're way too young to be this cynical."

"Hey, I earned these cynic stripes." I adjust my left shoulder, reminding me that it and my neck also took some of the impact earlier when I fell on my ass. "Ryan, there is nothing on the island that she can do that won't put our other guests at risk."

"If we give her something to do that's a team effort or that requires her to be in the company of other staff members—washing dishes or helping in the kitchen or housekeeping chores not in guest rooms. You know there's never a shortage of things to do."

"Do you honestly think she's going to want to chip in?"

"She will if she wants to stay on the property until the wedding. Otherwise I'll call and have her escorted off. Trespassing laws and all that."

"You know she won't pay for a room."

"So she sleeps in the staff quarters. We have a vacant room she can use." The staff quarters are small, "quaint," as Tabby describes them, nicer than college dorms and outfitted in the same décor as the rest of the hotel, but the bathrooms have showers only, no tubs, single beds, dressers and small writing desks, and two employees per room.

"You have to tell her. If I tell her, she'll try to bully her way into a full-size guest room."

"I'll tell her," Ryan says. "I'll pull Thomas in if I have to—he looks menacing with all those muscles and his Mafioso-wannabe suit. He'll scare her right."

"And if she doesn't agree?"

"Then she leaves. Simple as that." He pushes the button on the GPS to make sure we're still on course.

"Why are you so good to me?" I ask, all of a sudden feeling a little weepy. "From the moment she showed up, you've been nothing but patient and understanding. You cannot be such a nice guy, Ryan. It makes me look more like a jerk."

He laughs. "I did a lot of shit in my twenties that I have to atone for. And age has mellowed me out."

"Yeah, on second thought, I'm not sure I can marry a thirty-two-year-old geezer. That's way older than me."

"I spent the better part of a decade taking my anger about my dad out on other people's heads. Either on the ice or in the bar after we were done on the ice. I was always looking for the next fight because I was so *angry* that he could've been so selfish, knowing that the smoking was going to kill him, knowing that he was going to leave my mother alone with four kids to raise on her own."

He looks forward again, eyes seeing but not, his hand making small adjustments to the steering wheel as we glide atop the water. "That night when the accident happened with my knee, it was rock bottom. I wasn't in the shape I should've been in so it was my fault that the injury was a career-ender. Worst night of my life, and also the best. It made me realize how transient everything is. You just think you've got your shit made, that you've arrived, and then, bam! Life has other plans for you. When Alyssa left and I knew that my life in the NHL was over, I had a lot of time to think. And I had to finally forgive my father."

I push the blanket off and groan out of the chair so I can snuggle into Ryan's side. "You think I should forgive her?"

"I think you should first give yourself permission to be angry with her, and then take the baby steps forward to find that place where you can forgive her. It's a process, Porter. It won't happen overnight, and it certainly won't happen in the next fourteen days." He kisses the top of my head.

"Fourteen days ... technically, it's thirteen days now because it's after midnight," I say, nodding at the dash clock. "You sure you still want to do this?"

He pulls my engagement ring out of his pocket and positions so my right, cast-free hand rests in his palm. "Babe, your fingers on this hand are—"

"Don't say 'fatter.'"

"They're *bigger*."

"Right-hand dominant."

But thanks to the cut in the band, the ring fits, if only temporarily. "I hate that they had to cut it. I'm so sorry."

"I'll get it fixed this week. When we go to Victoria to buy *my* ring."

"Oh! Shit! I totally forgot about that! I thought this wedding was all about me ..."

"Of course it is. But if you want me to continue to service your needs, you're going to need to put a ring on it." He lifts his left hand and wiggles his wedding finger.

"I love it when you service my needs."

"I knew you were only marrying me for my penis."

"'Tis a nice penis, I will admit."

Two hours later, snug in our apartment, me doped up on the happy pills the ER doc was so generous to share, Ryan practices his husbandly duty of servicing my needs, proving my point once and for all: orgasms are, in fact, excellent pain relievers.

22

Hollie Porter, Goat Whisperer?

In one of the psych or sociology classes I took before I accidentally didn't finish college, the professor lectured how humans, possessing a trait unique among other species, find satisfaction and even inner peace when they are given a purpose for their days, how productivity can lead to harmony as a person feels a sense of accomplishment when his or her head hits the pillow at night after a long day spent doing meaningful work.

If you had asked me to provide a case study for this theoretical framework, Lucy Collins would not have made my short list of viable candidates.

But something weird happened: we gave her the option of going home, or she could stay at the resort, in the staff quarters instead of a regular guest room, until the Monday after the wedding, if she agreed to take on tasks as they were assigned, without causing a scene or a fuss, without stealing so much as a Revelation Cove pen, in exchange for meals and a room.

It worked.

That's not to say that she hasn't continued to be a thorn in my side, especially when she came along with me on a nature walk the other day, thinking (incorrectly) I'd need help because of my casted left hand and then she shared with the kids a story about one time when she was employed at a strip joint where they had live baby tiger cubs in the VIP Room, if you wanted to pay extra to see them, and how she made so many tips that night because she showed everyone the giant "pussycats" in nothing more than some pasties and a tiger-striped G-string. Or night before last when one of the kitchen staffers thought it would be fun to feed her endless Jell-O shots and then, even plastered, she cleaned everyone out at the rousing, all-night poker game held in the common room. This wouldn't have been such a problem except for the staffers dragging their sorry asses around the resort the next day, too hungover and sad about losing their shirts to do their jobs effectively. *That* pissed Ryan off.

But as long as we keep her busy, Lucy Collins is manageable. With a constantly refreshed list of chores to keep her away from the temptation of guest rooms, surprisingly, she has chilled out. A little. Miss Betty's calming influence has been remarkable, plus I think getting away from Ernesto Finklestein has done Lucy a world of good. I can't be responsible for what happens to her once the wedding is over—dear lord, she cannot stay here indefinitely—but walking into Miss Betty's apartment last night and seeing Lucy Collins, sans all the garish makeup and fake nails, holding a cup of tea while the two of them watched TV ... Even though it was *Real Housewives* and the distress on Miss Betty's face was palpable while Lucy schooled her in the finer points of these women's disastrous lives, it was nice to see Lucy being normal.

Also: I can't believe I just used "normal" and "Lucy" in the same sentence.

Which means, this early Thursday morning, coffee in hand, donut stuffed between my lips, I'm calmer than I might have been a week ago as Ryan and I leave the Cove for forty-eight hours. Must knock off more items on Miss Betty's Wedding Checklist of Doom.

We're en route to Seattle—to his preferred jeweler to get my engagement ring fixed and pick out his wedding band, to the clothiers owned by the uncle of one of his hockey buddies, and down to Portland to see Dad because he has a big union election dinner event tomorrow night, and he thought it would be fun for us to come along as his +2s.

Poor Dad. He misses me now that I live so far away. If Ryan and I hadn't had the long list of things to take care of in town, I wouldn't have been able to make his union banquet, but I think a bit of Nurse Bob is feeling neglected, and even jealous, that Lucy Collins has gotten so much of my time lately. When I was little and I'd get sad about not having a mommy like the other kids, Dad would say that he was glad she was gone because then he didn't have to share me, that I was too much fun to share with anyone else. It always made me feel better that Dad cherished me like he did, even if I had a mother who didn't. Loneliness didn't have time to blossom with Nurse Bob around.

Because the other planes are needed for guest use, we fly the world's scariest floatplane, Miss Lily, usually reserved for supply runs, down to Lake Union, and then rent a car. The visit to the clothiers is easy enough—Ryan isn't having a tux custom made, plus he's a guy, so we didn't have to spend eight hours trying on every single tux in the store. He wants something traditional—black coat and pants with a subtle pinstripe, gray vest, dark purple tie to match our flowers. And because Rex, the shop owner, does a lot of business with hockey players, sizing is never an issue here. He's used to long legs, broad shoulders, and thick thighs. That sounds so delicious when I say all those things together ... and I'm gonna *marry* that, ladies. Hold your applause.

The jeweler, Sal, is happy to see Ryan again, welcoming us into his extravagant shop with all the Turkish hospitality he can muster. When we show him what happened to my ring, I try not to get emotional—but Sal gently pats my cast and promises he can have the gold patched up before we return northward, and that he will size it for my right ring finger for now. When the cast is off and we again visit the big city, he'll resize the ring for the proper finger.

Clearly these two have been working in cahoots. Sal steps into the rear of the store, its access point controlled by a keypad-locked door, and returns with a small silver tray. He and Ryan share a conspiratorial smile as Sal sets the tray down on the gleaming glass countertop and Ryan retrieves the velvet box resting atop. "You needed a matched set," he says, opening the lid.

The wedding band to match my engagement ring. More diamonds, more sparkle. And naturally, more tears.

Sal demonstrates how the two rings fit together—the wedding band seats right under the center diamond of the engagement ring, hugging it in a broad U-shape so that the band disappears under the engagement stone. It's ridiculous how much I love it.

"I want to get married every year. Can we do that?" I say, laughing as I try on the set. Sal and Ryan talk about sizing and pricing and pickup times but who cares about all that businessy stuff when I have starlight glimmering from my finger. Even if it's not the wedding finger.

We scan tray after tray of bands for Ryan. With our occasionally rugged lifestyle, he doesn't want anything with stones, and the metal needs to be durable enough that it won't scuff or show signs of wear. He finally decides on a seven-millimeter-wide band in sandpaper-finished platinum with polished twenty-four-karat yellow gold edges. It looks so handsome on his hand, I tease that we should just go to the justice of the peace and get it done right now.

But his ring also needs sizing, so Sal the Turkish jeweler has lots to keep busy from the Porter-Fielding party. Hearing my stomach growl over the shop's soft music, Sal promises to see us on Saturday before we return to the Cove and shoos us down the block to his brother-in-law's restaurant. "He's Persian, but I forgive him," Sal teases.

I don't care what part of the world the brother-in-law comes from because once the food hits my tongue, I know with certainty that wherever it is, I need to go there post haste. This food, man ... I haven't eaten like this in forever. Which naturally leads to more Ryan jokes about Hollie's unbridled expertise in the kitchen.

"You're not dead yet, right?"

"Only because I have Joseph making sure I don't starve or burn to death in the flames of your culinary rage."

"It was one fire."

"One that you've admitted to."

"That's why we have extinguishers."

"Yeah, and I bought about forty more after you moved in," Ryan says, shoveling a bite of Persian chicken with pomegranate stew into his face, moaning to translate his taste buds' pleasure.

"Keep that up and the people at the next table are going to complain."

"What? The moaning? But it's sooooo good."

"This is a family establishment, Fielding. Stop making love to your food."

"Oh, don't you worry. There's enough of this," he sits tall and gestures to himself, "to go around."

"Maybe not at my dad's house." Which is where we're headed next, three hours south. Once we're done having erotic relations with this mind-blowing meal.

"Oh, I am so nailing you in your old bedroom."

"You are not."

"I so am. I can't stop fantasizing about it—I could sneak

in the window and pretend like I'm your pimply high school boyfriend coming to do nefarious misdeeds to your hot bod under your Spice Girls posters."

"I do not have any Spice Girls posters!" I throw a chunk of bread at him.

"Sorry. Otter posters." His cheeky grin begs for a solid, under-table nudge. "Ow! Don't be mean. Payback's a bitch."

"I have never had sex in that bed."

"Liar."

"My dad's room is right next door!"

"So you don't deny that there were opportunities to have sex in that bed."

"We will sleep on the hide-a-bed in the family room like we always do."

"But we've already had sex on the hide-a-bed."

"So, what, you want to hump me in every bed in that house?"

He shudders. "Not every bed."

"Ryan, we cannot have sex in my childhood bed in my father's house."

"Why not? Last time we did it in the shower."

"Yeah, because my dad was out *fishing*. Not sleeping in the room next to us."

"What if I promise to be quiet? Oh, wait. It's not me who has to be quiet. My little screamer."

"Ryan!" I whisper-hiss at him when the man at the table next to us looks over. My cheeks burn and I hide my face in my napkin for a beat until I can make sure I'm not going to laugh and spew half-chewed rice across the table.

He leans forward and lowers his voice. "Admit it, Porter. You know you want me. In that bed."

"If you sneak out of the house just to climb in through my window, the goat will get you."

"Mangala? No way. We're bros. That goat loves me."

"That goat wants to eat you."

"No, that goat wants to eat *you*. Which I don't blame him for. I'd want to eat you too if you fed me all that codeine."

"He also got all the cupcakes. Jerk."

"He wouldn't have gotten the cupcakes if you'd not tried to murder him with codeine."

"I should've given him the whole bottle."

"See? That's why the goat hates you," Ryan says, tearing seared meat off a bamboo kebob skewer. "It's so weird that you have issues with the goat, but not with any other creatures."

"Oh, like Yorkies? Or how about how I whispered Chloe the Cougar into submission?"

"Wow. You're right. You're a terrible animal lover. What a snob."

"Hey, otters are the best. End of story."

"I'm just sayin'—if you tried a little harder, I bet you and the goat could be friends."

"The only way that goat and I will be friends is if he's soaking in curry on a buffet table and I'm lined up with my plate."

"I didn't know you were so ... evil."

"Have you ever had goat curry? It's brilliant. With cucumber and yogurt and naan? Seriously. We should have it at the wedding. We could give Mangala whatever drugs dad has in his medicine cabinet and then the main course is set."

"But then wouldn't the guests get sick from the medicines that would work their way into the goat meat?"

"Judging by what I saw in Dad's medicine cabinet last year, guests would either feel really happy or have really big boners."

It's Ryan's turn to cough into his napkin, shaking his head, begging me to stop. "I do not want to think about the reasons your dad might need medications that do either of those things."

"You started it."

"I think we should go with unmedicated meats only for the wedding meal."

"You're no fun," I say, handing Ryan the bill folder when the server sets it next to me on the table. "If you want to get laid tonight, you have to buy dinner."

Ryan leans forward, a twinkle in his eye. "Only if it's in the room where Hollie Porter listened to Celine Dion and wrote angsty poetry and dreamed of her future husband."

"Fine. But you have to sing to me before I will take off a single item of clothing," I whisper, holding my water glass aloft. "I want 'My Heart Will Go On,' the whole thing. With the Celine chest-pound."

Ryan picks up his beer bottle and taps my glass, sly smile twisting his lips. "Get your Heart of the Ocean ready, Porter, 'cuz this ship don't sink."

~ ~ ~

A half hour from Dad's, he texts to say that he just got off shift and is stopping for beer and breakfast makings but to let ourselves in: *"Key's under the mat."* My dad is too trusting. Even though he lives in the boonies, mere feet from the line where the sheriff's office takes over from the municipal police, he still leaves his damn key in the very first place a bad guy will check.

Although, what the bad guys don't know is that Dad keeps an evil bearded beast from Hades patrolling the grounds. If you're stupid enough to trespass while Mangala's on duty, kiss your nut sack goodbye.

Solar-powered yard lights stabbed into the earth cast warm shadows across the goat-manicured yard as we pull around the half-moon driveway and park along the waist-high fence that could use some paint.

"You have to go first," I say to Ryan. "If that bastard smells me, it's game over."

"He's no different from a dog. Just give him a good scratch on the head, and he's your best friend."

"If by dog, you mean Satan, then sure. You first."

Ryan releases the lever on the gate and steps through, closing it behind him. I won't take a step onto the yard until the goat is distracted so I can run for it. "Mangala! Here, buddy! Come on! Come say hi to your favorite Hollie in the whole world!" Ryan snickers.

We listen for the telltale jingle of the heavy bell around his neck, meant to provide fair warning for potential victims. "Hey, demon god of war, where are you?" I yell.

Ryan looks over his shoulder. "Don't insult him. That's why he hates you."

"I didn't insult him. That's what his name means."

"*Hindu* god of war. Not demon."

"If the shoe fits …"

Ryan continues up the walk, calling for the goat. He strolls around the side of the house, unafraid, clicking his tongue like one might do for a horse—it works on the idiot goat too. "Hey, which window belongs to your room? For future reference."

"Last one from the back of the house. Good luck getting the screen off."

"Nothing will stand between me and my conquest."

"Nothing will stand between your face between my boobs, is more like it," I say. "Goat!"

"What?"

"He's there!" I yell, pointing as Ryan jogs toward me. The blasted beast is in the house, his snotty nose and rectangular-pupiled eyes pressed against the mesh of the unlatched wooden screen door. His horns look freshly sharpened and I swear flame flickers out of one as the screen door knocks and bounces ever so slightly under the force of Mangala's head pushing against it, jaw masticating in all its slobbery glory. "Ryan! He's in the house! And he's chewing on something!"

Something white? He's been known to snap the wash off the clothesline and finish an entire set of 400-thread-count bed sheets in a single sitting, but he must've yanked loose a tablecloth or kitchen towel because through the screen, he's definitely making short business of whatever textile product he's found.

Ryan hops up the porch steps and opens the screen door, stooping over to pet the goat. "Hey, Mangala—" Ryan freezes. "Oh ... fuck."

"What?"

"Oh no ..."

"Ryan, what? Jesus, hold onto his collar." I grab a long stick out of the thicket in the wilder heart of the driveway's curve.

"Hollie, wait—"

But I don't know what the man's lost all his color over so I'm definitely not waiting and I will beat the shit out of the goat if he comes at me.

"What is going on—"

The white thing?

Is my wedding dress.

Or what's left of it.

23

Tragic Kingdom for the Win

Dad tries to calm me down by shoving my head between my knees to slow the rage-induced hyperventilation.

Ryan already had to tackle me to get the fire poker out of my hands. I ran for the butcher knife but my hockey player is naturally faster and bigger than I am so he beat me to the knife block, threw me over his shoulder, and deposited me on the couch in the family room so the goat wouldn't come after me, even though I really wanted the goddamn goat to try it because that was what the butcher knife and/or fire poker would've been for had my mission not been thwarted.

BECAUSE HE ATE MY WEDDING DRESS.

My beautiful, perfect, breathtaking, heart-stopping seven-thousand-dollar wedding dress.

Is now in the acid grinder known as Mangala's stomach.

When I'm finally allowed to put my head up—signaled only by the fact that I can breathe without gulping for air—Dad hands me a shot of whisky. "Down the hatch."

"I don't want—"

"Drink it, Hollie," Ryan says, my phone pressed against his ear. "Keith, hey, Ryan Fielding here. Yeah ... I know it's late. Super weird I'm calling you, but listen, I need a favor ..."

And thus, this very bizarre and tragic night proceeds with my fiancé talking to my ex-boyfriend who in turn talks to his current (pregnant) girlfriend, Felicia, the saleswoman from the bridal shop, to arrange for us to come down first thing in the morning to see about replacing my very perfect wedding dress with either the same dress or a less-perfect dress.

And then when he's done saving the day on that count, Ryan calls his credit card carrier to see if there is any insurance on the beautiful organza and silk gown that is soon going to be fertilizing Nurse Bob's garden.

No insurance. Nothing they can do. Seven thousand dollars down the literal shitter.

Ten days before the wedding.

"Seven thousand dollars, Dad!" He hands me another shot, his cheeks blotched and ruddy.

"Hollie, I am so, so sorry. Goddamn goat," he says, wiping his hand over his face, massaging his brow, pacing across the living room to look out the window as if to check on Mangala's whereabouts. "Hollie Cat, I swear, I'll fix this, kid. I am so sorry. We'll get your dress replaced."

"DAD! Seriously! It's not like effing Target where they have forty-two of the same dress on a rack!"

"At least he didn't eat the bridesmaids' dresses too," Dad says, face sheepish. I glare at him. He zips his lips.

Ryan hangs up and moves in behind me, happily taking and downing a half-full glass from Nurse Bob before settling in to rub my shoulders. "Felicia said she will help us first thing tomorrow. She says they will put the word out to the dressmaker and other local shops to see if they can find the same dress," he says, using his calm-and-quiet voice to soothe the crazy out of my body.

I yank forward, away from his hands, and stand before both of these men who would do anything to make me feel better. But I am so angry that feeling better isn't an interesting solution. I want to kill the goat. *That* is an interesting solution.

"We are not spending another seven grand on a dress." I hold up my casted arm. "It feels like the world is conspiring against this wedding. Am I the only one who sees the bigger picture here? I mean, shit, what bigger hint do I need? Lucy Collins shows up. I break my wedding finger, which means I can't even wear my ring on the correct hand but the ring already has to be fixed because they had to cut it off and it's been on my body for, what? Two weeks? My face looks like I'm a botched science experiment. Now my wedding dress has been eaten. Is anyone else noticing a pattern?"

The look on Ryan's face as I rant causes a fissure to open in my heart. I'm hurting him. He's gone to all this trouble and I'm raving and carrying on like a selfish crazy person.

Like my mother would.

Before either of them can protest or try to talk sense into my senseless head, I stomp down the hallway and slam the door of my childhood bedroom hard enough that a framed picture of me at Sea World falls off the wall. From when I was a little kid and Sea World was still considered cool and not the terrible bringer of corporate-sponsored terror for all my ocean-dwelling buddies. Sorry, guys. I didn't know then.

I collapse onto my bed, curling around a tattered stuffed otter, to cry myself to sleep with the proper level of melodrama given current circumstances.

I really, really hate that goat.

But more than anything, when I wake up a few hours later and the house is quiet, and Ryan hasn't, in fact, sneaked into my childhood room to take advantage of me and I'm cold because I'm sleeping alone, in my clothes, I hate that I was the cause of the look on his face earlier when I questioned the sanity of us getting married at all.

I open my bedroom door and tiptoe into the bathroom to get ready for bed and to apply a slimy new layer of Neosporin to the healing crow scratches. Back in the hallway, the light from the family room television flickers through the crack under the closed door. Ryan's still awake, probably watching hockey highlights. Shit, I think his team was playing today. And he didn't even peep about missing the game.

The creaking hinges announce my arrival.

"Hey ...," I say, testing the waters.

"Hi." He smiles, but it's not the broad toothy greeting I usually get.

"How'd they do tonight?" I click the door closed behind me.

"Anaheim won. Five-four in overtime."

"Who you think will take the Cup?" I ask, curling my legs under me on the couch next to him.

"Hard to say. These teams are so evenly matched." He clicks off the TV, erasing most of the room's light, and turns to me. I reach for his hand, relieved when he doesn't resist.

"I'm sorry. About earlier."

"I get it. I'm upset that you're upset."

"It was a lot of money for the goat to eat."

"Hollie, it isn't about the money—"

"But it is. I know you aren't an endless source of gold. I feel gross and wasteful and terrible that this stupid goat did this."

"He probably smelled you on the dress," Ryan says, his lip lifting in the tease of a smile. "Which meant he needed to destroy it."

"Too soon, Fielding."

He turns and clasps his free hand around my cast. "It's only a dress. And your dad feels absolutely horrible about the goat getting in. It happened. In the morning, we will go and see about replacing it, either with the exact same gown or another one."

"It's too much."

"Did the dress make you happy?"

I nod. "So happy."

"Then, that's all that matters."

My eyes sting. "I didn't mean to imply that we shouldn't get married. Earlier, when I was ..."

"Hol, there aren't any signs. I don't believe in that stuff."

"Says the guy who won't shave his beard because his team might lose?"

"Hey, now, that's different," he says, smiling. "Seriously, though, I believe in this—" he lifts our joined hands—"I believe in you and me and our future together. I already told you that. But if you think there are signs pointing against us getting married, we can slow down."

"No. No, I was just lashing out. My mouth got away from me. Sometimes I worry that you will grow tired of how I'm always finding trouble."

He laughs. "It's one of your most endearing qualities."

"Then there is something wrong with your brain."

"Probably. One too many concussions."

"Of course. My perfect boyfriend has underlying brain damage."

"Your perfect *husband* does. You think I'm a good boyfriend, just wait until you're legally obligated to wake up next to me for the rest of our lives."

"It gets better?"

He pulls me onto his lap and bites my earlobe. "This party is just getting started, Porter." Before I can wiggle free—it tickles when he bites me there!—the world's worst singer launches into heartfelt song:

"*Every night in my dreams, I see you, I feel you ... That is how I know you ... go on.*"

He tilts me back far enough to give his chest a mighty, one-handed chest pound that would bring Celine herself to tears, and serenades me out of the family room, down the hall, and into my childhood bedroom, whispering that Nurse Bob has had enough whisky to knock out a horse.

For the first time since this bedroom became mine, it is pillaged and plundered in the unholiest fashion when my future husband makes good on his earlier promise and plumbs the depths of my ocean, all the while the smiling face of Gwen Stefani, rotten orange aloft, and her No Doubt crew look on.

Spice Girls. Puh-leez.

24

It's a Dress, But...

I should be prepared to find a different dress. Ryan swears he didn't see it, not really, because Mangala ate too much fabric to have spoiled the wedding-day surprise for my groom.

This morning before we left the house, Dad made sure the goat was in the small barn, chained in his stall. No more mishaps. It also means the goat will stay alive another day, kept away from my potentially murderous hands. Plus, Dad doesn't think Ryan will appreciate his bride in a body cast.

Ryan would probably love nothing more than his bride in a body cast. Means I can't move and cause any more trouble.

Felicia, the darling, unlocks the storefront an hour early and whisks us through to a private room. Knowing that she is Keith's baby momma is still a bit surreal—she seems way out of his league—then again, there exists a legion of people who've said the same thing about Ryan and me. The heart wants what it wants, I suppose.

While today is nice because I don't have to babysit Lucy Collins, Ryan is here, and superstition dictates that I won't be parading dresses around in front of him. I'm adamant about him not seeing it, whatever dress I end up with, until the actual wedding day.

Once were situated in the private suite—fresh orange juice and coffee rather than champagne this early in the day—Felicia takes my arm and escorts me into the curtained dressing area.

"I wasn't able to find your dress yet," she says. My heart falls. "But don't panic. I'm going to bring in a few others that are similar, and we can go from there. I have the girls upstairs trying to reach the designer. They're also double-checking our warehouse and a few local stores. Hope is not lost!"

She pats my shoulder as she hands me the satiny robe, but I can't hide my disappointment.

My disgust for Mangala is so far gone that there aren't words yet invented to describe my emotions. Strangely, I am craving curry.

And so the process begins anew of trying on dress after dress, making do with the single mirror in the curtained change room so Ryan doesn't see. Exacerbating my disappointment, when we find one that looks like it could work, Felicia has to kick Ryan out to go upstairs and wait so Dad and I can discuss yes versus no in front of the bigger mirrors.

The first one's a no. I don't like the feeling of the fabric against my skin.

Three more dresses down, all noes.

Then two more noes, one maybe.

The eighth dress I try on is the closest thing to a yes so far—quite a similar feel to my original dress, with the same white silk and organza but without the three-dimensional flower effects and the fantastic train that I so loved. I didn't want a poofy ball gown but Felicia says without the petticoat, the skirt's girth diminishes as it flows from the natural waist. The sweetheart neckline has embroidered white floral appliques on the tulle and the ruched bodice does make my boobs look bigger than they are. Plus this one fits. Very little will have to be altered. And since time is of the essence …

Seriously, I am trying really hard not to be a spoiled brat, but I'm getting married in nine days and it was such a lucky break to find The One on our last visit.

Dad stands behind me in the mirror after Felicia has zipped me into the ninth dress, but immediately I know it won't work.

"The one before this—you looked like a princess."

"Yeah. This one-shoulder thing is too eighties for me."

"What's wrong with the eighties? That was a good decade—I had nice hair." Dad smiles and pats his thinning coif. He pauses, our eyes meeting in the mirror. "It's just a dress, Hollie Cat."

"I know." *But it isn't, Dad.*

"Ryan's going to marry you whether you're wearing this or otter pajamas."

"Otter pajamas would be cheaper," I say.

"We are going to keep looking for a replacement for your first dress," Felicia says. "And my manager said that if you buy another gown, and we *do* end up finding the replacement, we'll do an exchange so you're not buying three dresses."

One bride = three dresses: sounds like Hollie Math.

Felicia helps me back into gown number eight so Dad and I can make the final decision. Ryan has been more than patient upstairs doing whatever he's doing—I need to be an adult and get on with it.

"Antoinette is going to push everything aside and do any necessary alterations on whatever gown you get today so you can have it with you to take home," she says, offering a hand so I can step into the borrowed heels. "Although this one won't need much. When are you going back?"

"Tomorrow morning."

"Perfect. Probably best you not keep it at your dad's again, though. Keith told me about that goat," she says, hiking an eyebrow. "If it were me, I'd eat it."

I offer my hand for a high five. "Thank you. A voice of reason amongst all the demon-goat-loving bleeding hearts."

She straightens the short train and calms the tulle in the skirt, remarking that it's a good thing we found one that doesn't have sleeves now that I've added a cast to my ensemble. I waltz out for one final Dad approval, stepping onto the low, round pedestal so we can get a three-sixty view of the whole gown.

It is awfully pretty. A little bigger than I wanted in the skirt but the fabric and bodice are what sell it. Well, that and the price tag: four thousand less than the other dress. Done.

And I am relieved that I won't have to get married in the aforementioned otter pajamas.

An hour later, the new gown is downstairs on Antoinette's huge white sewing table, stabbed with just a few pins along the bodice to remedy the extra room in the bust.

"Just wait until you get pregnant," Felicia says, giving her ample bosom a two-handed shake. "Boobs for days."

"Yeah, I've been watching my sister-in-law with her pregnancy, and I think I'm leaving that one to the experts."

"No kids for you?"

"I can hardly take care of myself," I say, lifting my cast and pointing to my scratched face. "Perils of living in the wilderness."

"You should definitely get married indoors," she teases, leading me back to the elevator. "Hollie, I hope you don't think it's weird ... you know, Keith and me. Having a baby, so soon after you guys were together."

"Why would I think that weird? It's incredible. He's a new man. You guys are perfect for each other. And I have Ryan. Like my dad says, everything works out the way it's supposed to." I hold the doors until she's inside and hit the button for the first floor.

"I never thought I'd have kids. Ever. But then I met Keith

through my idiot brother—a miracle Keith would ever be friends with Joe—and we had so much fun together. The pregnancy was a surprise but it's been incredible. Really brought us closer together. And he's going to be a great dad."

"I saw how loving he was with his dogs, so I can only imagine what he'd be like with a kid," I say. This conversation is beginning to feel weird. I know what's coming.

"His dogs—they're so adorable!" she says. *Yeah. Super adorable. Ever fed them nachos?* "You shouldn't say no to having babies. Look at who you're marrying!" She fans herself. "Ryan seems like a total sweetheart. And it's obvious he adores you. I'll bet he'd adore your kids too. Bunch of little hockey players ... so cute!"

The doors ding, and when they've opened not much more than a foot, I squeeze through. The combination of confined space and the sudden spike in my anxiety-related body temperature has me five steps ahead of Felicia, so relieved that Ryan and Dad are sitting on the white couches in the lobby, waiting for me.

"Thank you so much for your amazing help," I say, shaking Felicia's hand, ready to skedaddle before she oozes baby love all over my fiancé and my father who very much wants to be a grandfather. "I suppose we need to pay now?"

Dad wraps his arm around my shoulders. "Thanks again, Felicia. We'll see you tomorrow morning for pickup?" he says, nodding his head and turning me toward the front doors, Ryan a few steps behind.

So they took care of paying while I was downstairs? To

save me the embarrassment of Ryan forking over more of his retirement to pay for wedding dress number two? Was he relieved that it was less expensive?

We toy with the idea of heading to the Oregon Coast for the day, but we won't be back in time for tonight's banquet. As such, we play tourists in downtown, a few delightful hours spent at Powell's Books, lunch at Jake's Famous Crawfish, a stop at Nordstrom—Dad and Ryan go in search of a wedding tie for Dad while I sneak into the lingerie section to find a little something for Ryan for the wedding night. No saggy, faded Hanes for Her with tired elastic under my dress. I'm a swanky bride, baby, all satin and lace for my undercarriage. Ooh la la.

Spending time in the city of my youth reminds me why I love this part of the world so much. After dreary, rainy months spent indoors, Portlanders emerge to soak up the sunlight, blossoming and blooming alongside the trees and floral tapestries planted in the city's vast flowerbeds and parks. Pioneer Courthouse Square fills up with families desperate to get out of the four walls of their apartments and houses, the light rail deposits car after car of suburbanites excited for a day in the big city—even the cops on horseback smile occasionally. A sunny day in Portland is akin to a deep breath, a satisfying stretch after a long sleep.

We've reconvened, walking toward the car a few blocks away, Ryan's arm lazily draped over my shoulders, Dad a few steps ahead talking on his phone. "Thank you," I say, looking up at my bearded god. "For buying me another dress."

He smiles playfully. "I didn't buy you another dress."

I stop.

Ryan nods toward my dad.

"He paid for the dress?"

"He'd do anything to make you happy, Hollie."

"Ryan, no—no! He can't afford to do that!"

A young couple beeps at us with their baby stroller—we're blocking the sidewalk. "Sorry," I say, stepping aside, knocking my cast into a parking meter pole. Ryan is across the concrete from me.

"He insisted. I tried to tell him we'd cover it, but he wouldn't listen." Ryan steps forward and pulls me into his side, propelling us forward again. Dad is far enough ahead that he's already at the car parked along the street. "Just thank him. Men like taking care of their women. Let him do this." Ryan kisses the side of my head and squeezes me closer.

I love the way that sounds: *Men like taking care of their women.*

My men take such good care of me.

When we reach Dad at the car, I hug him tightly. "Thank you, Daddy. Thank you for the dress." He returns my hug, and when he pushes me away from him, his eyes shimmer with maybe a little sappy-dad condensation that he wouldn't quite call a tear.

"You're a good egg, Hollie Cat. I'm sorry about the goat. I really am. I'd do anything for you, you know that." And when his voice cracks, he wraps me up again so I won't see the bona fide tear sneak out of his eye. "Couldn't have my little girl walking down the aisle in a half-eaten dress, now could I?" I love how his laugh rumbles in his chest when we hug.

He clears his throat. "Now let's get gussied up so I can show off my strapping new son-in-law. Manjit's son has his new bride in tow so we need to show 'em that we Porters are no slackers, right?"

25

"O! for a muse of fire..."

The one thing about a nurses' union banquet: those people know how to party.

And for the record, my dad's coworker, Manjit? Her new daughter-in-law isn't some sweet-faced, timid lass from a quiet family in Mumbai, obeying her family by agreeing to an arranged marriage. She's a molecular biologist who did her PhD thesis on genome sequencing who has known Manjit's son since they were kids and who also has an amazing laugh and a frightening understanding of the game of hockey.

But my dad was the real belle of the ball, parading Ryan and I around to his many coworkers. Hugs and handshakes, cocktails and cougar jokes aplenty.

Which means this morning, my concierge and I are doing a little nursing of our own—of skull-crushing hangovers. We choke down Dad's surefire post-drunk remedy—something with tomato juice and ibuprofen and possibly a raw egg. I don't even care. As long as it makes me find my will to live again.

Mangala grazing out in the front yard means I get a piggyback ride to the car. "Asshole," I mutter as we pass him. He stomps the ground and bleats, jingling his bell in warning, and then returns to eating the heads off the marigolds. I don't even know why Dad plants flowers with that diabolical fiend around.

Dad, fishing vest already atop a pair of old blue-green scrubs, exchanges a manly shoulder bump with Ryan before a lift-me-off-the-ground Hollie Hug. "See you in six days for a wedding?" I ask.

"Wouldn't miss it for the world."

As we're exiting the half-moon driveway to head downtown to pick up my new dress, a giggle bubbles out of my lips.

"What's so funny?" Ryan asks, nuzzling his hand under my casted arm.

"This is the last time I'll be at my dad's house as a single woman. Next time we're here, we'll be married."

"You still have time to back out," he says, his cheek pulling into a half grin.

"What, and miss the opportunity to eat that cake? You should see the cake. Not even joking. Plus, any man who sings Celine Dion to get in my pants deserves to get laid every day of his life."

"Every day?" His eyebrows almost touch his hairline. "I'm pulling this car over at the next courthouse."

"But you know what they say—once you're married, you don't do it as often."

"Who have *you* been listening to?"

"It's true. All the magazines talk about it. How marriage kills your sex life."

"That's because none of those people have ever been married to me."

"Sarah says she and Tanner don't do it very often anymore."

"That's because Sarah is forty-two months pregnant."

"See? Another reason we should stay *sans enfants*."

"The fun is in making the babies, Porter. Practice, practice, practice. And don't you worry," he says, picking up my casted hand and kissing the back of my two exposed fingers, "we will practice until the moon crashes into the sea."

"That sounds rather cataclysmic, actually. Moons crashing and such."

"Don't tell me that when I made you scream into your pillow the other night that you weren't thinking about crashing moons and exploding stars."

"You're so sure of your abilities, aren't you, ice jockey?"

"Hey, I've been bestowed a magical gift. It will be my life's purpose to share that gift with you until the wand loses the magic."

"And then there are pills for that."

My phone buzzes in my jeans pocket. A flicker of excitement tickles my insides when I think it could be a text from Dr. Little at the Aquarium—I emailed yesterday afternoon to check on our little otter baby but I haven't heard back. I hope that's not a bad sign, that the tiny sweetie is sick, or worse.

But then again, the text could also be from Lucy Collins.

Which makes me not want to look. I love it when it's just Ryan and me against the world. I also love it when I don't know what trouble she's causing.

I'm not great with suspense. I pull out the phone, hoping for the best.

"Good thing we're going home today." I sigh.

"Do I even want to know?" Ryan's content grin slides off his face.

"Your fire and flood insurance is up to date, right?"

~ ~ ~

Tanner and Thomas, with the help of two other staffers, have moved the major pieces of Miss Betty's furniture onto the grassy area behind the resort. It looks like an antiques bazaar out here, the grass covered with throw rugs, wooden dressers, coffee and side tables, and two armoires. It took four men each to lift her loveseats, which is what happens to wood and fabric and stuffing when it becomes waterlogged.

Depending on whom you ask, the story goes something like this: Miss Betty was giving Lucy Collins a cooking lesson—teaching Lucy how to make homemade scones to go along with Miss Betty's earth-shattering, secret-recipe jam. Miss Betty realized she needed more shortening and went to the main kitchen, only she got sidetracked while in the main building. Two hours later, the sprinklers in her apartment were triggered because Lucy Collins fell asleep watching reality TV and two large trays of baking scones actually caught fire and spread outside the oven and then took fiery hold of the backsplash, surrounding flooring, and two cupboards adjoining the oven.

Who knew scones were so flammable.

Everyone is okay, although Lucy won't stop complaining that she almost died from smoke inhalation and there apparently was some debate about whether she should be transported to Nanaimo or Victoria to get checked out, but Dr. James came by per Sarah's urgent request just after the fire was extinguished and he said Lucy is fine, if not perhaps suffering from a touch of hysteria.

I didn't even know doctors used that diagnosis anymore.

Miss Betty, though, like the momma duck she is, hardly seems ruffled, though she does pause for a moment to touch the framed wedding photo of she and her late husband that may or may not be salvaged. Under her careful and patient guidance, Ryan and his brother and a couple staffers clean out as much water as they can—an insurance adjuster will come up first of next week but the biggest pain in the ass is the renovation and restoration that will have to be coordinated. Good thing my future husband and his brother are handy fellows.

I help carry out what I can, which isn't a lot given my hobbled arm, but I'm more in the way than anything. And when Ryan stands pinching the crooked part of his nose, his jaw ticking and grinding, it's time for me to excuse myself. Perhaps my presence in another part of the world is safest all around for the time being. My family has caused enough damage at the resort for two lifetimes.

I send Lucy to her room in the staff quarters with strict instructions to rest and stay away from flames, knives, open water, wild animals, and hot dogs. Knowing her, she will find a way to choke to death, or worse, she will feed said hot dog to someone else and he or she will choke to death while Lucy applies the topcoat to her blood-red nails and shrieks at her TV about the rich, overstuffed harpy in Orange County who has just wrecked another Mercedes.

I then corral Tabby and make her help me unload Miss Lily of my latest treasures. I have to get the dress and our rings off the floatplane before the damn thing decides to sink to the bottom of the sound for no other reason than out of pure spite.

In the interim during our brief Portland sojourn, I swear Sarah has grown another foot in circumference. She looks like a water balloon stretched over the bathroom tap right before it splatters its innards all over the sink and counter. I settle her onto the couch in our thankfully dry apartment while Tabby helps me unsheathe my new goat-free wedding dress, regaling them with the sad tale of Dress #1 and how a goat pooped out of the bowels of Lucifer himself decided long ago that the complete ruination of my life was his one true mission. "Forget milk, forget cheese, forget amiable companionship—I am a goat of destruction. And I am coming for you, Hollie Porter."

The whole incident is *sort of* funny—now—two days after the fact. And by *sort of* funny, I mean it's only a tiny bit funny that a goat ate my wedding dress, now that I have another dress safe and sound in my apartment. It's *not* funny that I am still mourning my first very perfect dress, but then I feel like a brat bemoaning such a first-world problem so I should shut up about it.

And only hellfire or apocalypse, or Lucy Collins, will stand in the way of me marrying the man of my dreams a week from tomorrow.

I didn't just say that out loud, did I?

Hellfire and apocalypse, I was only kidding. That was not a challenge, I swear.

A brief debate happens concerning the best place for the dress to live for the next eight days, but consensus is that with my luck as of late? The dress stays here. Ryan will just have to behave himself and not peek.

Sarah twinges and oohs, a hand gripping the side of her swollen abdomen. "What? What's wrong?" I ask, heart freezing for a beat.

"Nothing. Baby gymnastics. In my rib cage. Super fun."

"Watch her belly, Hol. It's supremely gross," Tabby says, snapping open a pop can.

"It's not gross, Tabitha," Sarah reprimands.

"Seriously, I am so glad you're home. I thought she was going to have that kid while you guys were gone and I don't know how being a makeup artist qualifies me to deliver a baby, unless he or she wants some really nice eyebrows." Tabby settles onto one of the barstools.

"She's going to have that little bundle of chaos in a hospital where people who are not us will help her, aren't you, Sarah?" I give her an exaggerated cheesy grin, heavy on the fear.

"Don't you weenies worry. I won't trouble you with my bloody show or amniotic fluid."

"Oh god. I don't know what either of those things are but I'm going to barf if you keep talking," Tabby says, her face paling. "IN OTHER NEWS ..."

"Yes, Tabby, why don't you share your other news?" Sarah says. Tabby's eyes widen. "Tabby and Thomas, sittin' in a tree, k-i-s-s-i-n-g."

And thus begins story time where Tabby the makeup artist finally confesses her true feelings for Thomas the security hulk. "Why you no tell us?" I ask, throwing Ryan's laundry from the last two days into the closet stacked washer/dryer.

"You've been a little busy. Wedding planning, absentee mother corralling, *et cetera*."

"Is it serious?"

"Serious enough that she woke up in his bed," Sarah teases.

"If you weren't in a medically delicate position, I'd throw this pillow at you," Tabby says, migrating from the bar stool to a comfier side chair. "He also has a nicer bed than I do. I plan to file a complaint with management."

"Please wait for a week or two. Let Ryan rebuild his mother's apartment first," I ask, squishing in next to Sarah so I can rub her swollen hands.

Miss Betty knocks and lets herself in, a familiar flowered notebook under her arm. "We need to finalize the menu for Joseph. Are you busy right now?"

Once she's settled, the notebook spread open on the coffee table, I again apologize for the scone-fueled fire, for leaving her on Lucy Collins duty while we were in Portland. She pats my cast and says she's glad no one was hurt. Again. "Your mother means well. She just seems to have a bit of a shadow following her around."

"If by shadow, you mean a Category 5 hurricane, then yeah. Did she seem better without Ernesto here?"

"A little. A bit calmer. Although she sure can drink," Miss Betty says. "I tried to keep her busy because I was afraid she'd light a candle or something in her little room and then forget about it."

"And you ended up with the same result. Only with scones."

"I must say, I've baked those my entire life and I've never once seen them catch fire."

"This disaster stuff—it's a rare genetic anomaly. Some people have naturally straight teeth or curly hair or an affinity for math; my mother has the opposite of a Midas touch. It seems to have leaked into my DNA."

Miss Betty laughs and reassures me that my anti-Midas touch is a little less pronounced. I hold my cast up as evidence to the contrary.

But my soon-to-be mother-in-law is a woman of action, a gentle taskmaster, despite the fact that her entire apartment is soggy. Her pencil eraser taps a soft rhythm against the page as she talks: the menu and seating arrangements are handled, as is confirmation with the photographer (the same chickenshit who hid from the crow last weekend), flowers will be here Saturday from Victoria, and Joseph has the cake managed.

Plus, fun news, a surprise for Ryan: his brother Brody arrives in Seattle on Wednesday morning, Tanner and Ryan will fly down to meet him, and then the three Fielding sons, together at last, will join up with some of Ryan's hockey friends for his bachelor party. She promises no strippers, but Sarah guffaws, her whole belly jiggling like Jell-O freed of its mold. "With Brody around?" she says. "There will be strippers."

"And then Ryan's sister, Hailey, will be coming in with her kids and husband on Friday," Miss Betty says, unmatched joy on her face.

Because of the short notice, our very fancy wedding invites went out via email, and nearly all were to Ryan's family and closest friends. Dad invited his sort-of ex-wife Aurora and Hippie Barbie the Non-Sister, but even after she spammed the Revelation Cove Facebook page advertising her ridiculously successful organic cupcake business and how she just *had* to bake my wedding cake, she emailed to let me know she's in LA that weekend helping a new franchisee launch one of her cupcake shops. Hence, neither she nor her alien-fearing adoptive mother can make it to the Cove for the wedding. Gosh, are you sure? I'm so heartbroken. (I am not heartbroken.)

I'll have Dad—I don't need anyone else. Lucy Collins will be present whether I want her here or not. And everyone at the Cove—they're my family now. The people I love most will be in attendance, my point again proven when we show Miss Betty the new gown in all its white silk and tulle and organza glory. She chokes up and hugs me and thanks me for marrying her son.

Even without The Dress—any dress—it is the love of these people and the warmth I've found since ditching Keith and the Yorkies and 911 and almost falling out of Miss Lily last year—that's really all that matters these days.

It was always just Dad and I, until Aurora came along. No extended family with grandparents and aunts and uncles and all that madness. Quiet Christmases and Easters, no big get-togethers or massive family reunions over hot summer weekends in some random park where nametags were required to keep everyone straight. Dad has a sister somewhere in California but they're not close. We didn't need to surround ourselves with lots of people to feel loved.

But I didn't know friends and family could be like this.

Miss Betty helps me zip the dress back into the garment bag, remarking that we'll need to get the steamer out the night before to smooth the tulle.

"Hollie," Sarah calls from the living room. "Knock at the door. I'm too fat to move."

"I'll get it," Tabby says, hopping to her feet.

Probably a staffer come to retrieve Miss Betty for some apartment-related need.

"Is Hollie here?"

Hearing her voice, I want to hide in the closet until she goes away. Alas, I am not seven years old. "Hi, Lucy," I say from the bedroom doorway.

Lucy looks from Betty to Tabby to Sarah and then back

to me, face annoyed. "Am I interrupting?" She's adorned in so many animal prints—like she crashed into a safari or a blackjack table filled with Florida retirees escaped from their convalescent home. My poor, aching eyes.

"Come in," I say.

Tabby steps aside to grant her entry. Sarah quietly sits forward and closes Miss Betty's wedding notebook just as Betty emerges from the bedroom.

Lucy Collins pinches at the fabric of her tiger-print culottes. "I wanted to apologize, again, about the fire and everything."

"Accidents happen," Miss Betty says, though she doesn't sound wholly convincing. "I'm glad you weren't hurt. Are you feeling better?"

"Yeah, I'm fine. Throat's a little sore but that could be allergies too."

An awkward moment passes, quiet except for the tick of the small desk clock near the sliding glass door. "Well, Sarah and Tabby and I were just heading down to the kitchen for a little snack. We'll give you two some time to chat." Miss Betty helps Sarah off the couch. As Sarah passes, she squeezes my cast-free wrist.

Lucy Collins helps herself to the loveseat. "Have you got anything to drink?"

"Non-alcoholic only. Sorry."

"Diet Coke would be fine."

"Ice?"

She nods. *Your wish is my command.*

Once she has a frosty, booze-free beverage in hand, I

sit across from her, not sure what she wants, uneasy about what might be coming at me.

"You got your dress?"

"I did."

"Sucks that the goat ate the first one."

"Yes. That did suck a little."

"Did the bridal store give you a new dress, then?"

I am not going to engage Lucy in a discussion about my finances. "Thank you for apologizing to Miss Betty about the apartment."

"It's the least I could do, right? Is that what you were gonna say?"

Yes. "No. But everything is soaked and a lot of her personal effects are ruined from the ceiling sprinklers."

"Yeah, and I could've died in a fire but as long as her couch isn't ruined."

Deep breath. "That isn't what I mean, Lucy."

"Mom."

"Excuse me?"

"Why don't you call me Mom?"

"Because to me, you are Lucy."

"What do I have to do to become Mom?"

"Rewind about twenty years. Be around. Be a part of my life. In a contributing, nondestructive manner."

She smiles. It catches me off guard. "I didn't mean to suck at being a mother, ya know. It wasn't like I set out to have a baby and take off."

"But that's what you did."

Her grip tightens around her sweating glass. "I loved

your dad. I really did. Bob was the most amazing thing that ever happened to me. I'm not going to bore you with my tales of woe about my upbringing—but then there was your father, my own knight in shining armor. He looked at me the way I see Ryan look at you ... For two years, it was me and Bob and nothing could stop us. He was in college, and I worked at a restaurant in the college town where he was studying so much, so hard. He was going to be a doctor, you know."

I nod.

"He was too good for me. He was too good *to* me. He'd do nice stuff and it would make me mad. Like, I couldn't figure out what the hell he wanted at first. He'd come in to the restaurant with a stack of books as high as his hip to pull an all-nighter away from his partying roommates, and I'd serve him coffee until the wee hours, nudge him when he'd doze off on an open book. And the next night, he'd bring me flowers or some novel that he loved that I just had to read or a pastry from the town's best bakery or he'd bring me a sketchbook and nice pencils so I could draw animals—I loved to draw the critters. Can you draw?"

"Stick figures only."

She smiles briefly. "Then one night, he asked me on a proper date. I said yes. It was the biggest mistake of my life."

"What? Why?"

"Because I didn't deserve him. He wanted me to believe in myself as much as he believed in me. But I knew who I was, where I came from. I pretended for a while. I even married him because I thought he loved me enough to make up for how much I hated myself. When we got pregnant with you, he was over the moon. I've never seen a man so happy about a baby. In my world, babies meant trouble—just another mouth to feed, another brat to take care of. You know I have seven brothers and sisters?"

I shake my head no. I have that many aunts and uncles?

"We were like seeds in a strong breeze, though. Blew to different corners of the world. Some of us were in foster care, although never together. The others ran away as soon as they were old enough to stay hidden. I haven't seen or heard from any of my siblings in over a decade. Probably for the best."

"I had no idea."

"It doesn't matter," she says, sniffing. "What does matter is that you know this: I never meant to hurt you. But I didn't want to screw you up the way I was screwed up. I knew Bob would give you the perfect childhood. I knew he would love you to the stars and back, and that he would do anything and everything to make up for what I lacked. It was just easier for me to leave."

My head throbs with years of pent-up frustration and anger—and sorrow for what she went through in her own life. Hers are aches I cannot relate to because Bob *did* do everything in his power to give me a first-rate childhood.

"That day we met at the aquarium in Monterey, when I brought you the otter toy? That was the happiest day of my life. Just seeing you sitting there, smiling and so animated and talking a million miles an hour about all the fish and turtles and those floating things that look like giant bats—"

"Stingrays."

"Yeah. Those." Her quiet laugh sounds sad. "I knew that Bob had done exactly what I thought he would. He made you perfect."

"I'm not perfect."

"You are to your parents. All children are, if their parents give a shit. And now look at you—all grown up and about to start on your own big adventure as a wife. Maybe even a mother someday."

"Ha. Not likely."

"Don't say that. Bob wants to be a grandpa," she says. "Hollie, I knew if I stayed around, I would've messed you up. Things wouldn't have turned out as good for you."

"It was hard. Not having a mom." My throat burns as I force my voice to work.

"It would've been harder having me as a mom. In and out of jail? In trouble all the time? How embarrassing would that have been for you?"

"I would've liked to have been given the opportunity to decide that for myself. And you didn't have to make the choices that landed you in jail. You could've made different choices."

"Easy for you to say," she says, looking away and quickly brushing a tear off her cheek. "I'm sorry, kid. I honestly was doing what I thought was best."

I want to believe her. I want to believe that her tears are real and not another elaborate Lucy Collins con.

"Why did you wait until now to come back?" I ask, tucking the emotion back into its pocket in my heart.

"I already confessed this. I know what it must look like to you—"

"Then give me a reason to think otherwise."

"I'm not after Ryan's money, not now. I told you that."

"Yeah, and you blamed Ernesto. Didn't take any responsibility for your part in it. If you know he's such a dirtbag, why are you with him? Why did you agree to marry him?"

"Because we deserve each other." Her voice hardens as she sets her glass down a little too hard on the coffee table. "You don't know what my life has been like, so don't judge me."

"I'm trying, Lucy, I really am, but you come into *my* life, into the resort that my boyfriend and his partners and family have worked so hard for, you cause all this trouble—did you know the people you stole from were close friends of Ryan's? That the woman is his ex-fiancée? You're lucky that they were so cool about the whole thing or you'd be in jail right now."

"Yeah, I know, I know. And I said I was sorry." She exhales and slaps her hands atop her bent knees. "This isn't what I wanted to talk about. I just wanted to come and apologize for screwing up and hope that maybe somehow, someday, you'd find it in your heart to let me in."

"You're going to have to earn it. You're going to have to earn my trust, and the trust of everyone who is going to be my family in another week's time."

She snorts, the smart-ass look back on her face. "And how does one go about doing that?"

"Leave Ernesto. Stop letting him boss you around. Stop

stealing from people. I don't know, Lucy. I'm not a shrink. But I know that under all this?" I wave a hand at her. "There has to be a good person. Because the Bob I know, my father, the man who raised me to be a strong woman? He wouldn't have loved you if you weren't worth it."

She stares at me, anger dissolving as her eyes well with tears, and her shoulders slump.

Ryan's card key clicks in the lock and he pushes the door open with his ass, his arms full with a cardboard banker's box.

"Oh—hey. Sorry. I can come back." When he sets the box down, it's full of Miss Betty's trinkets and photos.

"No, no, I was just leaving," Lucy says, wiping her cheeks on her sleeve. She stands and pauses before Ryan. "I told your mom and now I'm telling you—I'm sorry about the fire."

"We'll get it sorted out," he says, his attitude evidence enough that he's not quite ready to forgive her.

"And thank you. For allowing me to stay here, to be a part of my daughter's life. And your wedding."

Ryan looks at me standing near one of the side chairs, and then he looks at Lucy. "You're welcome."

She gives me a final tight smile and quietly exits.

"You okay?"

I fall against his chest and inhale the smell of sweat and fire smoke and damp. He holds on until I'm done plowing through this unexpected emotion, and then tucks me under a blanket atop our bed, caressing my hair without another word until I drift off to sleep.

26

Water, Water, Everywhere

Peace is a relative concept, technically defined as "freedom from disturbance; quiet and tranquility." If I've learned anything in the last couple weeks, it is that such definitions are fluid, especially when one adds a dash of Lucy Collins to the highball.

Over the last four days, we have had zero fires, zero broken bones, and zero thefts. Which means Lucy is behaving. Except for those poker games. Saturday night, Ryan tried to shut it down but they sucked him in and he won fifty bucks. The next night he resisted (during my Portland shopping excursion, I may have bought an extra pre-wedding set of lingerie to entertain him) but he warned the staffers to not drink so much. The resort was full and Monday morning checkouts were going to hurt for the hungover.

But peace with Lucy Collins on the premises is not accompanied by the soothing, sweet sounds of a harp or the pleasant aroma of fresh flowers or even the charming chirp of morning birds. It mostly means she hasn't verbally abused any staffers (except during poker) or accosted guests or flashed inappropriate body parts. Even during yesterday's nature walk with a new batch of kids, she modified her story about the tiger cubs to omit the bit where the tigers lived at the strip club. Then she went so far as to induce actual shock and awe when she helped an injured butterfly onto a daffodil and sat with the kids to draw them impressive pictures of their favorite creatures.

Who is this strange woman and what have you done with Lucy Collins?

Whatever. Today is Wednesday. We have five more days to get through, and then she can return to her real life. Whatever that life entails. She even joked at dinner last night about me being her jailhouse pen pal. It's really not funny, but it made her laugh.

This morning, my fiancé is so excited to be leaving for an evening of debauchery among his brothers, those of the biological and hockey ilk, it's like trying to tie the shoes of a two-year-old who really wants to join his buddies in the bouncy castle. While I don't have to tie Ryan's shoes, I do need him to finish a few important work-related tasks before he jumps onto the plane with Tanner to go ogle strippers.

"If you come back with any diseases, the wedding is off, Fielding." I scoop his breakfast plate from the stainless steel worktop in the resort's main kitchen, but he takes it away and lifts me off the floor to gnaw on my neck.

"The only disease I have is lovesickness."

I squeal and push free. "You're such a dork."

"Tanner will keep Brody in check, don't worry," Sarah says, shoving the last bite of jam-covered toast into her mouth before gathering our plates and waddling to the giant double sink.

"Are you shaving before you go?" I tug on the thick, dark hair covering his chin.

Ryan puts a hand on his full beard, feigning insult. "Do you see my team carrying the Stanley Cup on their shoulders yet? Are you asking me to jinx the whole thing? Do you have no heart, woman?"

"Ryan. Please. You're shaving for the wedding," Sarah says. "Your mother will never let all that mountain-man crap stay on your face."

"But what if my bride likes it?" He towers over my shoulder, leaning down to rub his beard on my cheek. I slap him away.

"Oh my god, are you always this spastic when it's playtime?"

"Hol, just wait until all four Fielding brats are under one roof," Sarah says.

"Doesn't Hailey chill them out?"

"Hell no. She's the worst of all of us. Don't feed The Hailey any tequila!" Ryan warns, hands pushing open the kitchen's swinging doors.

"You are not leaving until you sign those checks in the

office! I need to pay the flooring guy this afternoon," I call after him. New laminate goes down in Miss Betty's living room today, now that everything's dried out after the flaming-scone mishap. Given the rush job and weird circumstances of having to transport flooring and underlayment via boat, I want to make sure the Mr. Carpet-and-Laminate is happy. And I don't want to be dealing with any resort business from Friday on because I will be in wedding mode. You hear that, Fate? NO MORE DISASTERS.

Rivaling Ryan's excitement, though, is Tanner's anxiety about his very pregnant wife. Sarah has had what she calls minor contractions since Monday evening, but she refuses to go into town until they actually hurt and/or are happening consistently. Miss Betty had Dr. James pop by yesterday on his way into Victoria to visit his ailing mother, and his assessment—which involved poking and prodding in areas only vibrators and/or sexual partners should see—reassured Tanner that everything is closed up tight, and the baby, though head down and engaged in Sarah's pelvis, is not ready to make his or her appearance yet.

"Go enjoy yourself while you still can," was his prescription, stated with a wry smile and a hearty laugh. "Once you're a dad, life as you know it is over."

My thoughts exactly. Uterus? Take note.

We're dockside, waving to our men as their plane finally lifts off the water into the stratosphere. Sarah exhales loudly. "God, he was driving me nuts. I hope he burns off some of that nervous energy. Let's go eat frosting out of the tub," she says, looping her arm through mine.

"Aren't you supposed to be monitoring your blood sugar?" I ask.

"One tub of frosting won't hurt," she says. "Oh, none for you, though. Your dress needs to fit. I'll eat. You can watch."

I call down to laundry to see if Lucy Collins made it in to help per our agreement, but before Marilyn, our head of housekeeping, has a chance to answer, Lucy's uproarious laugh trickles through the phone line. "She's regaling us with stories about the laundry rooms in various jails along the West Coast," Mary says. "It's actually quite funny."

"Fantastic." So proud of you, Lucy. "Just don't let her near anything flammable."

I check email while Sarah spoons enough vanilla frosting into her mouth to service a Dunkin' Donuts and Tabby rambles on about a nagging spa guest this morning. Something about waxing near labial piercings. I don't want to know.

"A message from Dr. Little!" I announce, although neither of them is listening, still entrenched in their own conversation. The good vet says our baby otter is doing so well. She tested negative for a bunch of scary otter-specific diseases and she's gaining weight and she's starting to get the hang of swimming, and if I want to arrange a visit, they'd love to have me. The ten-year-old in my heart backflips.

"Hollie, what time is the floor guy coming?" Sarah asks, pushing the frosting aside. "I want to go to the cabin. Grab some clothes, water the tomatoes, stare at how cute the nursery is. You could stare too. Maybe you'll feel some maternal stirrings, then."

My fallopian tubes tie themselves in knots at her waggling eyebrows. "Floor Dude is supposed to be here at one," I say, not giving her a moment to continue, "but his check is ready so Miss Betty can show him where he needs to be. You're not going to the cabin alone."

"Duh, which is why I asked you."

Tabby checks her phone and smiles. "I have to go. Duty calls."

"Duty? Ha. More like Thomas. Don't touch his penis in front of the guests. It's considered rude," Sarah says.

"Very funny. No, really, I have a lady in foils under the dryer. Thomas is for dessert," Tabby says, winking as she slips out.

"All you young people in love is giving me heartburn," Sarah says, wiggling a hand in front of her so I'll help her up.

"No, your forty-pound fetus is giving you heartburn." Because pulling her out of that chair? The fetus has to weigh at least forty pounds.

"Text Betty and let her know we're gonna go. We'll be back in a few hours tops."

I oblige and then grab boat keys and an extra sweatshirt from the apartment. So far, June hasn't shown us too much of her sunny side, and the brisk breeze fluttering through is enough to necessitate long sleeves to combat goosebumps.

The trip to Sarah and Tanner's is beautiful in the daytime, passing smaller islands, some inhabited by storybook cabins, some boasting seasonal yurts or small tents from adventurous kayakers, these grand rocks thrust out of the water decorated by varying trees showing off their new growth in bright green foliage and needles, small beaches with untouched patches of lithe grasses and multicolored wildflowers. Though the wind gets a little persnickety the farther south we go, whitecaps dancing in the wider part of the waterway, the combination of trees and freshwater and late springtime smells so good. Wild British Columbia is intoxicating.

Every time we're out here, I scan the water's surface for orca blow. The three orcas I saw last year were likely members of our southern resident community, from J, K, or L pods, although Tanner says that unless he could see dorsal fins or the grayish-white saddles of individual whales, it would be impossible to identify if they were members of the northern or southern resident communities. To me, any whales out here are mine, and I love them. Especially because they didn't eat me.

Motor slowed, I ease alongside the dock and wake Sarah from her short nap so I can tie off. The flower planters lining their cabin's porch aren't as grandiose this year, given the amount of time Sarah has spent at the resort. But Tanner has been adamant that she not be left to her own devices this far from civilization and/or our watchful eyes. And despite the rather formidable fence now bordering what passes as their yard—we can thank Chloe the Cougar for installation of that wood and steel monstrosity—there is no telling what has come in off the water or climbed the fence when the air horn-packing humans weren't around.

I've been to this cabin a hundred times in the last year, and it still freaks me out. I can't see the dock without seeing Ryan's blood all over it ...

Even though she is carrying a dwarf planet in her midsection, Sarah is surprisingly agile getting on and off the boat. "Just think, Hollie-Berry," she says, locking her arm through mine as we move up the dock, "next time you're here, you'll be my sister-in-law for real."

"Thanks for being my maid—matron—of honor."

"Hey, thank you! I'm ridiculously excited Ryan is marrying you and not that other thing."

I laugh. "Me too."

"I knew she was wrong for him. The whole time. But Tanner and I had to shut up. None of our business. I tried to talk to him about Alyssa when Tan wasn't around, you know, sisterly advice kinda thing. As soon as the plans for the resort were solidified, though, I knew their relationship was doomed. Alyssa never would've lived out here. Too prissy. She needs her shopping malls." Sarah digs in her bag for the house keys, pausing only to grab her side and wince.

"What? What's wrong?"

"I told you—this kid thinks my ribs are his personal jungle gym."

"His?" I ask, raising a brow.

"His. Hers. Whatever." The deadbolt releases and Sarah pushes the door open. We're instantly hit by the smell of dead food. "Shit ... Tanner didn't clean out the fridge. I swear, that man better listen to me once this baby is here because I cannot mother him forever."

Dead food can attract local wildlife, so we make quick work of opening windows and the patio doors to air out the house, cleaning the fridge of offending items, stuffing what we can down the garbage disposal, and rinsing clean all the containers. Rotten food that can't go down the disposal gets double-bagged for transport back to the Cove for composting or deposit into the dumpster.

With that stinky grossness handled, Sarah disappears into their bedroom to pack clothes for the next few nights. "Don't forget a strapless bra for your dress," I holler after her.

Rather than risk getting sucked into a moment where we stare with starry eyes at their dangerously cute nursery, I step outside and set to watering the tomatoes, zucchini, and sweet peas, as well as the planter boxes and hanging baskets. Every time, without fail—seeing these garden baskets along the front of the cabin, I relive those moments when I thought my life with Concierge Ryan was over before it had even begun. How he flopped over off that big rock on the yard's edge after I dragged him out of the woods, how his lifeless body slumped on the ground while I looked for boat keys, the fear of not knowing if the cougar would follow the blood and come back for us, the deafening pound of my heart in my ears as I hobbled our broken bodies down the dock and onto the boat.

What a difference a year makes.

The soaked garden dirt squishes under my work-issue hiking boots as I bend to pluck a few ripe tomatoes from the vine. A luscious red one held against my nose makes my mouth water when I think about biting into Sarah's famous salsa—

"Hollie?"

"Out back watering the garden!"

"Um, can you come here?"

Her voice doesn't sound right. I release the spray nozzle and drop the hose into a planter box, hustling around to the front porch.

Sarah stands half bent over, the fabric of her maternity jeans darker down the middle, along the inside of her legs—like they're wet—a small puddle forming atop the porch's wooden surface.

"Sarah ...?"

She giggles nervously and looks up at me, eyes wide. "My water just broke."

27

Sugar and Spice and Everything Nice

The next sound out of her face should rightfully belong to a howler monkey.

"What IS it with this cabin?" I ask, flying onto the porch to help her into the house. "Shit. SHIT." Absolutely her water has broken.

Sarah tries to stand up straight, one hand against the kitchen island, her other hand in a death grip on my cast. I swear she'll break the plaster if her white knuckles are any indication of her strength.

"How? How is this happening? You were fine ten minutes ago!"

"I guess those contractions meant something. Owwwwww!" She bends in half again, dripping on the floor.

"I need towels. I don't want you to slip." I move her hand onto the counter edge so she so she's anchored to something other than me. "Towels, towels, towels ..." Opening cupboards, in the hall, in their huge bathroom. "Towels!" I grab a stack and rush back into the kitchen to find Sarah stepping out of her pants. "What are you doing?"

"They're wet! It's gross!"

"Do you have maxipads?" She's going to need clean underwear, some sweats, and maxipads to soak this up until we can get help. I hurry back into their bedroom/bath to find everything we need so I can get her on the boat and—and—and what?

"Sarah, did you and Tanner have a plan for this?"

"What? For my water to break while I'm here at the cabin alone? NO! That is why—" She can't talk through the pain.

This shouldn't be happening so fast. From my medical training in my former life, I know that laboring women can often go into hyperdrive once the water has broken, but this is a bit nuts. This is her first baby. It shouldn't be coming this fast. Sudden births usually only happen with women who've had prior children. And usually when someone far better equipped than me is present to help.

Phone in hand, I step outside the front door for a better signal and so I can hear over Sarah's shrieks.

The front desk clerk answers, which means Miss Betty has her phone forwarded. "Find Betty! Sarah's water has broken and we're at the cabin!"

I need to call Tanner. And Ryan! Oh my god, they have to turn the plane around and come home immediately.

"Ahhhhhhhh!" Sarah screams again from the kitchen. "Hollie! Where are you?"

"Right here! I'm right here! Don't worry! I'm calling Miss Betty so we can—hello? Shit, Betty, Sarah's water broke and we're still at the cabin and I think she's in full labor, judging by the screams. What do I do?"

"Can she get on the boat?"

"I don't know! But where do I take her? I don't know the way down to Victoria without Ryan or Tanner here!"

"If you can get her back to the resort, I'll call the Coast Guard and see if they can send a helicopter."

"Gahhhhhhhhh, Jesus Chriiiiiiiiiiist!"

"Oh, oh, oh, this does not sound good," Miss Betty says.

"What? WHAT? What do you mean? Betty, I cannot deliver this baby. I need your help—"

"Hollie, listen to me—you are not allowed to hyperventilate. Sarah needs you."

Miss Betty says more words but between the roaring in my head and the screaming coming from the laboring woman in the kitchen—"Hollie, this is what you're going to do."

"Okay, okay," I say, practicing my own hee-hee-hoooo breathing. "I'm listening."

"Go back in with Sarah. Ask her if she can walk. See if you can get her to the boat."

"Okay." I rush inside. "Sarah, can you get on the boat?"

Oh. Oh, now that is a devilish look. "Miss Betty, I don't think she wants to get back on the boat."

Sarah's preggo-jeans are in mushy heap next to the dishwasher, and the towels she's now sitting on—"Miss Betty, there's blood."

WHY DOES THERE HAVE TO BE BLOOD? What *is* it with this family?

"Sarah, sweetie," I say. She looks up at me, my own death grip on the edge of the granite countertop so I don't faint. "What's going on? Do you think we can get you on the boat?"

Instead of words, a low moan comes out of her bright red face, her lips pursed like she's blowing through a straw. "Hollie ... Hollie, you have to help me. We have to do this. Now. Right now, right here. I can feel something."

"What did she say?" Miss Betty asks. "Put me on speakerphone."

I do. And then I set the phone on the floor near us. "Maybe we should move. Do you want to move onto your bed? It might be more comfortable—"

Sarah shakes her head violently no. "New bedding. It will ruin the bedding. Ohhhhhhh!"

"Girls, can you hear me?" Miss Betty's voice floats out of the speaker, excited but calm, in control. "Hollie, get her underpants off. Get as many towels under her as you can. Blankets, some hot water, a shoelace if you can cut one out of a shoe quick-like, extra towels and blankets for the baby—"

"Betty, I can't do this. I cannot deliver this baby."

"HOLLIE, you can and you *will*. You've trained for this. You know how to handle these situations. You've helped with babies at 911. You saved Ryan and yourself last year. You saved that baby otter. Delivering your niece or nephew is going to be a breeze. I will talk you through it."

Sarah howls again and kicks free of her underwear, hiking her sweatshirt up over her very tense, very huge abdomen. Wow, that is a lot of anatomy I never thought I'd see on another woman outside of a Discovery Channel reenactment. But it's not just hair and blood and angry skin.

There is something round and bulging. Down there.

"Holy fuck, is that the head?" I say.

I really could use a period of unconsciousness right about now.

"Hollie! Do you see the head? Are you moving? Get going!" Miss Betty shouts and snaps me back to the moment. Blankets, towels, giant pot of hot water, shoelace yanked out of my boot, extra towels and blankets for the baby.

Sarah sounds like a freight train chugging toward the station, interspersed with moans that would make Dracula shrink away in terror.

"Sarah, keep breathing. Do you feel the urge to push?"

"Yeeeeeessssssss!" she shrieks. "Why is this happening so fast? Tanner is going to miss everything!"

"I have Tabby calling the boys right now, don't you worry about a thing," Miss Betty coos. "We're going to do this, us girls. We're going to have a baby!"

I wish I could find a second to appreciate the excitement

in Miss Betty's voice but mostly I'm freaking out about what the hell to do with the snake of poo that is eking its way out of Sarah's compressed bottom. I snag the paper towels off the counter and handle that little bit of business.

"Oh god, I am so sorry, Hollie. Please don't tell anyone I poooooooooped!" Sarah moans through another contraction. There is no way we could've gotten her on that boat. I wouldn't even have had time to get her off the soggy porch.

"Okay, so Sarah," Miss Betty's voice crackles, "you—push—blood—tear—" And the phone goes quiet.

"No! NO, NO, NO!" I redial and redial but the screen flashes and it won't connect and why all of a fucking sudden am I out of range? This confounded island! "Sarah, where's your cell?"

"On the boat! I left it on the boat!"

"You don't have a house phone?"

"Nooooooooooo!" I don't think Sarah wants to debate at this particular moment why the hell they don't have a house line like a normal house.

"I gotta go to the boat and get your cell—"

"If you take one step out of this kitchen, I will kill you with my bare hands!" she growls. "Hee hee hooooooo, hee hee hooooooo. Hollie, I think I need to push!"

Okay. Okay. I can do this.

I close my eyes, stand with my head against the cool stainless fridge, and inhale a deep cleansing breath. Invoke my inner Polyester Patty, hear her voice in the training session where we covered what to do with laboring women, see the images of new babies squishing out of their mother's sad, torn, tired bodies, covered in goo and blood—

"HOLLIE!"

"Yes! I'm here! I'm here," I say, dropping to my knees onto the unforgiving kitchen tile.

"What's happening down there? You have to tell me—I can't see it!"

Sure enough, that round bulging thing is bulging even more and the taut skin around it looks angrier than a snakebite. "I think your baby has a lot of hair," I say, forcing a smile that radiates confidence—even if it's false. "We're gonna do this. You and me, okay, sis?"

She nods aggressively, tears spilling out of her squinted, pained eyes and over her scared smile. "You and me, sis." She grabs my hand and squeezes so hard. "Oh dear Jesus, that huuuuuuuuurts!"

The tightly stretched skin looks like it's going to tear. I grab washcloths and dunk them in the hot water. Gently, I place the cloth around the skin, not only to wipe it clean but in hopes of easing some of the obvious discomfort. "On the next contraction, I want you to push. Okay, Sarah? I can see the top of the baby's head."

I leave her long enough to scurry into the living room and grab couch cushions to prop her up. "Sarah, I need you off your elbows so you can grab your knees and really pull your legs back. You've gotta open up your pelvis so that baby can ease its way out."

"Hollie ..." She leans back for a moment in between contractions. "First-aid kit in the bathroom. Under the sink. There are gloves in it. Go grab it to protect your cast."

"I don't care about the cast."

"Get the gloves. There will be a lot of blood and icky crap. And on the changing table—a snot sucker. It's a rubber blue bulb thing—owwwwwww! You'll need it to suck out the fluid from the baby's mouth and nose! Go!"

I find the first-aid kit right where she said it would be and slap a glove on the not-mangled hand. Next, snot sucker at the ready, I fly back into the kitchen.

"What a story we'll have to tell this kid, hey?" I say, dropping back into catching position. Another contraction overwhelms Sarah's voice. Her abdomen squeezes down so tight, more fluid leaks out around the baby's head.

"Puuuuuuuuush!" She does, hard, and the skin of her birthing bits pulses against the pressure of the round cranium fighting its way to freedom. I ease a finger under the skin's lip, which makes Sarah scream, but I think if we can ease the head out, she won't tear. The contraction wanes and the baby's head sinks back ever so slightly.

More warm cloths.

More massage of the tight perineal skin with my knuckle.

Push.

Push.

PUSH!

Sarah's shrieks override my urging her to push. "God, it burns! Make it stop burning! I can't do this! I am going to die! This stupid kid is going to kill me!"

"You are not going to die! You can do this! You're almost there! You're a rock star, Sarah! Keep going—another strong push, babe, come on! Give it all you've got! PUSH harder than you ever have before!"

She thrusts her chin against her chest and wails through the next contraction, but the baby's head pops through the skin like a cork out of a bottle. Oh my god, it's a face. It's a human face! With hair! Dark, wet hair slimed with white waxy gunk and squishy eyes and a button nose and little red lips and—

"Okay, shoulders are coming. The cord is around the neck. I'm going to loop it off ..." I do, but it's tight, pulsating under my finger, and almost doesn't want to unloop. "Ease up, ease up, don't push too hard. Slowly, Sarah, slowwwwwly ..." The first shoulder slides out, although the tear in Sarah's skin above her rectum is bleeding pretty good now. She's hissing backward, the sound that a girl makes when she falls on the crossbar of a boy's bicycle. "You're doing so well. Another shoulder! Here we go! Legs are out! Everything's out!"

"Ahhhhhhh," she moans, flopping back against the pillows, breathing like she's just run a marathon.

"It's a girl! Sarah, it's a girl!"

She pushes up again, tears streaming down her face. "Let me see her!" The baby is super slippery and a scary blue color but I grab hold of the bum and around the neck and hoist her floppy body on to Sarah's belly, pausing only long enough to grab the snot sucker and clean out her airway.

"Come on, baby, give Auntie Hollie a good scream." I

pull a towel from the stack and rub the baby's back good and hard, my own heart thudding because the baby isn't squeaking or howling yet. The arms and legs are limp and the color isn't right.

Sarah pushes herself up higher. "Give me the sucker!" I hand it to her and she sucks more fluid out of the baby's mouth and nose and then gives the baby a light smack on her rear end. Still limp.

I pick up another towel and again massage the back and chest, cradling the slack infant in my hands and blowing on her face.

"Come on ..."

"Hollie ... why isn't she breathing?"

I put the baby on the blankets and cover her mouth and nose with my lips. Five quick rescue breaths, watching the chest for rise. Then, a squeak.

"Do it again!"

I do, and the baby takes over, a gurgling cry coming out of the back of her throat. My hand out, Sarah gives me the bulb sucker and I extract more crap from the mouth and nose, and then I lift the infant's body upright.

"Hooooowaaaahhhhhhhhh! Hooooowahhhhhhh!" Thank the stars in the sky, her entire tiny body flushes bright red with a big inhale and scream.

"Oh dear lord, I thought she was dead," Sarah says, tears streaming down her face as she takes her new daughter and cradles her against her chest. "Thank you. Thank you so much. We did it, Hollie ... we did it." I hand her more towels so we can wipe off the little thing and keep her warm. "Oh my sweet Jesus, we did it."

"On the kitchen floor, no less."

While Sarah tries to catch her exhausted breath, I tie off the umbilical cord with the shoelace. She and the baby are still attached but we need to get some medical help before I start cutting things apart.

"More cramping," she says, grimacing. "I still have to deliver the placenta."

"Yeah, and you're bleeding pretty good down here."

"Did I tear?"

"A little."

"If you stitch it up, throw in a couple extra. For Tanner's sake."

"Ha ha, very funny," I say, grabbing yet another towel. "I'm going to apply pressure here until that placenta comes out."

"Grab a garbage bag from under the sink. We'll need to keep it so the doctor can inspect. And you have to massage my gut."

"Won't that hurt?"

"It doesn't feel awesome, but the birthing class video showed the doctor massaging the uterus right after to get the placenta to detach. So I won't bleed out."

"Please don't bleed out." *Jesus, please don't bleed out.*

Thirty minutes of massage later, the world's most disgusting biological process makes its rather uncomfortable escape from the innards of Sarah's body, a gelatinous, life-giving blob of purple and red and veins and tissue and yeah,

I actually do step outside and barf a little in the bushes. I apologize to Sarah while I'm swishing with Listerine, but I really have no control over what adrenaline does to my stomach.

Once I'm relatively confident that Sarah and the baby are not going to bleed to death on the kitchen floor, I wash my still-shaking hands—noting I am definitely going to need to get this cast replaced—and sprint out to the boat. I get Miss Betty on the two-way immediately.

"It's a girl!"

The cheers from Revelation Cove echo through the radio on this late afternoon. The sun has dipped behind the taller mountains surrounding the cove where their cabin sits, painting the air in a subtle orange-purple, the huge trees almost blue except for the top thirds that still stretch into the sun's shrinking blaze. Bugs flit above the water, skimming for a sip before zipping off, and soft waves quietly lick the side of the boat where the easy tide moves toward shore.

"I've got the Coast Guard coming to you. Stay put, okay? Tanner is heading back—he's going to meet Sarah and the baby at the hospital in Vancouver."

"Is Ryan not coming?" I ask, a little disappointed.

"Brody's plane was delayed, so Ryan is in Seattle to get his brother, and then the two new uncles will drive up to Vancouver late tonight." Miss Betty sniffs. "Are you okay? You sound a little shaky."

"I'm fine." Lie: I'm freaking the hell out. That baby almost died in my arms. I can't stop shaking. The world looks sharper, like someone outlined everything in black

Sharpie. And my heart won't stop pounding, like I've sprinted too far, too fast and I cannot catch my breath.

"I knew you could do it, Hollie. You underestimate yourself, but I knew you could do it."

"It would've been easier if I'd had you on the phone. They have got to get this phone situation fixed."

"Nonsense. You did it. We are all so proud of you!"

The radio receiver goes quiet for a beat and then booms loud again. "Good work, kid!" Lucy Collins cackles. "Miss Betty and I are gonna have some champagne to celebrate, aren't we, Grandma!"

"Lucy—behave. Don't get Miss Betty drunk," I scold, but when they open the receiver on the other side, everyone is hooting and laughing.

"Hollie, it's me again," Miss Betty says. "Does the baby look good? Color and everything? And is Sarah okay? Not too much blood?"

"Baby's nice and pink now. It was scary for a couple minutes but once she got a solid breath, her little blue body changed colors. And she's got all her fingers and toes. A good bit of dark hair. Sarah tore a little so there's some blood, but I think everything will be fine. I should really go back inside with them."

"Thank you, Hollie. Thank you so much. I absolutely adore you. Kiss my new baby and I can't wait to see you soon!"

Ninety minutes later, a Coast Guard vessel pulls alongside the dock and two medical officers carrying a padded stretcher between them follow me into the house to our new momma, still curled on the kitchen floor, exhausted but drunk in love with her little girl.

The first officer introduces herself as Dale and then gives Sarah and the baby a medical inspection to assess them prior to transport, relating information via her shoulder radio to what I assume is the hospital. She also does the gruesome duty of inspecting the placenta, replacing my shoelace with a proper clamp closer to what will eventually be the baby's belly button, and then cuts the newborn free of her nine-month tether. The second officer, a male whose British accent is the only thing I can remember, asks me a million and one questions about the labor and birth and then asks me to pack a bag for Sarah and the baby.

"Rather incredible, yeah? Seeing a new life come into the world? It's a high that will stick with you for a while," he says, eyes twinkling as he pats me on the shoulder. "You did a fantastic job today. Congratulations."

"Yeah. It was something else." Wait—what high? I don't feel a high. I'm scared. What if I did something wrong? The baby could've died in my arms. What if she's okay right now but when they get on that cutter, all hell breaks loose and I will have screwed up somewhere and the baby or Sarah will have a medical crisis—

"Okay, we're about ready to go. Are you coming with us?"

"I think I should stay here and clean up so we don't attract any wildlife with what's left behind."

"Hollie, you don't have to do that. Tanner can come home and clean."

"Absolutely not. You go—he's en route to Vancouver right this second and then Ryan and Brody will be there later. Brody's plane was delayed."

"Only if you're sure," Dale says. I nod and then she and the cute British medic carry Sarah and her tiny lass (and her bagged placenta) out the door. I wait until their vessel has pulled away and then, on autopilot, I get laundry going, pull out the mop and bleach, grab more garbage bags for paper medical waste left behind by the medics.

By the time I'm done, there is no evidence that a new life was brought forth on this very floor.

I lock up and with dead food and medical garbage in hand, it's back to the boat for me. I untie, and thankfully, the engine turns over just like it's supposed to. Bottled water from the fridge refreshes my anxiety-tight throat, and I steer into open water so I can recalibrate the GPS. Sun's down far enough that the shadows are long and the solar-powered lights on docks I pass are lit up to welcome the evening. Bats swoop from the trees, chasing after mosquitoes and termites caught out past their bedtime.

I can't stop thinking about that limp baby in my hands.

Something is clearly wrong with me. I don't know what the "high" is the polite Coast Guard dude promised. I still don't feel high. I feel electrocuted, like my nerve endings are vibrating and oversensitive. When water from the plastic bottle in my shaking hand spills down my shirt, I know I'm in trouble. I felt the same thing last year after the cougar attacked us. But I'm not newly injured, so this can't be proper shock.

The baby could've died.

She could've died in my arms while her bleeding mother watched, and there was nothing I could've done.

I don't even know the baby's name.

Rather than nausea, tears accompany me all the way home, sobbing because instead of euphoria, I can't shake the fear of knowing that, for the longest three minutes of my life, I was solely responsible for the future of that tiny, tiny life. It's not like it was with the otter—if the otter baby had died, yes, that would've been awful. But if Sarah's baby hadn't taken that breath that turned her from dusky blue to rose-petal pink, this day—their lives—would've had a completely different outcome.

The rational, adult side of my brain spends the next hour of travel trying very hard to convince me that I did everything right—funnily enough, that side now sounds like Miss Betty. But the impulsive, scared girl who lives on the opposite side, the side with the band posters and the too-loud music and the hair glitter, she's really kind of losing her shit.

The resort at night never loses its beauty, huge windows lit by inside lights like a hundred candles in a Jack-o'-lantern. As I pull along the dock, music filters from the pool patio. Sounds like a party. Which means I will be going around the opposite side, away from the happy humans. I need quiet. I need to think. I need Ryan.

I actually might need to leave.

28

Serenity, Where Art Thou?

The garbage quietly tucked away, I sneak into the resort, the air-conditioned hall nearly the same temperature as the cool outside air. I slide the card key into our apartment door and once inside, I pause to look at the life Ryan and I have built in the last year. My lovely corner curio cabinet he built for me, now filled with otter collectibles; the cozy throw we snuggle under to binge-watch TV on rainy nights; the eclectic collection of work from local artisans, picked up during our trips to surrounding islands along British Columbia's wild West Coast.

I love it here.

Then why does it feel claustrophobic?

Bathtub tap on, I strip out of my clothes—my sleeves

are crusty with the leftovers of the unexpectedly fluid-filled afternoon. I dial Ryan, but it goes to voicemail.

I'm relieved.

With a fingernail brush, I scrub my engagement ring, seated temporarily on the right hand, and then immerse my left hand's cast in the water, despite doctor's orders, but it's gross. If I don't soak the blood out, it's going to stink to high heaven tomorrow.

Tomorrow. Thursday. Three days before the wedding.

Once the faucet's off, I go under, eyes closed, water bubbling into my ears so I'm trapped in a silent world, only the tink of my ring as it scrapes against the fiberglass tub.

Does the new baby have a name yet?

Did they make it to the hospital?

Should I go downstairs and check in with Miss Betty? I'll text her instead: *Exhausted. Going to bed. See you in the morning.*

Through the crack in the half-open bathroom door, the garment bag holding my replacement wedding gown calls my name.

I finish washing and climb out, wrapping an extra towel around my soaked cast so I don't destroy the bedding. Ten minutes later, I have a bag packed, enough for a couple nights until I get my head on straight. Passport, credit card, emergency cash.

When tomorrow's flight returns guests to Vancouver, I'm on it.

~ ~ ~

My alarm wakes me at seven—my phone shows three

missed calls and multiple texts from Ryan throughout the night. Not quite dry-eyed, I listen to his voicemails and read the texts, each one gushing with love and how proud he is of me and how amazing I am and how he cannot believe Sarah went into labor early but she's so lucky that I was with her and how "Porter saves the day again!" He's in Vancouver with Tanner and everyone, staying at the Fairmont, and he can't wait to get home to see me so he can squeeze me and thank me proper for helping bring his gorgeous little niece—named Elsbeth Leilani, "after my mom and their affection for Hawaii"—into the world.

I disconnect from voicemail and dial Tabby. "Hey ..."

"Hey! Omigod, you're a hero again!"

"Tabby ... I need you to do me a favor."

"Yeah. Anything. What's wrong, Hol? You sound rough."

"I need you to keep an eye on Lucy Collins for me. Just for the next day or so. And if Miss Betty asks what's going on or where I am, just let her know I'm fine and I'll be in touch."

"Hollie, what the hell is going on?"

My throat tightens, my eyes on fire. "Nothing. I—I'm going to Portland real quick."

"You can't leave!" she whisper-yells into the phone. "The wedding is in three days!"

"I know. It'll be fine. I'll be back in time." *I think.* "Just tell Miss Betty that I needed to go see my dad."

"Do you have cold feet? Is that what this is?"

Do I?

"No. I don't think so." *There's nothing more in this world that I want than to marry Ryan Fielding.*

"Then what is going on? Why are you leaving?"

I cannot explain this to her. I'm having a hard time understanding it myself. I just know that the resort will be crawling with Ryan's friends and family over the next eight to twenty-four hours, and everyone will be abuzz about what happened yesterday and then the questions will start and I really need my dad but he won't be here until Saturday. If I wait that long, my heart might implode.

"Just keep Miss Betty at the front desk this morning. Can you handle that?"

"Yeah, shouldn't be hard. It's busy up there already since the golf tournament guys are coming in today. And she's like a bee on fire now that she knows the baby is here and her kids are going to be arriving for the wedding. I haven't seen her this happy since you and Ryan met."

"I know ..."

"And I am really looking forward to that cake, so you'd better get your ass back home, wherever it is you think you need to go."

"I'm not doing this to be hurtful, Tabby."

"I trust you, Hol. I'm just worried."

"Well, don't be."

"Too bad. That's what friends do, so suck it up, princess."

I laugh under my breath. "This morning's outbound flight to Vancouver is at 9:45?"

"Yeah. Are you really going to Portland? I really want to

be your bridesmaid because my boobs look amazing in that dress so promise me you're coming home," she says.

"I'll see you later, Tab. Thanks again."

Next up: Dad. "Hey."

"Hey! Wow! You've been a busy girl. Again. That's my rescue hero. How's the baby?" His smile echoes through the phone.

"I think she's fine. I haven't heard otherwise this morning."

"What's up? You sound tired. Rightfully so. I'm all packed up for this weekend! Got my tux. I look like a handsome devil, I must say. Can't wait to see you, Hollie Cat."

"Dad …" But then I can't talk anymore much beyond strangled yeses and noes, so he does the talking for me.

Instead of me going to Portland, he's going to meet me in Vancouver. "I don't want you getting too far south. You might not ever go home."

Home. This place. It is home. Ryan is home.

"What's wrong with me, Dad?"

"Nothing is wrong with you."

"I was fine … until yesterday. Until that baby …"

"We can talk when I see you. I'll leave in the next hour, so that puts me in Vancouver this afternoon, probably two or three, depending on border waits. I have to feed the goat first."

"The goat should still be full from eating my wedding dress," I say.

"You'd be surprised. He ate another tarp yesterday. We

got some rain and wind and I was attempting to protect my new shoots in the garden. He's invincible."

"And me, fresh out of nuclear warheads."

He chuckles. "Hol, are you going to be okay until we meet up? Where can I find you?"

I don't know Vancouver as well as I should, given I've only gone as Ryan's copilot and he does all the major navigating. But I know the perfect place to meet Dad. Non-threatening, and maybe I can pop in and see *my* little girl.

"The aquarium."

29

It Means Bright

Our backup pilot, William, looked at me funny when I eased into the line along the dock, backpack over my shoulder, head down as I mingled with outbound guests returning to their real lives. After a quick word, I reassured him that everything was kosher and I needed to go see my dad and "here's twenty bucks if you promise not to tell anyone anything more than that."

So Jason Bourne of me.

Thanks to my iPod, I drown out the world during the short flight. No one knows what happened yesterday and thankfully, no one recognizes me or brings up the cougar attack of last year. You wouldn't believe the legs that story has—Ryan and I have relived it through a thousand retellings for well-meaning guests seeking the inside scoop.

Today, though, I'm just a girl, hunched down in a window seat, heading toward an uncertain future. Although given that the lining of my cast is still damp and squishy, that future will definitely include stopping by a proper hospital to get this bad boy traded out. Preferably before it stinks. My skin itches so badly under the plaster and padding, I shove a pen through the gap and scratch when no one is looking.

I ignore the calls buzzing my phone against my hip, a stab to the heart when Ryan pops up on the caller ID. Seeing his name still makes my insides swell with affection, but it's also tinged with uncertainty. A new and unwelcome emotion.

Once we're on the ground, I snag a taxi. The driver takes one look at me and mentions I could get to the aquarium cheaper by using public transit—must be the holey jeans and the mangled cast and the patch-covered backpack—but I don't have time to figure out buses and SkyTrains. That's what emergency cash is for.

The crown jewel of Vancouver, Stanley Park, selected by *Trip Advisor* in 2014 as the World's Best Park, is hopping with families and couples under a blue sky smattered with big, fluffy white and gray clouds; my destination, the Vancouver Aquarium, sits right in her beating heart. I scan the surroundings of the gorgeous, newly renovated facility but it's still too early for Dad to be here. He's easily an hour or two away from the border yet, which gives me ample time to see a veterinarian about an otter.

After I read a flurry of text messages, that is—Miss Betty (*Are you okay? I came to find you and you were gone!*), Tabby (*Miss Betty is freaking out. I caved and told her you're going to Portland. So sorry. Come back soon PLEEEZ*), Ryan (*Porter, are you all right? WTF is going on? Call me immediately. I LOVE YOU*), and even Lucy Collins (*What the hell are you doing running away? Don't be a chicken ship*). I laugh. That's exactly what I am, Lucy. A chicken ship. Aw, autocorrect, you're so cute.

Everyone, except Ryan, gets the same return text: *I'm fine. Meeting Dad. I will see you all soon. Xoxo.*

I haven't figured out how to answer Ryan yet. Not with any depth. I type and delete twelve messages before a simple *I love you too. I just needed a moment. Don't panic.*

At the information desk, I introduce myself to the young staffer, Leslie, working the counter. When she hears that I'm the one who found the new baby otter, her eyes light up. "Dr. Little is here today! She would love to see you!"

As if spending time with a baby otter on a remote beach weren't the pinnacle of my wildlife experiences to date, getting the VIP treatment behind the scenes at the Vancouver Aquarium certainly is. Dr. Little's smile is wide and genuine as she gives me a place to stash my stuff in her office and then outfits me in a smock and booties. I'm also introduced to several of her colleagues, all of whom thank me for saving the little otter, even if I did break a few major laws to do it.

"Our little orphan is doing so well," Dr. Little says. "What happened to your hand?"

"Long story, involving an angry daddy crow."

She snickers and holds open the door into the nursery. "After you."

The familiar squeaks and squeals bouncing off the sterile white walls are music to my ears, even before I see the beautiful brown fluff floating near the felt kelp in her small, enclosed pool. "She's eating like a champ and is really getting the hang of the water."

Dr. Little talks more about eating and sleeping and swimming habits, how the otter is growing faster than they expected—she looks to have doubled in size since I saw her last week! Her blood tests are clear and though it would be ideal for her to be released back into the wild population, because of her age when she was found, the likelihood is that she will remain at the aquarium indefinitely. "Not having a mom to teach her the ropes in a wild environment is problematic. Otters learn absolutely everything from their mothers, and our females here probably aren't good candidates to be surrogates."

The trainer inside the pool enclosure scoops the baby out and scrubs her dry, cradling her tight in a towel. She then holds her to the glass partition so I can see my otter girl's magnificent little face. "I cannot believe how much bigger she's gotten," I say.

"She eats all the time! She's consuming almost two kilograms of food a day now, plus baby otter formula."

"Little chunker. Do you have a name for her yet?"

Dr. Little smiles. "Now that you mention it ... we were sort of hoping that you might be interested in naming her. Since you rescued her. You're her mom, for all intents and purposes."

"No, I couldn't. She belongs to Vancouver now."

"But she would've died on that beach if you hadn't intervened."

"Don't you guys usually have a naming contest or something? To raise awareness and funds?"

Dr. Little nods at the trainer inside the enclosure. The young woman waves goodbye to us, and just like that, the otter is whisked through the swinging stainless steel doors. "You want to go see Tanu and Katmai while you're here?"

The Vancouver Aquarium is home to four rescued otters—females Katmai and Tanu, and males Elfin and Wally. Have you seen the famous YouTube video of the aquarium otters "holding hands" while they float? Those were Vancouver otters, Milo and Nyac. They've both since passed on, but the two of them holding hands—that's what otters do to sleep safely in groups. It's called a raft.

Like Ryan and me. Our own little raft.

Sigh.

I join Dr. Little in feeding the girls their midday meal. What a rush! Tanu's blond head pops out of the water to grab the offered delicacies and then she stuffs everything into her mouth with those little padded paws and it's just about the cutest thing ever in the history of the world. She's a big girl, coming in at around fifty-seven pounds, but young Katmai is faster than her matronly tank mate, sneaking alongside the pool edge toward Dr. Little's bucket.

A name for the baby otter. This is a huge responsibility. I don't know any names that are reflective of local or First Nations culture. I don't have any dear friends or dead relatives I want to honor.

When Ryan told me about the child he and Alyssa never

had, he mentioned that he had a name picked out had it been a girl. Clara. "*After my grandmother...*"

"Dr. Little—for the otter baby. What about Clara? It means 'bright.' A family name," I say.

The vet smiles as she hands me a small limp squid to feed to a patiently waiting Katmai. "Clara. I like that. Good choice."

Clara it is. A family name.

Two hours later, I've said my goodbye to Clara through the glass partition with the whispered promise I'll come back soon, and reassurances from Dr. Little that she'll keep me apprised of Clara's progress. Hands scrubbed clean of the otters' lunch offerings, I float on my post-otter-visit cloud to the cafeteria in search of my own sustenance.

"Hollie! Hollie Cat!"

Dad! He's here!

He maneuvers around a selfie-shooting family and their double stroller and practically runs to me standing at the café's wide, light-filled entrance, a garment bag draped over one of his arms. Did he bring his tux already?

"Ohhh, my little girl," he says, folding me into a tight hug.

"You made good time."

"Speed limits are fluid." He winks. "Are you eating? What's going on? How's your hand?" He cradles my cast in his palm. "This looks terrible. Did you get it wet?"

"After helping someone through childbirth? Yeah. My cast got wet."

"Let's have lunch, and then we can go find a hospital to change it out. You know your way around this city?"

"That's what Google Maps is for," I say. "Dad, did you bring your tux already?"

"I'll show you in a sec. Have you talked to Ryan?" he asks. "He called me, Hol. He's frantic."

I loop my arm through his and pull him into the food lineup. I don't want to talk here in the chaos. We need to sit. I need Dad Advice, and right now, that will need to happen over french fries because I am starving.

We pick a seat near the vast, bright windows and Dad drapes his tux bag over the empty chair next to him. This new cafeteria is really something else, offering panoramic views of the aquarium's exterior environs—the famous Bill Reid Killer Whale fountain, grasses and perennials and hedges bordering the well-planned concrete plaza with built-in benches and open space for littles to run around and local vendors to sell their wares.

"The baby otter. She's healthy and growing so much. They let me name her," I say. "Clara. It's a Fielding family name. I figured it would make Ryan happy."

"Perfect name for a little sweetie," he says, dipping a few fries in the tiny cup of ketchup. "Time's up. You have to tell me what's going on."

I shrink like a deflating balloon and lean against the tabletop. "Sarah's baby wasn't breathing when she came out."

"And?"

"And I can't shake the feeling that she could've died in my arms."

Dad reaches across and grabs my uncasted wrist. "Hollie, she didn't die. She lived, because you made sure of it. Imagine what could've happened had Sarah gone into sudden labor without you there! What if it had happened with Miss Betty or other staff folks from the resort? You had the presence of mind to walk her through the whole thing, and you did beautifully."

"I get all that. But I can't shake this *feeling*. Holding the little body in my hands," I demonstrate, an imagined infant stretched between my palms, "her whole life ahead of her. In little more than a few seconds, I saw this tiny human turning into a child and then a grown-up, and I felt the weight of the world in my hands, knowing that I was responsible for not only her entire life actually happening but the eternal happiness of Sarah and Tanner who tried so, so hard to get pregnant with her. It was completely overwhelming. And I freaked out."

"But you performed under pressure. You have to turn this around, Hol—you saved them. You helped that baby come into the world safely, and you helped Sarah be strong and brave in one of life's most terrifying—and joyous—moments."

"Maybe that's all true, and yeah, it was joyous in the end, but what if it had gone the other way? The whole situation made me realize that being a wife—and possibly a mother—that involves a real commitment to protecting another person's happiness. Am I ready for that? What about Ryan's happiness? What if I'm the wrong woman for him? What if I screw up?"

"Do you love him?"

"What?"

"Ryan. Do you love him?"

"Of course, Dad. More than anything."

"You're marrying Ryan. That will make him the happiest man alive. And his number-one job will be keeping *you* happy, because that is how men think. If you guys decide that kids aren't in your future, so be it. You still have each other, and if Ryan is half the man I think he is, *you* are what he wants. Kids would just be a bonus."

"I don't want to be like her," I whisper, fighting back the emotion clenching my throat. "I can't have a kid, Dad, because I'm terrified I will mess it up. I'm terrified that I will be the worst mother in the history of the world, and Ryan will be so disgusted that he married me, and I will get scared and bail."

My dad leans back in his chair and laughs loudly enough to startle the old woman sitting at the table next to us, gumming a cinnamon roll. "My little Hollie Cat, you are a nut."

"It's not funny," I say, shoving another fry into my mouth.

"You are *nothing like her*. Do you hear me? Yeah, you have the adventurous side of Lucy Collins—she was a lot of fun when she was younger. She loved getting into mischief and finding new things to be excited about. You have that from her—her curiosity and love of creatures and her general enthusiasm about the world. But something went wrong with Lucy. Something very sad, very deep. I couldn't fix that for her—even when I thought having you would be the fix she needed, I was wrong. And she left. And it sucked. But you have to let it go, Hollie.

"You have to stop comparing yourself to her because you're *not* her. I've watched you grow from the wild, crazy, loving kid into a wild, crazy, loving woman. A little accident prone, yes," he says, nodding at my cast, "but it's because you're giving a hundred percent of yourself a hundred percent of the time. You give your whole heart to everyone who deserves it—and I didn't raise you to be a quitter. You've never quit anything in your life that was important to you."

"I quit 911."

"It was a job, Hollie! A job you hated! You only took it to make me happy, and even that says so much about your character, about how much you love me and how much you wanted to make me happy. It's what's in here," he taps hard over his heart, "—that is what makes people fall head over heels for you. Ryan loves you, come hell or high water, come babies or no babies. He doesn't buy into any of the nonsense going on in your head—if you'd heard his voice over the phone an hour ago, you'd believe me."

Dad leans forward and takes my hands in his. "You are who you choose to be, Hollie Cat."

"What if I choose to not be a mother?"

"Well, that is something you will need to discuss with your future husband. But I promise you that if you do decide to have kids with Ryan, you will be a fantastic mother. Naturally, because I was a fantastic father and I taught you everything I know," he says, cupping my cheek in his soft palm. "And you're not going to leave because I raised you to be better than that. You are not Lucy Collins because you weren't raised in Lucy's world. You were raised in Hollie's world, and what a grand, glorious world it is." Dad's eyes mist over. He clears his throat and hands me napkins. "Do me a favor—wipe your hands clean. Before I show you," he says, standing and pulling the garment bag to full height.

"Did your tux guy get the right tie and cummerbund—"

I stop speaking as the zipper parts to reveal the fabric encased inside does not belong to a black tux.

It belongs to a white dress.

THE dress.

"Dad! Are you kidding me?" I throw myself at him. "How—is this—what did you do?"

Nurse Bob laughs and struggles to balance the dress and the hug with my bouncing body. "Felicia called from the dress shop the other night. I called Ryan. We worked it out."

"*How* did you work it out?"

"I could tell you, but then I'd have to kill you."

"Dad, please," I say, checking my hands for errant ketchup before fully unzipping the garment bag and draping the world's most perfect dress over my clean, uncasted arm. "This is just the best. THE BEST."

"I'm torn up about that damn goat, Hollie Cat. And I know the other dress you got wasn't the one you wanted. This one has been altered to fit like the first one—we made sure of it. The manager of the bridal shop will take the alternate dress back."

"No, you can't afford this. It's more expensive than the alternate dress."

"Why don't you let me worry about my own finances, little missy? Who the hell else am I going to spend my hard-earned union wage on?"

I reseal the dress into the bag, careful to make sure there isn't a single centimeter of exposed fabric that I can maim. "Daddy ... thank you. So much. But what if Ryan doesn't want to marry me now? What if I've messed up already?"

"Now you're just talking nonsense."

"I love this dress so much," I whisper, hugging and hugging him because I really do have the World's Awesomest Dad.

"Hol ...," he whispers against my ear. I push back and see that his eyes are pulled left, toward the café's entrance.

I follow his gaze.

Ryan, playoff beard still in its full glory, eyes wild with fear, his rugged body looking more handsome than should be legal in a blue button-down and Levis.

"I'm going to take a walk and visit my grand-otter," he says. In the time it takes Dad to again drape the encapsulated dress over the neighboring chair, Ryan has moved to our table.

"She's still in the nursery," I say quietly. "Go to information and ask for Dr. Little. Tell her who you are. They might let you in to see her."

"There are other otters here, Hol. I'll see you kids in a

bit." Dad stands and meets Ryan's solid handshake before slipping out.

"May I sit?"

I nod.

Ryan's face is whiter than I've seen it outside a nasty bout of flu, his eyes pink-rimmed.

"Hey ..."

"Hey."

"Hollie, look at me."

I do. Without asking, he cradles my right hand between his palms, pausing only to adjust my engagement ring so the diamond sparkles in the sunlight blasting through the wide windows. He's touched me a million times in the last year, and every time, the same zing of electricity races from head to toe.

"What's going on?" he says.

"I just needed a little space."

"Are you having second thoughts? About the wedding?"

I pause. "No. I'm not. Not really." I laugh under my breath to hold off the sting in my eyeballs. "Dad brought me THE dress." I nod at the garment bag.

"We knew what it meant to you."

"That's what he said."

"So then what's happening?"

"How is Elsbeth?"

"She's fine. Healthy and beautiful. You did so well," he says. He reaches over the table and brushes my cheek with his thumb. "Is this about the baby? Is this about what happened yesterday?"

I nod. I sniff and sit taller, swallowing the lump so I can speak. "It's about a lot of things. The last few weeks have been overwhelming. Yesterday at the cabin, when Sarah's water broke, I was sucked back to a year ago when the cougar attacked. And then the baby—she came so fast, and then there was a dicey moment when she wasn't breathing ..."

"Sarah said you were perfect. She's in awe of how cool you were under the circumstances."

"But it stirred up so many conflicting emotions. I couldn't be excited about what I'd just witnessed because it freaked me out so much."

"What part?"

"All of it! Have you ever delivered a baby? Have you ever delivered a baby that looks dead?"

He shakes his head no. "You have every right to feel these emotions," he says, rubbing my arm. "But you did amazing. And Sarah and Elsbeth are here in Vancouver—they're both doing so well that they will be out and back home in time for the wedding ... if we're still having a wedding."

"I want to marry you. I do."

"Why does it sound like a 'but' belongs at the end of that sentence ..."

"I want to marry you *but* I am terrified of having kids."

"We talked about this before, Hollie. We don't have to have babies if you don't want to."

"But *you* want to, and what right do I have to withhold that from you?"

He stands and seats himself in the vacant chair next to me. "Your dad said that this is about Lucy Collins."

"I probably need to talk to a shrink," I say, looking down at our conjoined hands.

"So, we'll get you a shrink," he says, finger tipping my chin so our eyes connect.

"Your whole family is going to be at the Cove for the wedding. They're all going to be staring at us when we're getting married, me walking down the aisle and you waiting—"

"That's what happens at weddings, Porter."

"I know, but all those eyes watching and judging and putting their expectations on us, even before the vows have been exchanged—"

"What expectations? No one's judging you. Shit, you're a hero to my family!"

"But then, watch, we won't even get to the part where we're cutting the cake before the questions and teasing starts about when we're going to start popping out junior hockey players."

"Yeah. Probably."

"And what am I supposed to say?"

"The same thing you say when someone asks you who you're voting for in the next election. 'We'll see what happens' is always a safe answer."

"But in my head, it feels like the whole world is pressuring me, and that's when I start to panic because all the anxiety about being a terrible mother comes rushing in." My breath shortens just thinking about it.

"No one is pressuring you. Asking about kids is just a thing other humans do when people get married. It's considered polite conversation."

"Why couldn't we stick to talking about hockey or conflicts in the Middle East?"

He laughs quietly. "Please, Porter, don't torture yourself like this. Don't torture me. You have to marry me, or I will have no reason to go on living."

"Stop making fun." I slap at his hand playfully.

"I'm not." He pulls me in for a kiss. "I love you. You are a remarkable human being. You saved me, and I'm not talking about from that nasty cougar." Another kiss, and then he speaks so close, his breath tickles my upper lip. "I don't care about babies. I don't care what anyone else thinks about us having babies. I don't care about hockey or conflicts in the Middle East—"

"You don't care about hockey? Now I know you're a liar," I say, tugging on his beard.

"The beard goes tonight. Detroit's out."

"Awww, I'm sorry, babe."

"No, you're not. Not if Anaheim won."

"You're right. Go, Anaheim."

"Traitor." He shakes his head and then pulls a thin square jeweler's box tied with a squished lavender ribbon from his back pocket. "I was saving this for the wedding night, but ..."

"No fair. I didn't get you anything."

"You can make it up to me with your hot bod," he says, the smile reaching his eyes. "Open it."

I untie the ribbon and lift off the white lid. Inside is a shining silver ID-style bracelet.

"I figured it would look nice with your gown," he says.

The engraved bar rests on my fingertips: "*Our raft, our rules*," I read, not bothering to suck back the tears. "It's perfect."

"Here ..." Ryan takes it from me and clasps the chain links around my right wrist, turning it so he can buff the fingerprints off the shiny surface. "It's our raft, Porter. We can do whatever we want. We just have to float together."

I kiss him this time, scooting onto his lap and wrapping my arms around his neck.

When we come up for air, Ryan looks over my shoulder and smirks. "That old woman at the table next to us just gave me a thumbs up," he says. "I guess that means I'm a keeper."

I slide back onto my chair. "Can we go see Elsbeth before we leave?"

"Absolutely."

I hold my cast aloft. "I also need to get this changed."

He pokes at it. "Is that what that smell is?"

"Be nice or I'll smear my germs on you."

"God, I hope so." Ryan cleans up the lunch leftovers and hands me the new dress. Then, arms wrapped around one another, we move into the aquarium's main building, emotional exhaustion slowing my steps a little. Through the glass doors, we spot Dad alongside the otter enclosure.

"Our little otter is doing really well," I say, pushing the door open. "They let me name her."

"Yeah? What did you pick?"

I stop him before we reach Dad. "Clara."

Ryan's eyebrow hitches and a slow, satisfied smile spreads across his face. He hoists me off the ground and buries his scratchy face against my neck. "Good choice," he whispers against my lips.

"It's a family name," I say. "From my new raft. I thought you might like it."

30

Enhydra lutris, Bridesmaid Edition

We're going to call yesterday Insanity Day, the day where all of Ryan's family and friends and hockey buddies plus my dad and Lucy Collins flitted about the resort, high on the pre-wedding euphoria we allegedly pumped through the ventilation system. It could also have something to do with the endless booze and Joseph's glorious buffets and the presence of a very tiny, very pink bundle of joy who is meeting every relative she never knew she had.

"Stop fidgeting," Tabby says, shoving another pin into my updo. "I've never had a veil give me so much trouble."

"Do you need help?" Sarah calls, though she's not moving very quickly, especially not without her inflatable donut. Lucy Collins graced last night's dinner table with her own postpartum horror story about how my giant head ruined her honeymoon vagina. She finally ceased embarrassing me when Thomas demanded she stop dancing on the table secondary to health code violations.

Miss Betty can be heard in the other room, cooing at tiny Elsbeth. She really is the cutest baby, and when she arrived home late Friday night with her beaming, exhausted parents, we spent a little time, just she and I, making our peace. Elsbeth agreed that she'd be a good baby and keep growing and breathing, and I promised her I'd teach her everything she'd ever want to know about sea otters. We shook on it. And then she barfed on me. So the deal is super-sealed.

There's a knock on the front door, followed by a glowing new daddy entering, decked out in his wedding finery. "Ladies, I will escort you down now. We should let the bride have a few moments to gather herself, yes?" Tanner plucks his new daughter from his mother and smothers her cheeks with kisses.

Last pin installed, Tabby, looking resplendent in her lavender off-the-shoulder dress, grabs my shaking hands. "Jesus, you're freezing. Are you still alive?" She air-kisses my cheeks and then adjusts the lovely white ribbon she used to decorate my new cast. "I will see you in a few minutes. You can do this. Right? Remember: don't focus on the people. Focus on your hot groom waiting at the front."

"Yes. Right. Hot groom. No people."

Dad tiptoes into my bedroom, which has been transformed into a grand changing area, the queen bed pushed far aside and replaced by a huge three-paneled mirror we usually lend to our guest brides. He's trying, and failing, to hold back his manly tears.

"My baby girl," he says, kissing my cheek. "I've got something for you."

"Dad, no. You've already given me too much."

"Zip it. I'm the dad, which means I'm the boss." From a long black box, he pulls an elegant string of tiny pearls. "Miss Betty helped me pick 'em. She said they'd go well with your dress."

I face the mirror as he fastens the necklace. "And?"

"Stunning." Dad's hands resting against my bare arms are so warm, I shiver.

"You ready to do this?"

I offer a fist bump. "Wedded bliss, here I come."

"That's my girl."

Miss Betty, Lucy Collins, and Sarah are next. A few more tissue-dabbed tears are followed by quick lipstick touch-ups, words of encouragement from Sarah, a question from Lucy about whether I shaved "down there" because "horny grooms like a clean workspace," and finally, more thanks from Miss Betty for making her son the happiest man in the world.

That remains to be seen.

And then the door clicks closed behind my entourage, and I'm alone, serenaded by the ticking clock and my thudding heart, to wait until it's time to head downstairs to the banquet room that has been transformed by an explosion of flowers, tulle, twinkly lights, and so much romance, a girl could get pregnant sitting in one of the white wooden fold-up chairs.

How long do I wait?

We text our brides and tell them when to come down, once everyone is seated.

This is taking forever.

I click on the TV. Look for a nature documentary to calm my nerves. Why is it Shark Week again? Watching a great white eat a seal is *not* relaxing.

When twenty minutes pass, my nerves are snacking on anxiety cakes. It's Shark Week in my gut.

What is taking so long?

A knock. They've come for me, rather than texting.

Shit, finally!

I sashay to the door, careful of my delicate train. Knowing me, I will snag and tear it and somehow accidentally trigger the Red Button that brings about the end of the natural world.

Unlock the door. Pull the handle.

"Ryan! Go away! You can't see me yet!"

I push to close the door against its stubborn hydraulic hinge, but he stops me, hand spread wide against the wood, mischief all over his radiantly handsome, clean-shaven face. "I won't look too closely," he says, eyes twinkling as he steps into our apartment. "Okay, I lied." He grabs my hands and pushes me back so he can see the whole thing.

"This is bad luck! You're going to ruin everything!"

"Ha. You look ... Porter, you're the most extraordinary, magical thing I have ever seen in my entire life."

"You're looking pretty delicious yourself," I say, "but whyyyyyy? Why are you here? I wanted you to be blown away when you saw me coming down the aisle."

"I will be. Don't worry. But I have a surprise."

"Right now? Couldn't it have waited?"

"You'll like this surprise. Trust me?" He holds out his hand.

I take it.

Instead of moving down the hall toward the main part of the resort, he scoops up my train and drapes it over my cast arm. We detour left, out the side entrance and around the rear of the resort, to the docks. "What is going on? Won't everyone be expecting us?"

"Remember: trust." Ryan helps me onto the cabin cruiser, arranging my train behind me so that it doesn't wrinkle, even in the limited space, and places my good hand atop an oh-shit bar so I have a place to hold on. "I am so glad we got you *this* dress," he whispers against my ear. "I cannot wait to get you out of it." And then he's at the helm, engine on, boat motoring away from the resort and what I assume will be some very confused wedding guests.

"You have to tell me what is going on," I say.

"No I don't. You'll see in a few minutes." He reaches a hand backward and helps me step closer to where he is, returning one hand to the wheel so he can keep the other wrapped around my waist. Instead of talking, he hits play on his iPod, and the song he used to propose to me at the Oregon Zoo, Etta James's *At Last*, snakes out of speakers he's wired through the boat's interior.

"You are a clever, clever lad," I say, swaying next to him.

"You have no idea."

Once we've moved south of the resort far enough that I know this isn't a prewedding pleasure cruise, it dawns on me where we're headed.

Otter Beach.

Ryan won't tell me a thing, the shit-eating permasmile affixed to his face.

When we round the rocky outcroppings that have become so familiar, ahead, moored alongside the quiet beach strip where we found little Clara, is another boat, one of our larger tour crafts. On the sandy beach, our tiny wedding party awaits—Dad, Miss Betty, Lucy Collins, Tabby, Tanner and Sarah and baby Elsbeth, Brody, Hailey and her husband and kids, Smitty the marriage commissioner, his wife Audrey, and the crow-fearing photographer.

Flickering candles wedged in glass cylinders in the sand demarcate our "aisle," flanked by just enough flower arrangements to remind everyone that two people are about to bind their lives together forever.

"How ... how did you do this?"

"Magic," Ryan whispers. "Don't move." Engine killed, he drops anchor. Tanner has come out to meet us in one of the Revelation Cove wooden rowboats, this one decorated with bright purple and white bows, the bench covered in canvas so my dress will stay clean. "Your chariot awaits."

My soon-to-be-husband and his brother help me onto the boat's middle bench, and then Tanner rows us to the shore, Dad and Smitty pulling the vessel all the way onto the beach so no one will get their toes—or their trains—wet while disembarking.

"Are you ready?" Ryan whispers against my head.

I nod and kiss his cheek. "Thank you."

Tabby scurries down to fix my dress and hand me my spectacular bouquet while the men get into position farther up the sand—Smitty in the middle, marriage book in hand, Ryan to Smitty's left, waiting for me, his smile glowing like a sun, his brothers behind him, and Dad walking down the beach toward me.

A light breeze picks up the end of my veil and it dances with an unseen partner, but I couldn't have ordered a more perfect day if I'd had the weather gods on speed dial. Blue skies with stripes of clouds that look fresh off a painter's brush, seabirds talking up a storm in the trees on the cliffs above, the swish and murmur of the tide coming ashore.

"Some surprise, hey, Hollie Cat?"

"Did you know?"

"Not until this morning. That Ryan, he's a crafty one. You should marry him," Dad says, kissing my cheek. "You look like an angel."

"The dress is perfect, yeah?"

"Like it was made for you."

"Hollie ... look," Tabby says, pointing. On the rear deck of the larger Cove vessel, two familiar otters are making short work of whatever is in the strategically placed buckets. Around the edge of the wide fiberglass deck shelf, a few others float, grooming themselves and watching curiously what the crazy humans are up to.

Wedding music starts out of the ether, and I laugh when I see Ryan's brother, Brody, standing aside, strumming an acoustic guitar.

"That's our cue," Dad says. Tabby straightens the train and fluffs the skirt and then gives my wrist one final squeeze before starting up the beach. We wait long enough for her to reach the first candles, and then follow.

"He loves you so much, my baby girl." Dad's voice hitches.

"I know, Dad."

Once we reach the front, Tabby takes my bouquet, and Dad pats the top of my hand draped over his tuxedoed forearm.

"Hello, Hollie," Smitty says. "You are a breath of the freshest air."

"Thanks, Smitty. Thanks for the crabs too. For the otters," I whisper.

He nods at Ryan. "Thank your groom." He winks and clears his throat, adopting the deep tenor of a proper wedding officiant and not the owner of our local general store. "Who gives this woman to be married to this man?"

My dad looks at Lucy Collins, and just for a butterfly's heartbeat, they smile at one another. "Her mother and I do," Dad says, offering my hand to Ryan.

And when my stunning groom faces me, our hands intertwined the best we can with plaster and ribbon and nervous jitters coursing between us like a completed circuit, his crooked nose and white, white grin and the way his emerald eyes wrinkle when he smiles and how he looks at me like he's never seen my equal in all the days of his life, the rest of the world falls away.

"Dearly beloved, we are gathered here today in the presence of family, friends, and otters, to celebrate the happy union of this vibrant twosome ..."

31

Epilogue: A Raft--or a Clan?

"Are your eyes closed?"

"Yes! For the sake of humanity, Porter, hurry up!"

I crack the door to the massive bathroom—we're in a proper honeymoon suite and not in our apartment tonight. Perks of owning the resort where you live.

"Are you still gonna call me Porter, now that I'm Mrs. Fielding?"

"Porter is more than a name with you—it's an adventure."

Stepping through into the dim light, I thrust out a hip and present myself in the slinky white two-piece lingerie. Ryan, leaning against his elbow in nothing more than loose cotton pajama pants, groans and falls flat against the bed, hand over his heart.

And then he springs to his feet and meets me halfway, clasping my fingers and spinning me around for a complete look, pausing to kiss my silver bracelet and then my new wedding band on my right hand. "This is exactly the kind of present I was hoping for," he says, voice low and playful. "Champagne?"

"You are a first-class concierge." He bows and then escorts me to the bed's edge, moving to the Moët chilling in the ice bucket.

"Are you annoyed that we're not rushing out for a honeymoon?" he asks, handing me a bubbly-filled flute engraved with our names and today's date. Ah, thanks, Miss Betty. Such a romantic.

"It's not like we had a lot of time to plan one. It's a miracle we pulled off a wedding." He clinks my glass and then pretzels his arms through mine to sip.

"Do you have any idea where you might want to go?" He sits next to me on the bed and it's all I can do to not chuck the glass and run my tongue over his muscled torso.

"Not a clue. We live in paradise. It's hard to envision another paradise somewhere else." I finish the glass and set it aside so I can climb onto his lap. "Was today what you'd hoped for?" I run my fingers down the patchwork of his damaged left arm, trace the muscles along his shoulders, brush the smattering of chest hair.

"Today was absolutely everything."

"The beach wedding ... thank you so much," I say, kissing him, hands cupping his strong jaw now prickled with late-day growth. "And the reception was so fun. But man, you have a lot of friends. I may have sprained my cheeks from so much smiling. I will never remember any of their names."

"They'll remember yours," he says, flopping me over onto the bed and pushing himself against me.

"Mmm, seems like someone wants to make this marriage legal."

"I think the word is 'consummate,'" he says, nibbling down my neck. "What do you expect when you come prancing out of the bathroom wearing this?"

"I'm so glad it's not like the old days when we had to have family or priests watching to prove that it happened."

He pushes up and stares down at me, fire sparking in his eyes. "I'd still nail you. Even if the whole world were watching."

~ ~ ~

Once Ryan has had a mildly restorative rest, he sets to bending the will of a roll of duct tape as he works to affix a plastic bag over my cast.

"That should do it," he says. "I'll hold your arm along the side of the tub."

"How the hell did you find duct tape at this hour?"

"I didn't. I thought ahead."

"You're always thinking ahead."

"Into the tub, milady. Do not slip. We are not going to the emergency room on our wedding night."

"Where's your sense of adventure?"

He holds my right hand as I step in and dip under the bubbles, left plastic-wrapped arm aloft. He then settles in behind me, his long legs coiling around mine, and exhales a satisfied sigh as he pulls me against him.

"So I was thinking ..."

"Uh-oh, should I be worried?" I ask.

"One of my buddies from the league—he left right around the time I did, for different reasons—he got tired of being bounced from team to team. Not every player can be a superstar."

"You're my superstar." I squeeze his thigh under the water, making him flinch. "Was this buddy here tonight?"

"No. He couldn't make it. We invited him—guy named Spencer Brooks—he took a job a few years back, coaching overseas in Scotland with the Elite Ice Hockey League."

"Oooh, Scotland. I've heard it's beautiful there."

"Funny you'd say that. He called me the other day—I talked to him in between picking up Brody and arriving at the hospital in Vancouver. Before you did your little runner ..." He pinches my ass under the water.

"And what did this call entail?"

"Just so you know, I will never make a decision without you, on anything. We're a team now."

"A raft," I say, touching my bracelet.

"The call entailed a job offer."

"Wait—what?" I spin around in the water, nearly dunking the cast arm.

"He's looking for an assistant coach. He couldn't make the wedding because his team is in their playoffs."

"Ryan, do you want to coach? I thought you were done with hockey. I thought that's why you opened the resort."

"We will always have the resort," he says, his face reflecting both excitement and apprehension. "It doesn't have to be the only thing we do."

"But ... coaching? Does that interest you?"

He laughs under his breath. "Hockey's in my blood. It will always be. I've never seriously considered coaching because the resort has taken up everything since I left the game, but if the opportunity ever presented itself, and now with the resort going strong like it is—it might be an interesting thing to think about."

"Fielding, you know that whatever makes you happy—I will support."

"Thing is, there wouldn't be a job for you right away, and certainly not anything to do with otters."

I laugh. "Scotland has otters. *Lutra lutra*—they look more like North American river otters than like our girl Clara."

"Little Clara ..." He smiles.

"So, does Spencer Brooks want an immediate answer, or ...?"

"No. Not at all. He knows we've got a lot going on right now and a decision like this is huge. He did, however, invite us over. To check things out, see what we thought. And I was thinking maybe it could be our honeymoon. See if we like the place, if it's a fit for this new life we're building."

"It rains a lot in Scotland."

"Says the Oregonian."

"Good thing I have webbed feet." I hoist one foot out of the water and wiggle my lovely painted toes. "Would you wear a kilt?" I close the gap between us to gnaw on his ear. "Kilts are ridiculously hot. Especially what's under the kilt." He shivers between my legs.

"I'd wear anything you want, as long as you promise me you will always do what you're doing right now."

"Scotland, hunh ... Scotland could be interesting."

Acknowledgments

As you likely are aware, books aren't birthed without a sizeable degree of outside help. It takes a team of support humans to act as labor coaches and story "midwives," helpers to massage the swollen fingers and clogged brain synapses and to encourage the writer to keep pushing through the pain. The saving grace of this book-birthing process? No terrifying bodily fluids.

My support humans come from every corner of this square planet, and if I could send them all celebratory (bubble gum) cigars right now, I would.

Thanks go to:

Dan Lazar, my charming, brilliant, eternally patient agent, who lets Eliza Gordon run around like a crazy person because it keeps Jenn out of trouble; his unrivaled assistant, Victoria (Torie) Doherty-Munro for laser-guided editorial assistance; Julie Trelstad, the Writers House digital rights manager and marketing guru, for being my right hand in New York and making sure we're getting All the Things done so we can make books happen; to Brodie Rogers, the Customer Experience Manager of the Chapters Coquitlam for stocking my books on so many shelves and for your incredible excitement about all things Eliza Gordon; and to the #1 Chapters bookseller, Aaron Beveland-Dalzell, for not only choosing *Neurotica* as a Staff Pick but for hand-selling the Eliza Gordon titles to the book lovers who frequent your store. (Also? I cannot wait to read your first novel. Get busy.)

Jim Covey of the Monterey Bay Aquarium (www.montereybayaquarium.org) for answering questions about what baby otters eat and for being a steward for California's sea life.

My supportive friend and very talented neighbor Larissa Meade with Bridal Beginnings (www.bridalbeginnings.com) for designing Hollie's perfect bouquet (I love it!).

Sarah Hansen of Okay Creations (www.okaycreations.com/) for my fantastic covers. I wish I could write a hundred books and have you design covers for every single one. You're the bee's knees, even if bees don't have knees. (Do they have knees?)

And Mariyam Khan of Oh Panda Eyes (find her on Facebook and Etsy!) for all the heart-squeezing swag and jewelry and Eliza Gordon quote graphics you make for my books—seriously, I get so excited every time you message me with a new treat! Your generosity and kind spirit is unbounded.

I couldn't write a book without the help of friends kicking my ass behind the scenes—Kendall Grey, you are the other half of my writerly heart. Your critiques see things I never consider and fix mistakes I would've glossed over. *Thank you forever and ever amen.*

To my darling cheering section, Angeline Kace, Amber Hart, Adrienne Crezo (I have a lot of friends whose names start with A), Jane Klassen Omelaniec, and Evelyn Lafont—you girls have listened to me whine, read my dumb ideas for other books, critiqued, encouraged, inspired, and supported me from the very beginning. My gratitude would fill the oceans.

Speaking of birthing, congratulations to my sister from another mister and birthday buddy, London Sarah, and her husband Sir Toby on the arrival of *their* new sweetie, Miss Ivy Bea. Ivy, your crazy American auntie can't wait to scoot over that big pool of water to kiss your cheeks good and proper.

Thanks to one of my very favorite bloggers and book friends (and a kick-ass English teacher working tirelessly to inspire a new generations of writers!), Shana Benedict of A Book Vacation (http://abookvacation.com/) for beta reading all of my prerelease drafts. You've been with me since the early days of *Sleight*, and I trust you implicitly. Thank you for sharing your bookish wisdom with the world.

Thanks to Candace Robinson of CBB Book Promotions (www.cbbbookpromotions.com/) for release and marketing support for all Eliza Gordon's books.

And of course, warm hugs and thank-yous to my loving and supportive super-readers and awesome blogger buddies—without word of mouth, authors don't sell books: Deb Hardy, LJ Ducharme, Carmen Jones, Tina Lykins, DeeJay Sakata, Liis McKinstry, Ali Hymer and Debbie Readsandblogs, Noemi Studie, Shelley Bunnell, Megan Furlow Broussard, Kay Howard, Nicole Miklavic, Christine Marie Jarrett, Deb Lebakken, Erin O'Brien, Alison Gaskin Bailey,

Toni Freitas, Karon Paris, Mandy Smith, Natasha Is a Book Junkie, Debbi Purcell, and Lynda Jeffrey. These humans help spread the word, and I am so grateful. If I've left anyone out, please accept my apologies. I love that you all love Hollie and Ryan as much as I do—or as Deb H. calls them, "Team RyLie."

Shout out to The White Dress Bridal Boutique (www.thewhitedressportland.com) in Portland, Oregon, for their fantastic website—you don't know it but you helped Hollie find her dream dress.

Thank you to the animal researchers, rescuers, veterinarians, volunteers, and global crusaders who protect our endangered and threatened marine mammals. I promise I will never pick up a wild otter, even if I want to give it a big, fluffy hug.

And of course, the fuzziest thanks go to the folks who own my heart—GareBear, Blake, Yaunna, Brennan, and not-so-little Kendon. Thanks for helping me breathe life into the lungs of these stories, for your ability to make your own food while I work, and for telling me I'm still the Best Mom Ever, even if we spent yet another vacationless summer. (Also, someone get Naughty Nuit out of the fish tank—I think she just gave Sushi a betta heart attack.)

A Special Note

REGARDING THE HANDLING OF SEA OTTERS (AND OTHER CRITTERS) IN THE WILD

Totally illegal. Dangerous for the animal and potentially dangerous for you too. Don't do it! Sure, we see videos all the time of heroic folks cutting sea turtles and whales free of ocean garbage, but if you are walking along a beach and you see a seal or an otter or a beached dolphin or even a bird in distress, best that you call the experts.

Hollie, as nutty as she is, is not a real person, and her choice to get involved with little Clara was done for entertainment purposes only. This story is fiction, remember, or as James Patterson calls it, "heightened reality." And just as Revelation Cove isn't a real place, what Hollie did to feed and later save that baby otter was not real life but rather a figment of my imagination, something I used to dream about doing when I was that sea-life-loving kid. (Yeah, I really wanted an orca in my bathtub.)

Please, please, please, if you find an animal in the wild you think might be in need of help, *call the experts.*

Sea otters and other marine mammals in the United States are protected by the Marine Mammal Protection Act;

the California sea otter population (a separate subspecies called the Southern sea otter) is additionally protected by federal law as a threatened species under the US Endangered Species Act; and marine mammal protection is afforded in Canada under the Marine Mammal Regulations as part of the Canada Fisheries Act.

If you are out along the pristine British Columbia coastline and you see a marine animal you think might be in distress, call the Vancouver Marine Mammal Rescue Centre at (604) 258-SEAL (7325). For information and resources for the American portion of the West Coast, visit www.marinemammalcenter.org for a comprehensive list of different marine mammal rescue authorities, including multiple listings for California and Washington. In Oregon, call the Oregon State Police Tipline at (800) 452-7888 or the Oregon State University Marine Mammal Stranding Network at (541) 270-6830.

The scenes written about the backstage goings-on at the Vancouver Aquarium (www.vanaqua.org) are pure imagination, derived from videos of rescued otters in a variety of aquarium and rescue/rehab facilities in the US, as I am a mere civilian and thus not granted access to such a mysterious and fantastic place. The folks at the Vancouver Aquarium Marine Mammal Rescue Centre, and other facilities such as the Monterey Bay Aquarium, do terrific, important work, and donations are always gladly received and most appreciated.

About the Author

A native of Portland, Oregon, Eliza Gordon (aka Jennifer Sommersby) has lived up and down the West Coast of the United States, from a small town south of Seattle down to Los Angeles. For the past thirteen years, home has been a suburb of Vancouver, British Columbia. Despite the occasional cougar and bear sighting in the neighborhood, there's no place she'd rather rest her webbed feet.

When not making words, Eliza can be found stalking the sea otters at the Vancouver Aquarium or keeping the local bookstores in business. And if you look lost between the stacks, she will probably follow you and recommend books. You've been warned.

Eliza/Jennifer is represented by Daniel Lazar of Writers House.

GET IN TOUCH WITH ELIZA GORDON

Website: www.elizagordon.com (Sign up for our newsletter too!)
Facebook: Eliza Gordon
Twitter: @eliza_gordon
Tumblr: onceuponeliza.tumblr.com

Must Love Otters

In case you landed at Revelation Cove with *Hollie Porter Builds a Raft,* treat yourself to the book where it all started!

MUST LOVE OTTERS

Hollie Porter is the chairwoman of Generation Disillusioned: at twenty-five years old, she's saddled with a job she hates, a boyfriend who's all wrong for her, and a vexing inability to say no. She's already near her breaking point, so when one caller too many kicks the bucket during Hollie's 911 shift, she cashes in the Sweethearts' Spa & Stay gift certificate from her dad and heads to Revelation Cove, British Columbia. One caveat: she's going solo. Any sweethearts will have to be found on site.

Hollie hopes to find her beloved otters in the wilds of the Great White North, but instead she's providing comic relief for staff and guests alike. Even Concierge Ryan, a former NHL star with bad knees and broken dreams, can't stop her from stumbling from one (mis)adventure to another. Just when Hollie starts to think that a change of venue doesn't mean a change in circumstances, the island works its charm and she starts to think she might have found the rejuvenation she so desperately desires. But then an uninvited guest crashes the party, forcing her to step out of the discomfort zone where she dwells and save the day ... and maybe even herself in the process.

Neurotica

Fans of geek culture, *Star Wars*, rubber ducks & food trucks — with a generous dollop of romance — apply within.

NEUROTICA

If you find yourself talking to Jayne Dandy, keep the conversation on *Star Wars* and rubber ducks—best not to mention men, dating, or S-E-X. Because Jayne is fine with the way things are: writer of obituaries and garage sale ads by day, secret scribe of adventures in distant galaxies by night. But her crippling fear of intimacy has made her the butt of jokes since forever, and hiding behind her laptop isn't going to get her lightsaber lit.

After her therapist recommends that she write erotica

as a form of exposure therapy, Jayne joins forces with pen and paper to combat the demons that won't let her kiss and tell. Unexpectedly downsized at work, she adopts a pseudonym and secretly self-publishes one of her naughty books to make ends meet. When her adorable, long-time friend Luke, co-owner of the popular Portland food truck Luke Piewalker's, hears she's been demoted, he insists on hiring her to sling éclairs and turnovers at his side. Her secret must be kept, but sparks ignite between them, sending Jayne and her X-Wing into a tailspin that will either make her face down her neuroses or trigger a meltdown of Death Star proportions.

Made in the USA
Charleston, SC
12 October 2015